Book 1

The Adventures of Sherlock Holmes' Cat

Patricia Srigley

WigglesWorth Press
Montreal, Quebec, Canada
SrigleyArts.com

Library and Archives Canada Cataloguing in Publication:
Please contact the publisher for this information

ISBN 978-1-9990511-1-2

Layout by WigglesWorth Press
Cover art and design by P. Srigley

Published by:
WigglesWorth Press
Montreal, Quebec, Canada

Additional titles by the author:

The Unreal Estate Series
The Storyteller Series

April-May June Series
Moody Gasping Middle School Series
Blue Wings
Deeply

Universe Idol
Fire-scape
All Planetary Shipping
Scarecrow in the Graveyard

Available at SrigleyArts.com and on Amazon

Table of Contents

Prologue

The tall man wasn't one to go out of his way to help an animal in trouble, yet, there was something about the little bundle of shivering black fur, so alone and abandoned. The creature's circumstance seemed to tug at his heart strings, not that a heart had strings. Silly sentiment.

The tall man's good friend and partner-in-crime-solving had recently gone off and gotten himself married, of all things. He had even vacated the rooms the pair had shared for many years, to live with the wife he had acquired. Truth be told, it had left an unexpectedly large and gaping hole in the place the man called home. Lonely wasn't an emotion he would have assigned to himself, yet he did seem to be feeling it of late.

Because it was out of character, the tall man was surprised to find himself stepping in front of the angry woman, who was wielding her broom like a weapon, determined to squash the little cat as flat as a flounder. "Madam, that is quite enough," he said in his coldest, sternest tone—the one that oft stopped criminals dead in their tracks. Alas, it did not stop the woman, only altered her target. She attacked him with the filthy broom.

"Stop that this instant," he sputtered, raising the walking stick in his hand in defense. "Explain why you are battering this kitten, Madam."

She lowered the broom and took a squinty eyed look at him. "Oh, so you's one of d'em la-dee-dah gentlemans, is you?"

The tall man gazed down his nose at the woman. "I am no such thing. Answer my question. What has this small feline done to deserve such barbaric treatment?"

"What's that you's saying," the woman asked, confused.

"Why are you attacking the kitten?" he asked more succinctly, trying to use smaller words.

"It took one of me fishies, dragged it off, you see. There it is." She pointed the straw end of her broom at a minnow of a fish on the ground. It stank, despite its minuscule size. It had tiny bites out of it. At a glance, the tall man knew the marks were caused by an animal with small pointy teeth. The pattern of chewing was not that of a rat or mouse. So, a cat was the most likely culprit, and a small cat at that. Evidence did not lie.

The shivering bundle of fur shivered harder, as if it knew it was the topic of discussion, and its fate hung in the balance. The man sighed loudly, greatly put upon it seemed, though no-one had impelled him to intervene on the cat's behalf, save himself.

Impatiently, he tossed back the cape of his long black Inverness cloak. The short cape was always getting in the way, yet it was ideal to repel the rain. And when was it not raining in London? Or if not raining, so thick with pea-soup fog, a man was soaked through by simply walking. He slipped a hand into his pocket and produced a coin. He held it up in the manner of a stage magician. "I shall pay generously for the fish, and take the cat with me."

The woman pursed her lips. She did not agree at once, perhaps wondering if she could milk additional coin from a man who appeared to have more money than brains. "Madam, to be clear, I shall not pay a halfpenny more," he said, proving himself not quite the fool she hoped him to be.

She sniffed, as though affronted. "As you wishes. I accepts your bargain for the fishes, mister sir."

Was she trying to make a clever rhyme? If so, the attempt was an abject failure. "And the cat," he added, questioning his sanity at that point.

"And the pesky cat." Clearly, the stray was not her cat to give, but that was no matter to her.

The tall man flicked the coin spinning through the air. A greedy hand snatched it with ease, and tucked it deep into an apron pocket. He picked up the black kitten by the scruff of its neck. He departed without another word, and without the fish.

1 – The Cat in Question

🐾 *from The Observations of Cat Watson*

The tall man who rescued me from the broom-wielding fiend of a fishwife, was none other than the famous detective Sherlock Holmes, although I didn't know it at the time. As soon as we left the fishmonger's wife behind, he tucked me beneath the cape of his cloak. He carried me all the way to his home. I didn't try to squirm free. His coat was the warmest, cleanest place I had ever known. I confess, I felt bad that I was not better groomed for the occasion, and soiled the fabric with my dirty paws.

In his cozy rooms, he fed me some fish. It was leftover on a platter, likely from his dinner. Nonetheless, it was delectably fresh, and not rotten at all. While I gobbled it up, he sat and contemplated me. By the time I had finished the yummiest fish I had ever tasted, in cream sauce no less, he had come to several conclusions.

He said to me, "You are a cat. A small one. I would estimate that you are six, or at most seven, months of age, unless you are the runt of the litter." He paused, as if waiting for some sort of confirmation.

As it so happened, I was the runt of the litter. I meowed to confirm his supposition. I had seen eight months, and had long ago reached the age of cat independence. I wouldn't get much bigger, yet I didn't mind being small. It meant I could squirm into places larger cats could not.

He continued. "I have never liked cats. I have always preferred dogs, but upon further observation and reflection, I have concluded that cats are less trouble, less work, far cleaner, and tremendously more intelligent than canines." I may have added that *tremendously*, but it's the kind of long word he liked to use.

I purred in agreement, and washed my face with my paw, proving one of his four points.

"And you, my young foundling feline, appear to be in need of a home. I can only hope you are a most intelligent representative of your species, as I do not suffer fools gladly," he said.

I had always thought of myself as smarter than your average cat, but don't we all like to think we are cleverer than our neighbours? Cats, as well as people? He wasn't finished. "I have no doubt you are far too intelligent to go off and get married, saddle yourself with a wife, abandon all whom you hold dear, for some buxom cleavage, rouged lips and bouncy ringlets."

Where had that come from? As far as humans went, the tall man didn't seem as clueless as the bulk of his kind, yet he was proving rather eccentric. I purred a bit louder, encouraging him to expound on his praise of cats. We like nothing more than to hear how superior we are to dogs. His rooms did smell unpleasantly of dog, but only faintly. I soon found out why.

"My name is Sherlock Holmes," he introduced himself. "I am a great detective, with an extraordinary sense of observation. I am reputedly the land's greatest detective, and I have no quarrel with that description. My good friend, Dr. John Watson, recently vacated these rooms. He is enjoying wedded bliss, such as it is. He took his dog with him. I do miss John, but not *the dog*." The way he said *the dog*, made it sound like a dubious designation indeed. His explanation also clarified his previous remark.

I padded over to his chair and jumped onto his lap. He started in surprise. After an awkward pause, he patted me on the head. Normally, one stroked a cat and patted a dog. Clearly, despite his reputedly great detective skills, he didn't know that. I rubbed against his hand, trying to clue him in.

His mind was on other things. "My home has felt rather empty, since John wedded *that woman*." *That woman* received an even more dubious designation than *the dog*. He continued, "If you, my small feline, would like to make this, 221B Baker Street, your home, it would be agreeable to me. I shall adopt you, and you shall adopt me."

I did like how he presented our arrangement as a two-way street. I curled up in his lap, agreeing to his suggestion. He half-patted and half-stroked me, his hand as big as I was. I had great hope that he would soon be stroking me as a cat should be stroked.

"I suppose you will need a name," he murmured. I sprang to my paws, excited by the possibility. Even though I was eight months old, I had never had a name to call my own. Yet, if I was going to have a home, I would need a name. I had always wanted one.

"What shall I call you?" the detective mused. He scooped me up in his big palm, raised me to his eye level, and studied me keenly. "You are black, furry, small, underfed." He ran a long, boney finger over my ribs, and continued. "You have blue eyes, one small white patch on your belly, and just a bit of white fur on the very tip of your tail. You are a male cat, often referred to as a tom." For a great detective, he was merely stating the obvious. "Shall I christen you *Lucky*?" He laughed as if at some private joke, a bitter edge to his humour.

I dug my claws into his hand, politely, not hard enough to draw blood. *Lucky* was not the right name for me. My short life had been anything but lucky, although I did hope that had now changed.

"I've had trouble sleeping, since John left me," the detective confessed. He did look very weary about his eyes, and deep within his eyes. I climbed up onto his shoulder, made wider by the caped coat he had not yet shed. Once there, I curled up beside his ear and began to purr. A cat's purr is a miraculous thing. It is soothing and relaxing and calming. Sherlock Holmes, reputedly the land's greatest detective, sagged deeper into his chair. His muscles relaxed and he heaved a great sigh, and another, then a yawn. His head drooped forward and he began to snore in a gentle rhythm.

Sadly, I did not yet have my name, but I would soon. I was sure of it. I was tired too, and my belly was warm and full of fish that was not rotten and rumbling restless inside me, as if it was still swimming in the sea. I fell asleep on the comfy shoulder. We both slept the night away, already at ease together.

2 - Dr. Watson's Case

Sherlock Holmes awoke to a pounding on his door. He was rather surprised to find himself sleeping upright in his chair, still clad in his cloak. Yet, he felt wonderfully rested for the first time in many weeks. He was even more surprised to find a small cat slumbering on his shoulder. He had slept so long and deep, his normally sharp mind was dulled by drowsiness. It took him a moment to recall that he had brought the scrappy little thing home himself. The why was a bit of a mystery in his somnolent state.

The pounding repeated, more urgently. He struggled to his feet, always such a long way up. His furry passenger didn't bother to rouse from its perch, so he opened the door with the cat on his shoulder.

The friend who had abandoned him in favour of *that woman* burst in, as if the hounds of hell were snarling at his heels. Dr. John Watson didn't even notice the cat on Holmes' shoulder. John was not the most observant of men, unless a pretty woman was within a hundred yards of him. John never failed to observe the fairest of the fairer sex.

Sherlock was relieved John hadn't brought his smelly dog along, as he was oft prone to do. "Come in," he said, with a sweep of his arm, despite the fact that John was already in. Sherlock simply wanted to make a point, that John Watson was now merely a visitor at 221B Baker Street, not a resident.

Being less than observant, since no pretty girl was sashaying about the sitting room, John didn't notice the gesture, and he still didn't notice the cat on Sherlock's shoulder. He really should have, as the cat had roused and sat itself up. It was now perched on Sherlock's shoulder in the manner of a pirate's parrot.

"Sherlock, I need help," John wailed, wringing his hands like a washer woman strangling a sodden rag.

Sherlock did not ask questions, yet. He raised one finger, signaling that he needed a moment. He opened the door John had slammed behind him. Mrs. Hudson was hovering just outside, her ear about to be pressed to the door for a good old eavesdrop. Her lip rouge was freshly applied, but not quite where it ought to be, and it was a bit smeared, as if applied with a hurried hand. Watson's panicked pounding on the door would have alerted the landlady to the fact that something interesting was afoot, and she never liked to miss out on her upstairs border's exciting cases. Hence the messy lip rouge.

"Tea, Mrs. Hudson, if you please. Perhaps a biscuit or two." The cat meowed and kneaded his shoulder with its front paws. "Oh, and a platter of cream, and a morsel of fish, if you have it. Chicken will do, if you do not. Or a dead mouse, if it is fresh."

Mrs. Hudson was far more observant than John. "You've got a wee kitty on your shoulder. Is it hungry-wungry?" she lisped, attempting to stroke the *wee kitty*.

Sherlock shifted aside. Mrs. Hudson ended up stroking his cheek, her fingers brushing over his lips. "Mrs. Hudson! Mind your hands," he cried indignantly.

"I was only trying to pet the wee kitty, not your bristled face. Settle down and tend to Dr. Watson. He's in a right state, isn't he? I'll fetch the tea and fish." She descended the stairs in a swirl of skirts, almost tumbling down them in her haste not to miss too much.

"Don't you believe her for a moment," Sherlock muttered to the cat. "She's always trying to lay her hands on me." He returned to his visitor. "Sit, Dr. Watson." He pointed to the client's chair.

"What? Sit there? And why are you calling me Dr. Watson. I'm John," he stressed, as if Sherlock was an imbecile who had forgotten his long-time companion's name.

"At the moment, you appear to be a client, and that is where clients sit, Dr. Watson," Sherlock annunciated, a wintery bite to his words.

"Sherlock!" Dr. Watson wailed. "Are you still holding a grudge, because I fell in love and got married, and now live with my wife?"

"Don't be ridiculous." Sherlock settled in his armchair. John claimed his usual upholstered chair with a *harrumph*, eschewing the client's hard wooden seat. He gazed straight at Sherlock with a frustrated aspect, and he finally noticed the cat.

"Why do you have a cat on your shoulder?" he asked.

"This is Watson," Sherlock announced, patting the cat on the head. "You have a wife. I have a cat, and it is named Watson. Not Dr. Watson, Dr. Watson, merely Watson," he stated.

"If you call me Dr. Watson again, I am going to throw something at your head," John said. "My name is John, as you well know. Or Watson, if you must. I am still your friend, even though I am now a happily married man. And I need your help greatly. Something dreadful has happened." He got back to wringing his hands.

Sherlock wished Mrs. Hudson would hurry up with the tea. It would give John something to do with his hands, before he sprained all his fingers. Sherlock leaned back, adopting a relaxed pose. "Describe in detail this dreadful event that has occurred, if you please, Dr. Watson," he said, all business.

John did not throw something at his head, as threatened, yet he did sigh so ferociously, it was akin to a growl one might hear when visiting the Zoological Gardens in The Regent's Park.

Sherlock's new feline companion, who was perhaps now stuck with the name Watson, leapt down from his shoulder onto his lap. The little cat sat there so alertly, he seemed to be all perked ears, eagerly awaiting John's tale of woe.

3 - The Naming

♥ *from The Observations of Cat Watson*

I was of two minds in regards to my new name being *Watson*. I liked the sound of it. It was rather dignified, for a cat. It was leagues better than Fluffy or Mittens or Whiskers, or, heaven forbid, PussPuss. Still, if this Dr. Watson fellow, who absolutely stank of dog, was going to keep turning up, two *Watsons* would be very confusing for all concerned. Watson the man, and I the cat, would never know which of us Sherlock Holmes was addressing, or speaking about. Hopefully Sherlock Holmes would come to the same conclusion, and right the situation, given that he was reputedly the land's greatest detective.

I stopped worrying about my name when Dr. Watson started telling his tale. The man rambled on and on, ad nauseam, but in short, the problem was this—his wife's bicycle was missing and presumed stolen. Oh, and she was very upset. Yes, that's the entirety of it, the *something dreadful* that had him wringing his hands as if he was in the process of strangling a chicken.

I admired Sherlock Holmes when he didn't laugh outright at his former companion's anguish, over a bicycle. It showed great restraint, or a lack of a sense of humour. I didn't know Sherlock Holmes well enough in our early days together, to discern which it was.

In the middle of the overly long tale of the mystery of the missing and presumed stolen bicycle, Mrs. Hudson brought the tea. The dear lady from downstairs hadn't forgotten my saucer of cream. She even presented me with a dainty little dish of fish. My new home was proving to have many luxurious perks. Alas, I did have to put up with more degrading baby talk and kissy noises. Why too many humans think cats wish to be addressed so idiotically, is a mystery to me. I doubt even babies appreciate it, not that I've ever met a baby. They smell worse than dogs and are best avoided. Now dogs, they lap up baby talk as if it was raw liver. Daft creatures.

While feasting on my fish and cream, I did not pay attention to Dr. Watson's blathering. I suspect I didn't miss much, if anything. I mean, how much can one say about a missing and presumed stolen bicycle?

Belly delightfully sated, I opted to sit on the client's chair, although I was no client. I was simply interested in observing how the two men interacted with each other, and that was best done from a seat where I could easily view both.

Sherlock Holmes was a picture of darkness. Midnight dark hair, the dark caped cloak, which he had yet to remove, a furrowed brow, and a broody, burdened countenance. Very dark indeed. He was cool, cutting, distant, and sarcastic, with his former companion, yet it was as plain as the fur on my face, that he was hurt. Nothing more. He was sad and he missed his friend, and resented Dr. Watson for abandoning him—which is how he saw it.

In the days that followed, as I came to better know Sherlock Holmes, I concluded that he was a man of the mind, not the heart. Don't get me wrong, he did have a heart. He simply did not share it with many. It was a guarded thing, perhaps to overcompensate for wounds in his past. The detective was rational, most of the time, and unused to messy emotions. On those occasions when emotion did grip him, it overwhelmed him. He was quite clueless about how to deal with *feelings*. Whether anger, or hurt, or distress, or even joy, he was at a complete loss. It was one of his failings. Sherlock Holmes, despite being the land's great detective, was still a man, not a cat, so of course he wasn't perfect.

Dr. John Watson was quite the opposite in both nature and appearance. He was shorter, fairer, and stockier than Sherlock. He sported a ghastly moustache that I craved to claw off his face. He appeared to have a nice face, and no need to hide behind the scraggily, wispy, whiskers that surrounded his mouth and dangled raggedly to his jawline. Unlike a cat, he hadn't even groomed his dismal whiskers properly, nor did he appear to have an inkling of how to do so. Enough about his horrible facial hair. I do apologize for digressing.

Clearly, Dr. Watson reacted from the heart. I suspected, rightly, that first time I observed him, that his heart was very big indeed. It was obvious, at least to me, that he knew his friend was hurt and lonely, though Sherlock would never admit to such human weaknesses. Dr. Watson was trying his utmost to mend their friendship, yet Sherlock was having none of it. As I would soon learn, he was stubborn. It was another of Sherlock's traits—sometimes a failing and sometimes a strength, depending on the situation. Luckily, that mulish streak did not oft rear its pig-headed head, only when Dr. Watson was involved. Or criminals. Sherlock could be very stubborn in his pursuit of justice and villains, which was a good thing indeed.

Alas, at this moment, Sherlock's stubbornness had the two men at an impasse. Sherlock was turning his back on his friend, rebuffing all his advances. And Dr. Watson was trying to mend the rift, and making no progress whatsoever.

It was very lucky indeed that the detective adopted me and welcomed me into his home. If not for me, I don't know if the two men would ever have reconciled their differences and become fast friends again, but I am getting ahead of myself. There was a bicycle to find, and yours truly was about to play a key role in solving that mystery.

4 - The Mystery of the Missing & Presumed Stolen Bicycle

Sherlock listened to John blather on and on about Mary's missing penny-farthing bicycle, and on and on about how distraught Mary was, and how she wouldn't stop crying, over a ridiculous big-wheeled bicycle that was almost entirely out of fashion, given how impractical it was to ride. Hare-brained woman.

In truth, it was nice to see John again. It had been two months and three days since he had last laid eyes on his former roommate. Although why John had grown the atrocious moustache was beyond even his magnificent mind to fathom. He knew John wanted him to comment on the hideous, hairy new addition to his face. Sherlock refused to do so. He pretended the ghastly moustache wasn't there at all. He suspected John had grown the thing merely to annoy him. Why else would a man want the worst moustache in the world disfiguring his face? Even the little cat seemed quite gobsmacked, and unable to look away from the scraggily, droopy, uneven, crumb-laden, ginger whiskers. The bright orangish colour, in contrast to John's sandy hair, only made the thing more disturbing.

Sherlock mulled over what he should name the cat, when John pulled a notebook and pencil from his pocket and began writing case notes about the missing bicycle, as if Sherlock didn't have perfect recall in all things. Even though he craved to call the cat *Watson*, which would annoy John no end, Sherlock knew it would be confusing to have two Watsons as associates. Perhaps his cat could make-do with the surname *Watson*, if Sherlock christened him with a given name that he would call the cat, unless John was lurking around. Yes, that was the perfect solution. The name that popped into his head was *Tom Watson*, since the cat was a tom.

"No, far too common and unoriginal," he muttered. He had taken to talking to himself, a bit, since John had left him.

John stopped scribbling notes. "What's that, Sherlock? Are you saying the bicycle is too common and unoriginal to be found amongst all the other bicycles in London?"

Sherlock was about to say *yes*, so he wouldn't have to take the case, when John continued. "Are you saying this is a case *you* can't solve?" There was a distinct emphasis on the *you*.

Sherlock was about to say, *Of course I can solve your case. I can solve any case presented to me, if I have a desire to do so*, which he did not in this instance, but John wasn't finished.

"Are you saying London's greatest detective can't locate a missing and presumed stolen bicycle?" John's tone kept increasing in pitch, as if he was astounded.

Sherlock was about to say, *Of course I can find your stupid wife's stupid bicycle*, when he realized that such words did sound rather petty, and yes, childish.

And John wasn't finished. "Because if this case is beyond you, I can contact the police. I am sure Inspector Lestrade, or Inspector Gregson, could find the bicycle in no time, since you cannot."

It was a low blow. Sherlock crossed his arms and scowled. "Fine, I will take your stupid case and find your ... wife's stupid bicycle." At least he hadn't called John's wife stupid, although it had been a close run thing, and a few other *stupids* had slipped out unbidden.

John didn't take offence. He smiled. "Thank you, Sherlock. I do appreciate your willingness to help a friend in need."

Sherlock raised one eyebrow. "Client, Dr. Watson. I have accepted your case, so you are a client. No more, no less."

"Yes, yes." John hopped to his feet with enthusiasm. "I will show you the crime scene now, as we have finished our tea and biscuits."

Sherlock rose, to tower over John, just a little bit. "Before I venture out in the world, I am going to freshen up. I slept in my cloak, in my chair, and I seem to smell of fish."

"I thought that was the cat," John said.

Sherlock did not hurry through his ablutions, and he changed his shirt. The fishy aroma lingered and he was forced to conclude the smell came from his cloak. Ah well, the rain would wash the odor away in time. He put his cloak back on, slung a clean scarf around his neck, and returned to the sitting room.

John and the still unnamed cat appeared to be engaged in a staring contest. "Where did you get it?" John motioned at the cat, as if Sherlock couldn't deduce what he was talking about.

"I rescued him from a vicious attack. He needed a home, and I have a place in mine, for him. Cat Watson is my new companion," he declared, needing to get in one more dig. Yet, once he spoke the name aloud, he did like the sound of *Cat Watson* immeasurably.

"Can't you come up with a better name than that, Sherlock?" John asked, opening the door.

Mrs. Hudson was outside. Her ear would have been pressed to the wood, if the door had still been in the closed position. She straightened stiffly, as if she had been slightly bent at the waist for a very long time. "Good luck with your wife's bicycle, Dr. Watson. So nice you've come to visit with Sherlock. He's been so very sad and lonely since you left. I've just come to collect the dishes," she added, although everyone present knew it was a bald-faced lie. Even the little cat probably knew it.

"I have not been so sad and lonely," Sherlock snapped, inclined to pout, until he realized what his lips were doing. He smiled slightly instead, just to make sure he wasn't pouting.

"At least you have the wee kitty-witty to keep you company now. Isn't that a treat! Oh, your scarf is uneven, Sherlock. Let me adjust that for you." Mrs. Hudson reached up around his neck with both hands. He couldn't escape, short of shoving her down the long flight of stairs outside his door.

His landlady took her time, straightening his scarf just so and tickling his neck, and running her fingers through his hair. She pressed the scarf flat, as if she was ironing it against his chest, which involved a lot of stroking his chest at the same time. She made sure to tuck it very deep inside his cloak, deeper than the scarf could possibly reach, as it was not an overly long scarf.

"Are you quite done, Mrs. Hudson?" Sherlock asked, when he had stood patiently for as long as he possibly could, under her too-tender ministrations. John was biting his lips, trying not to laugh outright. His atrocious moustache was far too thin and scraggily to hide that. Scarf adjusting, coat adjusting, and hat adjusting, were scenes that had played out too many times to count. And then there was the singular and infamous trouser adjusting incident, which was best forgotten by all concerned.

Cat Watson had followed them out onto the landing, apparently intent on accompanying them to the crime scene. He also appeared to be chuckling, or he was choking on a hairball.

5 - The Scene of the Crime

from The Observations of Cat Watson

I couldn't stop chuckling. Sherlock had spoken truth. Oh my, did Mrs. Hudson like to get handsy with him! It was one of the funniest things I had seen in a long time, yet I did feel some sympathy for Sherlock. If the landlady had been a cat, Sherlock would have been a little mouse she was toying with.

I guessed her to be about forty, or possibly as much as forty-five in years. She was doing her utmost to look younger, with curled hair, a clownish amount of face paint and powder on her face, and a flouncy, lacy gown with far too many bows. It would have better suited a girl in the schoolroom.

Scarf adjusted to within an inch of its life, Sherlock, Dr. Watson, and I, descended the stairs and made our way outside. When we entered street traffic, Sherlock scooped me up and carried me. Wheels, hooves, and even big boots can be perilous to a small cat.

A carriage was hailed. I got very excited. I had never ridden in a carriage before. The one that picked us up was pulled by two brown nags and had a lot of peeling paint. It wasn't the fanciest of carriages, but I didn't care. As we rolled through the streets, I stood up on Sherlock's legs, front paws braced on the window ledge, my head out in the breeze. The feel of the wind on my furry face was delightful. What a way to travel! All cats should be so lucky, but few cats were. None that I knew of.

Too soon, Dr. Watson banged on the roof with his walking stick. "Stop here, driver."

The carriage deposited us before a square brick house. I bounded out and had a look around, and a good sniff. The house was neither large nor small, neither plain nor fancy. The garden was fairly expansive and well-tended. It was a perfectly respectable and suitable home for a newly married doctor and his bride.

There was a separate side entrance, with a plaque affixed to it. As Dr. Watson was a physician, it was most likely his surgery where he treated his patients. Alas, I was not able to read. I had yet to meet a cat that could.

It must have been the first time Sherlock had visited his friend's new domicile, for he said, "You've come up in the world, Dr. Watson. Did you marry money as well as Mary?"

"Mind your manners, Sherlock," Dr. Watson chided him. "You are here to examine the crime scene, then we shall take tea and discuss your findings."

I was a bit alarmed about that. To take tea, one must enter the house. Dr. Watson's dog most likely lived in the house. It is a well-known fact that dogs and cats do not get along. And it's all the dogs' faults, for being so stupid and slobbery and needy. Roll over? Beg? Sit? Heel? You would never catch a cat behaving in such a humiliating and shameful manner. Cats have dignity. Not all cats, it must be said, but most cats. No species is without its black sheep, or black cats, as it were. While I was a black cat, I was not a black cat of a disreputable nature. Stealing the odd wee fish is not a crime, merely a matter of survival on the streets.

Dr. Watson led us toward the main door of the house, the one without the plaque. He pointed to the right. "The bicycle was leaning there, just around the corner. Now it is gone." He bypassed the door and stopped just around the corner of the house, announcing dramatically, "This is the crime scene."

I sat down to observe the proceedings. I had never seen a great detective at work, or any detective, for that matter. I was eager to observe how detecting was done.

Sherlock raised one dark eyebrow at Dr. Watson. "No pooled blood? No pistol rounds? We can only hope the bicycle is still alive. Has a ransom note been delivered?"

"Sherlock!" Dr. Watson reproached, without any true rancor. He was exceedingly patient with his prickly friend.

The detective gave an exaggerated sigh, before he lowered into a crouch, to examine the ground up close. He pulled a magnifying glass from the pocket of his coat and peered through it. I padded over, to detect with him. "What do you observe, Cat Watson?" he asked, giving me a nice little stroke on the head. He was learning.

17

Since my nose and scenting ability were far superior to his, and any given humans', I gave the ground, where there was an obvious bicycle tire mark, a delicate sniff. It smelled of rubber, dirt and horse manure, and perfume. The perfume was the most recent scent, dominating the others. I meowed loudly, to let the detective know I had discovered something.

He rose back to his great height, and said, "Let us follow the tire tracks, as far as they will take us." So we did, toward the road in front. Sherlock pointed out the small but distinctive nick in the left side of the solid rubber front tire. Despite the nick, the trail went cold as soon as we reached the street. Numerous carriages, horses, handcarts, humans, and other bicycles, had obliterated any trace of the missing bicycle's tires.

At that point, Dr. Watson declared, "Time for luncheon."

"I already had morning tea," Sherlock said. "There is nothing to find here, nothing to discuss. Buy your wife another bicycle. Get her one of those new safety bicycles, with air in the tires so her bones won't shake, and she won't get headaches from all the bumping along when she rides. I have even seen a new model, a step-through, manufactured to allow for women's skirts. Get her one of those. Given your new address, I'm sure you can afford it. I shall take my leave now. Come, Cat Watson," he ordered, as if I was a dog, which I did not appreciate one iota. He turned back toward the road, instead of the house.

I was watching Dr. Watson. With Sherlock's back turned to him, he had lost his positive demeanor and looked like he was going to cry. He truly did. Sherlock's slumped shoulders were looking no happier.

"I guess this case is too complex for you. I shall have to call in the police constabulary," Dr. Watson threatened.

"They will have no more luck than I. Do they ever?" Sherlock said wearily, and took steps toward the road.

I could not let him leave, I realized. Both men were miserable, although my allegiance was to Sherlock Holmes, of course. How could I persuade him to stay? Perhaps it was silly of me, but I only had seconds to act, so I pretended to faint. I had seen women faint in the streets, too many times to count. I knew how to do it well. I wobbled on my legs, staggered from side to side, and stumbled like a drunk human, before I collapsed to my side on the ground, eyes closed. I did not go so far as to let my mouth slacken and my tongue loll out, as I did not wish to be viewed at dead.

"Sherlock, something is wrong with your cat," Dr. Watson called.

I heard the detective's footsteps returning and I peeked, just a bit. Sherlock's boots were right there in front of me. "What did you do to Cat Watson?" he demanded of Dr. Watson. It seemed that was to be my name.

"Me? Not a thing. He just collapsed, right there on the ground."

"Well, you're the physician. Do something," Sherlock ordered.

"Physician, not veterinarian," Dr. Watson stressed.

"Surely you can do something. He has a heart that pumps blood through his veins, lungs that breathe air, as do humans." Sherlock sounded properly upset. I did feel bad for my ruse, yet it was necessary.

"Bring him inside. I will do what I can. And you will take luncheon with Mary and me," Dr. Watson said.

"Oh, fine, if I must. But I'm only doing it for Cat Watson's sake." Sherlock picked me up gently. He bore me along the walkway toward the house, as one would carry a fish pie to a table, most protectively and flat on his two big palms.

Dr. Watson opened the front door, rather than the side surgery door. The two men traipsed inside, and yours truly was carried like a precious pie into a house that reeked of dog. That is when everything went pear-shaped. It was entirely the stupid, smelly dog's fault.

6–Attack of the Horrible Hound

Sherlock carried his new companion inside, simply hoping the little cat wasn't dead. In truth, Cat Watson didn't seem dead. Sherlock felt tiny twitches of muscle and noted the eyelids flicker twice, as if the cat was trying to peek around. Was his cat feigning a faint, as women were inclined to do, when they wanted a handsome man to catch them in strong arms? And if so, why? Was the cat so smart that he could plot and act? If that was indeed the case, Sherlock had ended up with an exceptional companion. But what was Cat Watson about with this stunt?

John opened the door to his new home with something of a flourish, as if proud of how he had come up in the world. In Sherlock's opinion, he wasn't showing proper concern for poor Cat Watson. He stepped inside with the cat, and then everything went to hell in a handbasket, or handcart, or handbag, or whatever the expression was. It was all John's stupid dog's stupid fault.

With a great loud woof and a feral growl, Gladstone barreled into the foyer. It is an appropriate expression for how the beast moved, since he was shaped like a barrel—a barrel with four stubby legs and a bulbous head. Oh, and a poor excuse for a tail stuck on as an afterthought. It was an altogether ridiculous dog, and it had only gotten fatter since Sherlock had last laid eyes on it, two months and three days ago. Gladstone now had even more weight with which to attack Sherlock, whom he had never liked much, perhaps because Sherlock had performed the odd experiment on the dog when John was out and about doctoring, or observing pretty girls or some such.

Cat Watson proved he was very much not dead, or even fainted, when he sprang up with a yowl and a great deal of hissing. In typical cat fashion, he arched to look larger. The fluffy fur on his back rose up too, doing its part, despite the futility of making the small cat look much bigger than a well-fed rat.

Gladstone hadn't even realized, until that moment, that there was a cat on the premises. Alas, he couldn't help but realize it now. A rabid

20

look filled his droopy brown eyes. He howled and snarled like a hound shat from the bowels of hell. He kept coming at Sherlock and the cat, with the determination of a freight train on a track, under full steam.

John, stalwart fellow that he was, tried to intercept his dog, shouting, "Gladstone, no, no, no. Bad dog, heel, sit, stay. Gladstone, no, no, no!"

Gladstone was having none of it, and knocked John off his pins, enroute to Sherlock. Cat Watson had great survival instincts, and upon the dog's approach, sought a safer perch than Sherlock's hands. He sprang onto Sherlock's shoulder, and from there, his head. Sherlock could not say he appreciated the cat's claws digging deep into his scalp. He wished he had worn his deerstalker detecting hat, yet he had no time to dwell on it. Gladstone arrived. The beast leapt as high as he could, which was about a quarter of an inch off the ground, and sank his teeth into Sherlock's leg, just above the knee. Sherlock shrieked in a surprisingly high pitch, rather embarrassing really.

Cat Watson did not like Sherlock being attacked, or in pain, or perhaps he simply did not like dogs, for he yowled viciously. It was akin to a cat's battle cry. Sherlock was taken by surprise when Cat Watson launched off his head and landed on Gladstone's back, digging his tiny claws in, riding the dog as a man would ride a horse. Sherlock was most impressed with the cat's bravery, and grateful that his cat seemed set on defending him, and was no longer clawing into his head. Alas, Cat Watson's attack only made Gladstone sink his teeth deeper into Sherlock's flesh.

Mary appeared in the doorway at that moment. She took in the scene at a glance—Sherlock with a dog attached to his leg by its teeth, a cat riding on the dog, and John knocked on his bottom on the floor. "Gladstone, no. Release. Sit," she commanded at once.

To Sherlock's surprise, the dog freed his leg and plunked his ample bottom down on the carpet. Cat Watson must not have felt safe at ground level, and now that Sherlock no longer needed his defense, he sprang back up to Sherlock's hands. Sherlock caught him, but couldn't hold him. Cat Watson squirmed free, and again used his shoulder as a stepping stool to his head, by far the highest perch around.

Gladstone merely panted, wet tongue sticking out and flapping around. He wagged his poor excuse of a tail, adoring gaze fixed on Mary. So John wasn't the only one in love with her. Clearly, the stupid dog was as well.

John struggled to his feet, rubbing his bottom. "So sorry about that, Sherlock. Hello, Mary. We're here for luncheon."

Mary, who in truth did not have a buxom bosom on display, or rouged lips, or even bouncy ringlets, smiled at Sherlock. She was a woman that one could easily overlook, being of quiet countenance. Brown hair, average height and weight, straight nose, brown eyes— yet her eyes always seemed to hold a secret smile, as if she was happy, and considered life amusing. Sherlock found her most disconcerting, especially when she smiled at him. He frowned back at her.

"Good day, Sherlock. It is so nice to see you again. Welcome to our home, and I am sorry Gladstone bit you. That is not a very nice reception, is it? John will tend to your wound, while I arrange the meal. Why do you have a cat on your head? Is he your new detecting cap?"

Sherlock frown transitioned into a scowl. "Of course the cat is not a cap. If the infernal dog could be relocated to another room, or better yet, out of doors, Cat Watson will come down and calm down, I am sure. He is an exceptionally intelligent and most reasonable cat. He is my new companion and roommate, and defender, it seems," he announced grandly.

Mary smiled even wider, and bit her lip, as if trying not to laugh outright. Her eyes danced merrily. "Cat Watson, is it? Welcome to our home, Cat Watson. I will arrange tea for you, too. I suspect you enjoy fish. Come, Gladstone. Heel." Mary left the room, an obedient Gladstone waddling so close beside her, he might have been a conjoined dog. His poor excuse for a tail wagged a mile a minute. Although she tried to muffle it, Sherlock heard Mary's laughter burst forth once she had left the room.

"Ready to come down now, Cat Watson?" Sherlock lifted the little cat off his head. He was docile again, and in robust health, not fainted or dead at all, as it turned out.

John exhaled noisily, ballooning his cheeks as if he was playing a trumpet. "Gladstone is much more obedient for Mary, than me. I don't know how she does it. So sorry about the dog biting you, Sherlock. There's blood coming through your trouser leg. I'll treat you in my surgery, and you've got some blood dripping down your forehead. I'll tend to that, as well."

Sherlock knew dog bites could turn septic, and he didn't want to lose his leg. That was the only reason he followed John into his surgery. He set Cat Watson on John's desk.

The cat observed with keen interest as John cleaned and bandaged the dog bite, which wasn't too deep, and cleansed the claw marks on his scalp, which were rather deep. Sherlock refused to allow John to bandage his head. Bandages on heads always looked ridiculous. His hair would hide the marks well enough, and wounds tended to heal best when left to the air, despite what medical men claimed.

The cat meowed apologetically when John fussed over the scratches, as if he felt very bad indeed for clawing Sherlock's head. The little ears even drooped, and the piercing blue eyes looked bigger and sadder than ever before. Were they dampening? No, humans were the only animals who shed tears, yet Cat Watson was clearly distressed. Sherlock said, "I know you did not intend to scratch me. It was merely an accident. I forgive you, Cat Watson, and lay the blame at the dog's door, not yours. I do thank you for acting so bravely to defend me."

The cat's ears perked back up and he made a happy little chirping sound. John frowned. "Cats do not understand people, you know, Sherlock. They are animals. They are not even as intelligent as dogs."

Cat Watson gave a little hiss, as if to prove John wrong. Sherlock smiled at his new companion. "I am not so sure, John. I do believe Cat Watson is a most remarkable and exceptional cat. If you are saying Gladstone is smarter than Cat Watson, we do need to question your intellect."

John really couldn't dispute that. Gladstone was staggeringly dumb, even for a dog. John harrumphed a bit, and packed his medical supplies away. Sherlock rose and his leg didn't feel too bad at all. The same could not be said for his stinging head. John had insisted on using a newly discovered antiseptic called iodine. It stung like the dickens, and seemed to stain the skin purple on contact, but surely that would wash right off.

They left the surgery, settled in the dining room, and enjoyed a very civilized luncheon, with Mary, and without Gladstone, thank heavens.

J - A Cat on the Case

🐱 from The Observations of Cat Watson

I had yet another dish of fish, washed down with cream. It was a most satisfying lunch for a cat who had been traumatized. Dogs! I couldn't understand what people saw in them, or why they allowed them into their homes, to stink them all up. Gladstone was fouler, smellier, and saggier, than any canine I had yet had the misfortune to meet. Worst of all, he had attacked my Sherlock, and drawn blood. Yes, I had drawn blood, too, but that had been accidental. Sherlock had forgiven me. And he had complimented my bravery. I had done my best to defend him, despite the fact that I had been soundly outmatched against the hound, in size, certainly not intelligence.

Mary seemed very nice indeed, and a good match for Dr. Watson, if I was any judge of human relationships. Mary was friendly with the detective, probably for Dr. Watson's sake, but Sherlock wasn't meeting her halfway, or even a quarter of the way.

A most interesting thing about Mary was her perfume. I had noted the same distinctive fragrance at the crime scene, overlaying all the others. It was the freshest scent by far, and led me to suspect that Mary herself had made her bicycle disappear. But why would she steal her own bicycle? And then weep over its disappearance. She didn't even seem like the type to weep, unless a true tragedy had occurred. Perhaps she was one of those females I had overheard men discussing, the ones who were prone to female hysteria. Then again, from the way men talked, all women were prone to female hysteria. It made me extra glad that I was a cat, and a tom.

The humans sipped tea and nibbled little sandwiches, while discussing the missing bicycle, and making no progress in the case whatsoever. As soon as the sandwiches and tea and little cakes were cleared away, Dr. Watson produced a bottle of the strong liquor that some humans, notably men, crave to drink.

24

"Brandy for your injuries, Sherlock," he announced grandly. I couldn't abide the horrible smelly stuff myself. When imbibed in any quantity, it made humans, notably men, act even sillier than they were inclined to do naturally. Worse yet, Dr. Watson produced two cigars to smoke, along with the brandy. I think he was trying to prolong his time with Sherlock, but I truly couldn't stomach the smell of smoke. It wasn't as odorous as dog or baby, but it did make my nose sting and tickle something fierce.

I opted to make myself scarce, do a little bicycle investigating on my own, in the fresh out of doors. As long as I avoided the dog, curiosity shouldn't kill this cat.

Without being noticed, since cats can be very sneaky indeed, I slunk from the room. I found my way to the kitchen by following the delicious aromas wafting from it. As most kitchens tend to be, it was located at the rear of the house.

A cook was starting on supper, plucking feathers from a chicken, and a scullery maid was cleaning up the remains of lunch. I padded over to the door that opened out onto the back garden, exactly where I wanted to go. I sat down and gave a polite little meow, requesting someone let me out. One of the few disadvantages of being a cat is that we can't open doors.

The scullery maid was the one who heard me. She hurried over. "Oh, does the wee pusspuss want out, to do his business-wusiness?" I rolled my eyes at her. She didn't notice, but she stroked me very nicely, before she opened the door. I meowed a thank-you and scampered outside. There was no sign of the dog and I ducked into the shrubbery. I don't know why it's called ducked. Ducks are not at all stealthy, with all their quacking and flapping and fussing. It should be called catted, for cats are as clandestine a creature as exists. So, I catted into the shrubbery.

I like being black, as much as I like being small. At night, I am invisible. Daytime, I can slink through the shadows without being noticed. I used that to my advantage now, as I snuck around to the side of the house, back to the scene of the crime. Perfume was still the dominant scent.

This time, without human interference, I tracked the fragrance, not the tire tracks. Yes, the bicycle had been rolled to the street, or been ridden, although the tire tracks did not look deep enough for that. It wasn't easy, but I managed to follow the residual scent of Mary's perfume for several yards, whereupon the bicycle turned back onto the Watson's property. It had then traversed the short grass of the lawn, without leaving a track. Or its passage had been hidden by scuffing it away.

The perfume trail led to an outbuilding behind the Watson's residence. From the lingering odour, it was probably a former carriage house. The wide double doors were opened during the day, probably for the groundskeeper or some such. And, there were no dogs about.

I followed the faint perfume to the shadowy, cobwebby, back corner of the structure. I should add that it was a very crowded little building. A handcart, a wheelbarrow, a plethora of gardening implements, furniture in need of repair, several milk churns, barrels, bulging burlap sacks, a stack of logs for the fireplace, crates, planking, hand tools, even a battered washtub that had seen better days, haphazardly cluttered up the floor space. Hence, it was the ideal spot to stash a bicycle that one does not want found. But I found it!

The thing was concealed beneath a draped horse blanket. The nose-watering scent of horse made that abundantly clear, yet I could still smell Mary's perfume. Two tires poked out the bottom of the blanket, the back one small, the front one enormous. Curious and curiouser. Why had Mary hidden her own bicycle, declared it stolen, and cried buckets of tears, according to Dr. Watson, motivating him to seek out a great detective to solve the mystery? Mary's motivation was the true puzzle.

I sat down to have a good think, and to groom my fur at the same time. I had gotten very dusty while bicycle tracking. I had washed all my fur clean before inspiration struck. Mary loved her husband and wanted him to be happy, as I wanted Sherlock to be happy. So Mary had taken action. She had hidden the bicycle, raised a ruckus, and impelled her husband to seek out Sherlock, in the hopes of mending their friendship—not to find a bicycle that wasn't even missing, merely well hidden, except from one special cat.

I was sure my conclusion was the right one. I now had a tough choice to make. Did I lead Sherlock to the bicycle, to prove to him how proficient a detective's assistant I could be? Or did I keep my discovery a secret, so Sherlock and Dr. Watson would spend more time together. Perhaps they could mend their friendship, while trying to solve the mystery of the missing bicycle together. Oh, I was in such a quandary. How I wanted to triumphantly reveal the location of the bicycle!

As it happened, matters were taken out of my paws. It was the blasted dog again. Gladstone, who I had decided to think of as *Badstone*, as there was nothing *glad* about him, arrived on the scene. He had an entourage. I immediately sought higher ground, to avoid the dog. Luckily, there was a partial, overhead loft in the outbuilding. If I haven't mentioned it yet, cats are talented climbers. I silently scrambled up to the loft, and I had a safe perch from which to observe the events as they unfolded. And let me tell you, it was quite the to-do.

8 – A Frightful Affliction

Gladstone was tugging at his leash, almost pulling John right off his feet, as he lumbered into the outbuilding behind the house. Mary trailed close behind, looking more anxious by the minute. Sherlock brought up the rear, an unwilling participant in the little parade. "Cat Watson has not run away," he declared, for the fifth time, since no-one would credit his words. "He does not need tracking down, especially not by Gladstone. That is begging for trouble. My scalp can attest to that."

"No, Sherlock. Gladstone is an excellent tracker. I have no doubt he is on the trail of your missing cat," John insisted.

"Cat Watson is not missing. He is too clever to be missing!" Sherlock was at the end of his patience.

"I'm sure he's right, John," Mary said. "The cat has probably just gone for a little walk, as cats are prone to do."

"That is dogs, Mary, not cats. Cats are lazy creatures that lie about, serving no purpose whatsoever, except as decorations, I suppose," John said.

"Be that as it may, we should wait for the cat at the house. It knows where to find us. Come, John." Mary gave his sleeve a tug to stop his progress. She was no match for Gladstone.

Sherlock wondered, briefly, why Mary did not wish to traipse about the outbuilding. Then he realized, being a woman, the prospect of getting dirt on her slippers, and the hem of her skirt, would be most upsetting to her.

He thought he heard a faint scrabbling sound in the loft overhead. Mice perhaps? Or a wily cat avoiding a horrible dog? Sherlock squinted up, yet couldn't see anything in the shadowy loft overhead.

Gladstone, nose to the ground, kept bumbling forward. John was hauled along in his wake, tripping through a veritable obstacle course of items, all the way to the back corner of the building. The dog stopped when he could go no further, and planted his bottom on the grimy ground.

"What's that?" John motioned at what was obviously a blanket-draped penny-farthing bicycle. There was no mistaking that shape, the over-sized front wheel being almost as tall as a horse's withers.

"What is that?" Mary echoed, her bafflement seeming overdone. Had she known her bicycle was there all along? Was that the true reason she hadn't wanted to explore the outbuilding?

Tongue-in-cheek, Sherlock said, "My, my, what could that penny-farthing bicycle-shaped item, with one enormous wheel and one tiny wheel, possibly be?"

John tossed off the blanket with great excitement, filling the air with a thick cloud of dust. "Why, it's Mary's bicycle. Gladstone has found your bicycle, Mary, by tracking its scent. See how clever he is, Sherlock? Good boy, good job!" John patted Gladstone enthusiastically. Gladstone lapped it up, clueless.

"Yes," Sherlock drawled, not believing it for a second. A much smarter creature had tracked the bicycle. The dog had merely followed the fresh scent of the cat, to the bicycle. It was elementary. Sherlock glanced up again and thought he saw a small dark head with two perky ears peeking over the edge of the loft.

"What is your bicycle doing here, Mary?" John asked, every bit as clueless as his dog.

"Perhaps one of the gardeners stored it here for safekeeping, and forgot to mention it," Mary proposed.

"But we asked all the staff if they had seen the bicycle, or witnessed anyone lurking about it, eyeing it covetously," John said.

Sherlock rubbed his chin, studying Mary. What was she about? Why would she want to steal her own bicycle, hide it, and weep over its loss? Did she truly want a better bicycle? The newer safety models were far superior, and more pleasant to ride. Had she hoped John would purchase her a shiny new and modern bicycle?

Sherlock was fully aware that he did not understand women as well as he did men. He did not consider this a detecting weakness, per se, merely a surplus of logic, which was always a good thing. Only women and fools could understand the female mind, and that was fine by him. Most challenging crimes were perpetrated by men, after all, and he understood men. Women were so much more convoluted than their male counterparts, their minds a twisted maze of mystifying and unpredictable paths, leading to equally befuddling destinations.

Sherlock was still trying to deduce Mary's motivation, when he heard a distinct rustling overhead. He looked up. He could no longer see a small dark head. He did hear a squeak. Several pieces of straw wafted down from above.

John and Mary noticed, as well. "Mice are such resilient creatures," Mary said. "It's impossible to rid the place of them."

"Sherlock, why don't you put that great brain of yours to work, and invent a foolproof trap that will catch mice," John suggested.

"One already exists. It is called a cat," Sherlock said.

They were still gazing up at the loft when a mouse skittered off its edge. It plummeted through the air toward them in a rain of hay. Gladstone let out a great woof and lunged. John was yanked off his feet by the leash, and landed on his knees. Mary scuttled back, showing excellent reflexes, and judgement. Not so, Sherlock. He took too long to move. The mouse landed on his head. Again, Sherlock regretted not donning his detecting cap before he left home. In his defense, he hadn't deemed the mystery of the missing and presumed stolen bicycle a legitimate case. And he had been proven right.

The mouse squeaked its displeasure, not at all happy to find itself on Sherlock's head, so exposed. It opted to dart down his neck, into his shirt. Sherlock squealed, a most embarrassing sound. The mouse tickled his skin something awful and he danced around, yanking and ripping at his clothing. His shirt was properly tucked into his belted trousers, as every civilized Englishman dressed. The mouse could find no egress, but alas, it could descend. It squirmed beneath his belt and reached the nether region inside his trousers. Sherlock tugged more frantically, attempting to free his shirt from his pants.

Gladstone woofed and leapt at Sherlock, joining in the fray with great excitement. If Mrs. Hudson had been there, no doubt she would have been doing the same. She certainly would have lent Sherlock a hand or two, to strip him of his clothing. Sherlock might have even appreciated Mrs. Hudson disrobing him at that point, as a mouse in one's underpants is a frightful affliction.

John lost all control of the stupid dog. Even Mary's command of, "Sit, Gladstone," went unheeded. Gladstone was too frenzied to obey. He bounded about in circles, and his leash became tightly wound about Sherlock's ankles. It was a disaster in the making.

The mouse invading his underpants was the lesser worry when Gladstone knocked into him like a battering ram. Legs tied together,

Sherlock lost his balance. As he went down, such a very long way down, he knew the landing was going to hurt rather badly. And ye gods, was that a freshly sharpened thatch rake, knocked to the ground in the fray, and lying tines up? Alas, it was.

9 - A Frosty Parting

from The Observations of Cat Watson

From the loft, I was witness to Sherlock's unfortunate accident. I am sad to say, it was in part my fault. It is no excuse, but cats lack control where mice are concerned. Mice are our Achilles heel. If I see a mouse, I must pursue it. I have no choice in the matter. And in the loft, I discovered a whole nest of the vermin. I had a grand time, stalking them, closer and closer, until they scented me. I pounced. They fled, willy-nilly, racing about the loft. The dumbest of their number ran right off its edge.

I peeked down, to see what had become of the thing, and there it was, on my Sherlock's head. Neither of them was happy about the situation. The mouse disappeared into his clothing and Sherlock went a bit berserk. He looked like a scarecrow come to life as a marionette, long thin legs and arms jerking spasmodically, every which way. I had previously noted that Sherlock was a most graceful fellow, especially for a human who has no long tail to aid in balance, but you wouldn't know it to see him now.

His antics inspired the idiotic dog to go berserk, too. The end result was that Sherlock took a very nasty tumble. Entirely the dog's fault, of course. The part I played in instigating the happenings was so small, it barely needs mentioning.

My poor Sherlock landed on his behind, on an upturned and wicked-looking thatch rake. The hard metal tines were as pointy as fangs, biting into his bottom. He gave his head a hard whack, too, when he tumbled backwards, with the rake stuck in his behind. The blow to the head did not knock him out, as his shrieking proved.

Below, everyone was in an uproar. Even Dr. Watson, who should be a cool and collected professional in the face of wounds, looked quite undone. Mary was the one to take charge. She called over all the staff within earshot. One dragged the dog away. Two others wrenched the metal tines of the rake from Sherlock's posterior, where it was firmly impaled. There was a great deal more howling, before Sherlock was lifted into a handy garden cart.

At that point, I scrambled down from the loft. I raced over to Sherlock, to offer him my loyal support. I leapt into the cart and perched atop him as he was wheeled toward Dr. Watson's surgery. There was no doubt in anyone's mind that he needed medical treatment.

I was a bit afraid he would be angry with me, over the mouse. As a great detective, surely he would have deduced that I was the culprit responsible for chasing the rodent off the loft. Yet, he gave me a little stroke on the head, and said, "It was all the dog's fault."

I purred in agreement. Sherlock and I were of one mind.

In the doctor's surgery, Sherlock's trousers were dropped, so his wounds could be tended. A dead mouse fell out. The rake had decided its fate, it seemed. Sherlock endured Dr. Watson's cleaning, stitching, and fussing, and more stinging iodine, quite stoically.

I had listened to enough conversations in the street, to know that cats can't see the same range of colours that humans do. I could not see the red of Sherlock's blood. To me, it looked a dark gray, with a tinge of yellow, and there was a fair amount of it. I knew Sherlock's colour was high, too, from the dark hue of his face. His cheeks were so shadowed, they were likely as red as his wounded and exposed below-stairs cheeks. Yet he had grown so withdrawn, I began to worry. What was going on in his mind?

As soon as the last of Dr. Watson's neat little stitches was knotted in place, Sherlock replaced his trousers, ruined though they were. "Thank-you, Dr. Watson. I will take my leave now. Your home has proven most hazardous to my health, so do not expect me to call upon you again," he said haughtily. I think his dignity was as wounded as his bottom, which you will note, I did not actually describe. I wished to spare you the gory details, of not just the four deep puncture wounds, but the bottom itself. Humans, because they lack fur, are not attractive creatures. Thank goodness they wear clothing.

Dr. Watson's face fell. Even his droopy moustache looked particularly disheartened. "I don't think my home is to blame, Sherlock. I do believe it is something smaller and furrier that has caused your troubles."

"Yes, the blame can most certainly be laid at Gladstone's feet … paws." Sherlock tightened his belt with a jerk.

"Not Gladstone. Something a great deal smaller." Dr. Watson raised an eyebrow in my direction, where I was seated on his desk, observing the proceedings.

"Oh, do not dare to blame Cat Watson for this! Gladstone has caused all the pain and suffering I have endured this day. The mystery of the missing and presumed stolen bicycle has been solved, so I will bid you adieu, Dr. Watson." With that, Sherlock tossed on his cloak, which would also need some stitching to repair the tears. He scooped me up and limped from the surgery through the side door, to avoid revisiting the house proper.

I peered back, and could see Dr. Watson's woebegone face, watching Sherlock take his leave. Their relationship had not been repaired, but further torn asunder.

The carriage ride home was an ordeal for Sherlock, with his grievously injured bottom. He kept shifting and wincing, whilst trying not to sit, but half-crouch, and eventually kneel on the floor, as if he was in church, praying.

I could not enjoy the second carriage ride of my life, because I felt so bad for him. When we finally reached home, I trotted after Sherlock as he limped up the stairs like an old man, as if he had aged forty years in the scant hours we had been gone. He was not waylaid by Mrs. Hudson, a great relief to him, I am sure.

We entered his rooms and he immediately locked the door behind him. He poured himself a generous serving of liquor, and downed it in one great gulp. He shuffled into his bedroom, shed all his clothing, except for his socks, and eased himself gently onto his mattress, facedown, of course.

He made a feeble attempt to pull a blanket over himself, but could not seem to manage it. Luckily, he had me, his trusty companion. I gripped the blanket laid across the foot of his bed in my teeth and tugged it over him by degrees. It was no easy task. I had to go back and forth, from side to side, a great number of times, tugging by inches and being most careful not to step on his wounded bottom, but I managed it in the end.

He was not yet fully asleep and gave me an appreciative little stroke on the head. "You are a most remarkable fellow, Cat Watson," he told me. I curled up by his shoulder and began to purr. My Sherlock relaxed into sleep. Well, we both did. I was a cat, after all, not a watchdog.

10 - The Case of the Whacky Widow

Despite the pain of his injuries, Sherlock enjoyed a deep, dreamless sleep. If he had been a fanciful man, he would have believed his new little companion's purr to have magical properties that acted as a balm to the spirit. Alas, the restful slumber was interrupted by a rapping on his door, not overly loud, but a bit too firm to be judged polite.

Hazy light was streaming in through his window. Whether it was the same day or the next morning, Sherlock had no idea at that point. He sat up gingerly and whimpered in pain. Cat Watson was no longer on the bed, or anywhere in sight.

Sherlock rose and stretched stiffly. His bottom protested the movement, as did his bitten leg. Sherlock realized he was in no fit state to welcome any comers. Except for his socks, he was as naked as a newly incarcerated jailbird, post-shower, and made to walk from one end of the prison to the other without a stitch on.

"Easily remedied," he murmured, and donned his robe. It was handy, and softer on his four-times-stabbed bum than trousers. He belted the robe most securely, as a precaution in case Mrs. Hudson accompanied his visitor. A robe adjusting scene did not bear thinking about, when it was all he wore.

Sherlock left his bedroom and glanced at the mantle clock. It was ten, to the minute, the earliest acceptable hour for any civilized person to come calling without an appointment. "Ah, so morning then. I did have a long sleep, Cat Watson," he said. There was no answering meow or purr. Sherlock looked around and didn't see the little cat anywhere in the sitting room. "Cat Watson, where are you?" he called. Still no answer.

Sherlock opened the door to find a woman standing without. He blinked in surprise. In the recesses of his mind, he had been expecting John, and perhaps even looking forward to sharing tea with him. Face-to-face with a lady, he instantly regretted his disheveled state.

His caller was approximately twenty and eight years of age. She was tall and buxom, her hair a brassy shade of blonde. It was piled

35

elaborately high, with a crowd of ringlets draped down about her face for frivolous effect. Her eyes were as dark as burnt tobacco, her lips full and rouged. The gown she wore was a silky black affair, trimmed with purple lace. Widow's weeds. It was ill-fitted, as if she had recently gained a stone or two in weight. The lady was in mourning, which did not explain the weight gain. Widows were supposed to waste away, a bit. Or perhaps she was one of those women who reputedly ate in times of sorrow, though her face didn't droop mournfully, nor were her eyes red from weeping. She clutched no damp handkerchief at the ready, to stifle tears.

"Good morning." Sherlock inclined his head rather stiffly. That is when he noticed Cat Watson at her feet. His jaw may have slackened. He had no idea how the cat had gotten out of his rooms. All the windows had been closed tight against the chill of late autumn.

Sherlock did not like to think that his landlady had opened the door with her key, and come inside, perhaps to gaze upon Sherlock as he slept, especially since he hadn't been wearing his pajamas. He had caught Mrs. Hudson hovering over him once, in the dead of night. It had given him a most unsettled feeling, to be so vulnerable, laid out before her. But perhaps his landlady had merely opened the door to feed Cat Watson, and he had departed with her. Sherlock certainly hoped that was the case.

"Good morning, Mr. Holmes. I am in need of your professional services," the lady said without preamble, and shoved her card at him in an aggressive manner. Quality paper and print. The same could not be said for her hand, which was work-roughened—unusual for a lady of her supposed class.

Before Sherlock had a chance to actually read the card, she added, "I was pacing below, trying to work up the courage to call upon you, the country's greatest consulting detective, when this wee cat patted my foot with a paw, and meowed as if speaking to me. Fanciful, I know, but then, he started walking, glancing back over his shoulder, meowing all the louder, as if I should follow him. Isn't that silly? It was as if he was as intelligent as a dog, and truly did wish to lead me somewhere I ought to go, which was here, to you," she ended breathlessly, after such a long rush of speech. Add to that, the gown that was far too tight to allow for proper breathing, especially with a corset laced beneath.

36

Cat Watson gave an indignant little hiss, and stalked inside. His furry chin jutted pugnaciously, as though he was highly insulted. Sherlock couldn't help but smile. He motioned for the woman to enter. She did and Mrs. Hudson's head popped into view from the stairs, in the manner of a jack-in-the-box. His landlady trotted hurriedly up the last few steps and said, "I'll settle your guest, then fetch tea. You go make yourself presentable, Sherlock dearest, right this minute." An order, if ever he had heard one.

It was unseemly for a gentleman to entertain a lady whilst wearing naught but a robe, yet Sherlock suspected that was not Mrs. Hudson's motivation. More likely, she did not want the other lady ogling his calves, if the widow was the type to do so. He did not feel his calves merited any ogling, being stick-thin and as hairy as coconuts, but there was no accounting for women's tastes.

"Yes, Mrs. Hudson. Thank-you." He was content to make himself scarce, to wash and dress, leaving both women to fuss over Cat Watson. He also took the time to read the lady's card. What was written on it came as no surprise. Well, few things surprised Sherlock.

The name on the card, *Spoonwither*, was familiar. A photograph of Lord Spoonwither, dead in his casket, had appeared in the newspaper two days earlier. It had been a quality photo, making the lord appear alive. Eyes had been artistically painted on his closed lids, as if he was still viewing the world from the comfort of his coffin.

Sherlock had noted that there was something unnatural about the position of the head in regards to the body. The neck appeared overlong, and there had been an indent and bend, where there ought not to have been either. He had assumed the lord had suffered a severely broken neck, riding his horse to hound or some such. The newspaper story had merely reported that the man had died accidentally, one week earlier. Now, Lady Spoonwither had come to call. Sherlock did so hope there was a killing to investigate; nothing like a mysterious murder to lift his spirits.

Upon his return, he found his visitor seated in the client's chair. She was sipping tea with one hand, whilst munching on a scone with the other. It was not how a lady usually ate, but perhaps she was still trying to smother her grief in food.

The pot of tea was steaming on the nearby table, keeping company with a platter that was missing half its scones. Maybe more. Cat Watson was enjoying his fishy tea on the floor, purring as he lapped up what appeared to be sardines in cream. Sherlock suppressed a shudder at the sight of the oily fish floating in thick cream.

Mrs. Hudson lurked by the door, casting the other women suspicious glances behind her back. In turn, Lady Spoonwither was watching his landlady covertly, via a wall mirror. A hard scowl pulled at her mouth. It was not an expression one would expect to find on a newly bereaved widow. It shifted into a polite smile as soon as she spotted Sherlock.

"Thank you for the tea, Mrs. Hudson. I am sure Cat Watson thanks you as well. That will be all for the moment," he said in polite dismissal. Sherlock limped over to close the door with an apologetic smile, saying, "Clients have a right to privacy." Sherlock had no doubt her ear would soon be pressed to the wood on the opposite side, and privacy be damned.

He poured himself tea, and sat as gingerly as if on shards of broken glass, and that is how it felt when his stitches pulled tight. "How may I help you, Lady Spoonwither, now that my clever cat has escorted you to me?" he said.

Cat Watson paused in his eating and looked up, to chirrup happily. He did seem proud of himself for bringing the client to Sherlock.

"It is a sad tale, indeed," the woman began, her words sounding rehearsed. "My husband died recently, you see." She popped the last bite of scone into her mouth and chewed, mouth slightly agape.

Sherlock inclined his head. "I read Lord Spoonwither's obituary in the newspaper, and saw his death photograph. I am sorry for your loss, Lady Spoonwither."

"Yes, yes," she said dismissively.

"How did he die?" Sherlock was eager to get to the crux of the matter.

"He had an illness of the heart. He had been feeling poorly for several days, and on Sunday, late morning, soon after enjoying his breakfast, he suddenly clutched his chest and collapsed." The widow set down her teacup and mimed the chest-clutching action. Given her thrusting, heaving, amply endowed bosom, it was quite indecent. Sherlock hoped his eyes did not bulge at the sight, although he feared they did.

She released her chest and resumed. "Alas, he was poised at the top of our long, marble staircase at the time, so he took a rather nasty tumble backwards." She mimed an enthusiastic shoving motion with both arms. She reclaimed her teacup and continued. "And alas, he must have dislodged the pair of commemorative swords that were mounted on the wall, as he fell backwards down the stairs, for one impaled him through the chest." She set down her teacup again, to make a rather savage stabbing motion, as if holding a sword in two hands.

"How unfortunate," Sherlock murmured.

The widow retrieved her teacup, took a noisy slurp and resumed. "And alas, after rolling head over heels down to the bottom of the stairs, with the sword impaled in his chest, the second sword followed after him, clattering and bouncing down the marble steps. Can you believe, it chopped him clean through the neck, severing his head completely from his body." Her teacup clinked down into the saucer once again, and she mimed chopping off a head, in the manner of an enthusiastic axeman at an execution.

"Such misfortune," Sherlock said, for wont of anything cleverer to say.

Her teacup was reclaimed before she added, "Luckily, his head landed in a bucket of water. A servant had left it on the floor at the base of the stairs, for the purpose of mopping, I'm sure. The bucket's convenient placement did save the floor from a great deal of messy blood, as a severed head will roll around like a ball, I am sure. Heads are quite round, aren't they?"

Before she could add to the tale, which was simply ludicrous, Sherlock raised a hand for silence. He could not bear to hear another word of nonsense. Women! They did not have a clue how to give a proper account of a traumatic event. "Heads are more egg-shaped than round, but yes, they will still roll." Sherlock had seen it happen in *The Adventure of the Engineer's Head*. John had written up that tale for The Strand, but it had never been published. The editor had deemed it too gruesome for the average reader to enjoy reading over their breakfast eggs.

Cat Watson sprang up onto Sherlock's lap, to better watch the client, while he washed his face. He smelled strongly of sardines and Sherlock fed him a little bite of scone dipped in his own tea, to cleanse the cat's palette. He said, "Were you witness to your husband's fall, impaling, and subsequent beheading, Lady Spoonwither?"

"Why yes, I was indeedy. I saw the whole thing."

"Did you not faint at the sight of so much carnage and bloodshed?" Sherlock asked.

She thought about that for a moment. "No. Should I have done?"

"You are a lady, so yes, it would be expected."

"Well, I did not."

"I see. How brave of you," he commended. "Did anyone else in your household witness the accident?"

"No," she said quickly. "No-one else was about. Not a single soul. The servants attend Sunday service, midday, every Sunday."

"Yet, a bucket of water was left at the base of the main stairs?" That did seem odd to Sherlock.

"One of the young housemaids, she is a forgetful girl, head in the clouds. Always leaving buckets of wash water everywhere she goes." Lady Spoonwither flapped her hand around her own head, as if pestered by flies.

"I see." Sherlock steepled his fingers and propped his chin on them to think. Cat Watson meowed, managing to sound suspicious. The cat was in agreement that the tale was rather fishy, for want of a better word.

"Why have you come to see me? Do you suspect someone of murdering your husband?" Sherlock asked, perhaps a bit too eagerly.

The woman's eyes widened in alarm. "Oh no. No, no, no. He wasn't murdered. It was an accident. I saw it with my own eyes, as I have already told you, and the peelers. They agreed it was an unfortunate accident." *Peelers* seemed an odd word for a highborn lady to use in regard to the police constabulary. Her voice dropped to just above a whisper. "I have come to seek your detecting expertise on another matter."

Sherlock raised one eyebrow inquiringly. He had been much interested in the possibility of murder.

The woman leaned a bit closer. "He's hidden it all."

"He? Your late husband?" Sherlock surmised.

"Yes, him."

"And the all? What has he hidden?"

"Everything. Every coin and note, and the family jewels, they're all missing from our safe. My husband didn't trust banks, you see, and kept everything of value in our little vault, but now he's dead and the vault is empty. He has secreted it all away. I have no idea where, or why he hid it. But now that he's dead and buried, it must be found. By you, I am hoping."

Sherlock stroked Cat Watson. "I shall have to examine your home for clues as to where the missing items might be found."

"Of course," the woman said. "Can you come now?"

Sherlock looked down at Cat Watson, who meowed encouragingly. "I am available at the moment. Do you have a carriage waiting?"

"I do." The widow rose with alacrity. She was certainly eager to get her hands on her riches. Sherlock donned his cloak, and his detecting cap, since he was on a case. He picked up Cat Watson and headed for the door. She waited for him to open it, and said, "You are bringing your cat along?"

"Yes, he is my companion."

"I see," said the woman. "You should get him a little collar and leash then, so you could walk him like a wee doggie."

Cat Watson hissed and showed his pointy white teeth. "I don't think he would like to be put on a leash, like a dog," Sherlock said.

He was surprised to find the landing outside the door quite empty. No Mrs. Hudson. Then again, their departure had been announced, so she had had plenty of time to scuttle down the stairs.

The carriage that awaited them was a Clarence, as befitted a lady of standing. It was shiny and black with a polished golden coat-of-arms, and pulled by two gleaming black steeds. Cat Watson gave a long low meow. It sounded rather like an impressed whistle, not that cats could whistle, lacking lips that could pucker.

The coachman hopped down at their appearance. He opened the door, as no footmen accompanied the conveyance. They settled on seats that were so luxuriously padded, Sherlock had no need for the cushion he had been tempted to bring along. He had opted not to, for the sake of his dignity.

Half an hour later, they were stepping into an impressive mansion, which the woman identified as Wither Hall. Surprisingly, the coachman ran ahead to open the door for them. He even followed them inside. Lady Spoonwither explained. "I gave all the household staff, except for my coachman, the day off. I do not want them to know about the hidden riches. If they did, they would be searching the mansion from top to bottom, wouldn't they? And making off with whatever they could carry."

"A wise precaution." Sherlock eyed the coachman, who stood by the door, arms crossed. He was a strong, tall, rough-looking fellow. The livery he wore was ill-fitted, being far too small for his muscular frame. It was so small in fact, several seams had split.

"Oh, I trust Barns completely. He is aware of the situation," the lady said, observing Sherlock's gaze lingering on the coachman.

Sherlock turned to survey the grand foyer, and the long, wide, marble staircase that curved into it from high above. Halfway down the impressive flight of stairs, a pair of decorative swords were mounted on the wall. They were quite high up, at least eight feet above the steps. Sherlock had a hard time imagining how a falling body could have bounced so high, it would have dislodged those swords. Even flailing arms or legs should not have been able to knock them off the wall.

He pointed at them. "Are those the swords that impaled your husband, and severed off his head?"

"That they are," Lady Spoonwither said.

"Were they mounted exactly there, before the accident?" he asked.

"Yes, they have been cleaned, and restored to their proper place." She tossed the gloves she had been carrying, but had never donned, onto the nearest table, as there was no handy servant to take them.

Sherlock walked to the base of the staircase and looked up. "It is surprising that the swords had enough heft behind them to impale a man and chop off his head. Swords are not overly heavy weapons. Most are fashioned to be as light as possible. It makes them easier to wield and hold aloft in long confrontations." He turned back to face his client. "He fell down the stairs backwards, from the very top?"

"Mr. Holmes, I have not brought you here to relive my husband's tragic accident," Lady Spoonwither said sharply, spots of colour appearing on her cheeks. "You are here to find what he has hidden away. Jewels, coins, banknotes."

"Of course, Lady Spoonwither." Sherlock inclined his head. "You have already searched for them, of course?"

"Everywhere. Under his bed, beneath his mattress, in his wardrobe, in his trunk, in his tobacco tin, in his boots, in his shaving kit …"

While the lady continued to list the feeblest of hiding spots, not surprising given her sex, Sherlock removed his cloak and draped it over the bannister. He set his detecting cap on the post, for want of a better spot. As soon as she fell silent, he said, "Was your husband a clever man, Lady Spoonwither?"

"In truth, no. He was sound in business, rather pedantic, liked his routines, reserved, quiet …"

Sherlock stopped paying attention to her listing of lame attributes, when he noticed Cat Watson behaving oddly. The cat was sniffing along the base of the stairs in the manner of a bloodhound following a scent, but without all the baying and drooling and wild tail-wagging.

Cat Watson made his way toward Lady Spoonwither, nose to the ground. He circled her. She didn't notice, being occupied with describing her late husband in as many words as possible. Women were like that. What could be said in one or two succinct phrases, would take them a thousand words, if not an entire book's worth.

Cat Watson headed back to the staircase, and sat down at its base, as if waiting. Sherlock listened with half an ear to his verbose client, as she said, "He liked doing crossword puzzles, and he did like reading your adventures in The Strand, when Dr. Watson used to write them. He said how clever you were. What happened to Dr. Watson? Why doesn't he accompany you on your cases any longer? Or publish accounts of your adventures? Did you replace him with a cat?" She finally fell silent, waiting for an answer, or answers.

"Dr. Watson got married. I am not sad and lonely without him," Sherlock snapped, to be clear. "And my cat is proving to be a most agreeable replacement and companion, although he has yet to script a tale." It was meant to be a jest.

The cat in question meowed in enthusiastic agreement, as if he would indeed like to chronicle Sherlock's adventures. Barns took a step closer—too close. He didn't smell much like horse to be a coachman. "You should get to finding the missing loot," he said in a growl.

Sherlock glanced at his client for confirmation, since he was not about to take orders from her servant. She bobbed her head enthusiastically. "Barns is right."

Sherlock and Cat Watson shared a speaking glance, not that cats could speak. It was becoming clear to Sherlock that this case was not as straightforward as finding some misplaced valuables. Something more nefarious was afoot, he simply wasn't sure what as yet. "Well then, let me start by having a look at the vault," he said agreeably, turning away from the staircase.

The lady and the coachman shared their own speaking glance. It was not hard for Sherlock to interpret. The pair didn't want him to visit the safe-hold, and they seemed too closely allied for a highborn lady and a servant. Perhaps they were carrying on a torrid affair.

"No need to look in the vault," the lady said. "Nothing to see there. The safe is quite empty, and it's a bit broken, because I couldn't remember the combination to open the lock. Silly me. So we had to break in. Smashed the door right off the hinges." She giggled like a girl.

Sherlock looked quite aghast. "There was no need for such extreme actions. Why, opening safes is a hobby of mine. I could have opened it for you, with no damage whatsoever."

The widow shrugged. "Oh well, too late for that now. Why don't you start by searching his lordship's bedroom, and his study? I think he would have hidden the valuables—our valuables—near to hand."

"As you wish," Sherlock said, cooperating while he scanned for clues and mulled over what was truly going on. "Please show me to his rooms. The bedroom first, I should think."

The lady, who he was strongly beginning to suspect was no lady at all, led him up the stairs. The coachman, who was probably no such thing, walked behind Sherlock, as if herding him like a wayward sheep. No-one paid any attention to Cat Watson, who brought up the rear. Their little parade reached the top of the grand staircase and the lady turned right. The parade followed, minus one cat. No-one except Sherlock noticed Cat Watson slip away to explore on his own.

11 - The Haunted Armour

I had a very bad feeling inside, and it had not a thing to do with rotten fish. My diet had improved greatly of late, and I had no tummy troubles. No, the bad feeling had all to do with the so-called lady and her so-called coachman. As soon as we entered the mansion, it became obvious to me that both were imposters. Sherlock finally seemed to be clueing in. It had taken him long enough, given that he was a brilliant detective. I blamed that lapse in judgement on the previous day's hard blow to his head, if not the traumatic injuries to his bottom.

I will explain how I knew our client was a charlatan. Cats, as I have previously mentioned, have a nose that is far superior to that of humans, and dogs, of course. Each person smells inherently like their home, or the place where they spend the most time, if they do not have a home. This lady did not smell enough like the mansion to live in it. The coachman barely reeked of horse at all, so he did not spend a great deal of time in the stables. Both were lying, carrying out a ruse. Treasure hunting for treasure that was not theirs, I surmised.

If you are wondering what had become of the true lady of the house, and all the servants, I was, too. So when Sherlock and the imposters turned right at the top of the staircase, I catted away, to investigate.

I am a light-pawed cat, as are all of my kind, so no-one except Sherlock noticed when I slunk down the grand stairs we had just ascended. I had a good sniff around, starting in the enormous kitchen and dining room, progressing through the ballroom and music room and several studies and a library and a withdrawing room and a drawing room, etc. The place was enormous. I didn't know if all mansions are so huge, as it was my first time in one, but it could have housed hundreds of humans and thousands upon thousands of cats, with ease.

I picked up the recent scent trail of several humans, all moving in the same direction. I followed it to a closed door at the very back of the house, adjacent to a mudroom. I knew at once that it led to the cellar. Those below-ground spaces always have a distinctive damp, moldy, and earthy smell. Oh, how I wished I could have opened that door, for with my keen ears, I was able to hear a lot of peculiar noises. Human from the sound of it, yet muffled. I suspected there was a small crowd of bound and gagged servants below stairs, and possibly even Lord Spoonwither's true widow. A very dark plot was unfolding in the grand manor, and my Sherlock was in the thick of it.

I raced back upstairs, hoping he had not been harmed. I found him in a large bedroom. It was furnished with heavy, dark wood cabinets and a kingly four-poster bed. Sherlock was walking the perimeter, looking the walls up and down. He was being closely observed by the villainous pair of would-be robbers. I edged up to Sherlock and meowed once, quietly. He glanced down, brow furrowed.

"Where's your cat been?" the woman asked, rather suspiciously I thought.

"I have no clue." Sherlock scooped me up and held me protectively. I felt much safer in his arms. The coachman had very big boots, bigger than me, and he looked the sort to enjoy kicking small animals. "I see no sign that the items you seek are hidden in this room," Sherlock said, "or in the valet's adjoining closet of a room. I will investigate Lord Spoonwither's study next, if you will escort me to it."

"Of course, Mr. Holmes," the woman said.

Sherlock and I between them, the pair shepherded us down the grand staircase. We entered a room I had not been able to explore, as the door had been shut. Still holding me, Sherlock stepped inside and turned in a circle, scrutinizing Lord Spoonwither's study with his eyes. After taking it all in, he toured the perimeter at a snail's pace.

It was, in décor, much like the lord's bedroom. There was a great deal of heavy dark wood furniture, including an over-sized desk that put Dr. Watson's functional little writing table to shame. A bookshelf dominated one wall, from floor to ceiling. Its shelves were crowded with leather-bound volumes. In the corner beside it, stood a full suit of armour, as if there was a man inside. It was displayed holding a hefty great sword in both hands, raised high, as if about to cleave a foe's skull in two. It was probably a valuable antique and family

46

heirloom. The suit of armour, with its visor at half-mast, seemed to be looking right at me. It was eerie and I felt the fur on my back begin to rise.

In addition to the scent of paper and leather and furniture polish, and the metal of the armour, I could smell something else quite strongly. The ink used to print banknotes has a unique and distinct fragrance, and that's what I was detecting. I dug my claws into the back of Sherlock's hand, politely, to signal I had discovered something of import.

He paused in his tour of the room, appearing to read the spines of some of the books. The suit of armour stood beside him, as if they were keeping company. "Many of these volumes are well thumbed. Your husband liked to read, I take it," Sherlock commented to the woman.

"He did," she agreed, without elaborating.

"Which were his favourite books?"

"Oh, I don't know. He was always reading one or another. I didn't pay much mind. They all look about the same, don't they? And I'm not much of a reader myself, being a woman and all." Her self-deprecation did not ring true.

Sherlock nodded in full agreement. It was becoming clear to me that he truly did not hold women in esteem. I felt he was underestimating the threat his client posed, based on her sex alone. I squirmed so he would set me down. He did, and I paced closer to the suit of armour, as nonchalantly as possible, not that people usually pay attention to what cats are about, unless they have leapt onto the dinner table to gnaw on the leg of a goose, or lap up the cream intended for tea, or drag away a dinner fish by its tail.

The smell of the printing ink was definitely stronger by the armour's metal feet. I circled behind it and crouched low in the shadows, peering out from between the legs. The two imposters weren't paying me any mind at all. I think Sherlock was trying to see what I was doing, out of the corner of his eye, as he pretended to examine a book he had taken down from the shelf.

"I wonder if his lordship hollowed out some of the larger, less favoured volumes, in which to hide away his valuables," he mused. Was he attempting to mislead the pair watching him, and distract them from trying to spot me? Or was he simply way off track, because of that blow to his head?

47

While all the humans in the room proceeded to remove the largest books from the shelves and open them to look inside, I decided to infiltrate the armour. I was plenty small enough to do so. If I could carry out a coin, and I could smell gold coins as well as banknotes, hidden in my mouth, and drop it into the detective's palm, he would know I had located the treasure. If he produced the riches, Sherlock and I should be allowed to go on our way, unharmed, acting like we were clueless to what was truly going on. Once safely away from the mansion, if Sherlock had deduced the truth, he could summon one of the inspectors Dr. Watson had mentioned. Lestrade, or Gregson, I think it was, to capture the villains before they made their escape.

I hopped soundlessly up onto the desk, then climbed the curtains, my claws doing fair damage to the fine silk cloth, I am sad to say. From there, I leapt nimbly onto the suit of armour's shoulder. Things did not go as I had envisioned, I am even sadder to say. The metal of the armour was very slippery indeed, like ice. I slid against one of the upraised arms, posed holding the sword. The arms must have been very precariously balanced indeed. They were not held in place with wire, or mounted on armatures, or any internal structure at all. The arms, still holding the sword, began to drop fast. It was as if the armour truly was a knight in the flesh, slashing down at a helpless victim. Alas, the only victim before the armour was Sherlock, crouched low to remove a particularly large volume from the very bottom shelf of the bookcase.

Terrified of what was about to unfold, and not wishing to witness it, I darted into the helmet through the half-raised visor. It made it fall closed and it caught the tip of my tail. I emitted a tremendous yowl, which echoed around in the armour, sounding all the louder. Inside the armour was as slippery as outside. I slid right through the neck hole and dropped into the belly, as if the armour had swallowed me whole.

Outside the armour, there was a loud thud, followed by a squeal of pain. It sounded like my Sherlock. I howled in distress for his misfortune, hoping his head had not been lopped off. I thrashed around, trying to find an egress. Cats do not like being confined. As a species, we are claustrophobic creatures. The whole suit of armour rattled and shook around me, its metal joints making a boisterous clattering din.

The woman screamed, "It's his ghost! Lord Spoonwither has come back from the dead to kill us for killing him. He'll stick us with that blade, and haunt us into our graves and beyond." A great deal of hysterical shrieking ensued—the woman's, in concert with Sherlock's cries of pain. I was actually happy to hear his cries, as it meant that his head was still attached to his shoulders, and functioning. There was another, softer thud, then dead silence, but hopefully not *dead* silence. Hopefully not Sherlock's head sliding off his shoulders to thud to the floor.

I squirmed around, going a bit lower. I managed to peak out through the crotch, where there was no armour, merely a gap in the stuffing that filled the underpants area. The stuffing proved to be banknotes and coins and jewelry, in several cotton sacks, or perhaps they were pillowcases.

Sherlock was down, and bleeding from the upper arm, rather profusely. The woman was prostate on the floor, as pale as a ghost herself, eyes closed and face slack. She was out cold. Her big companion was nowhere to be seen, but I heard big boots clomping away, and distant cries of terror. Barns must have fled from the imaginary ghost, which had simply been a cat in a suit of armour.

No longer endangered, I clawed a banknote out of the sack. It was clasped between my teeth when I leapt out through the crotch of the armour and approached Sherlock. He was seated on the floor, clutching his arm, trying to staunch the welling blood. I laid the banknote on his knee and meowed most apologetically. He sighed and said, "Well done, Cat Watson, but I do wish you had not almost chopped my arm off. I will need Dr. Watson's services again this day, it seems."

I meowed in agreement, rubbed against him affectionately, and dashed away as quick as my four legs could carry me, which was very quick indeed. When I returned to him, he hadn't moved. I was carrying a kitchen towel in my teeth, and dropped it on his knee.

"Thank-you," he said and proceeded to bind it tightly around his wounded upper arm.

I could not help with that and checked to make sure the woman, who was no lady, was still unconscious. She was, and a key on a chain was visible, around her neck. I could guess what that key opened, and tugged hard on the chain with my teeth. Sherlock observed what I was trying to do and leaned closer, without standing.

"What does that unlock, Cat Watson?" he said through gritted teeth. He opened the chain with a great deal of fumbling, due to his injury, and freed the key. I padded to the door, and looked over my shoulder. I meowed for him to accompany me, if he was up to the task. Sherlock struggled to his feet, staggered a bit, and followed me.

To make a long tale short, I led him to the cellar door and he unlocked it. As soon as the household staff and the true Lady Spoonwither had been freed from their bonds, the imposter widow was tied up. The coppers were summoned, and the villain was turned over to one Inspector Lestrade, who seemed a very broody sort of fellow. The supposed coachman, Barns, was long gone. Constables searched for him, and he was nowhere to be found.

All had ended well. One of the villains had been captured, the prisoners had been rescued, and even Lord Spoonwither's riches had been found. It turned out the imposter was a recently employed housemaid, who was in fact a killer that the police had been hunting for some time.

Her method of operation, working with Barns, her accomplice, was to kill off the head of the family, and while the entire household was attending the funeral services, she and Barns would make off with all the family's jewels, money and riches kept in the house.

At Wither Hall, things had not gone as planned for the thieves. During Lord Spoonwither's funeral, they had broken into the mansion's vault, only to find it empty. They were still searching when the family returned and caught them red-handed. They had tied everyone up at gunpoint and stashed them in the cellar, then resumed their search of the mansion, without luck.

The faux housemaid must have read of Sherlock's detecting skills in The Strand, and she had had the brilliant idea of using Sherlock to find the missing riches. A big mistake on her part, as it turned out.

The true lady of the manor had thanked Sherlock most profusely for saving them, and finding her husband's hidden store of riches. She had rewarded the detective generously, even though she wasn't his actual client.

Banknotes stowed in his pocket, Sherlock was assisted to a waiting police carriage. It whisked him away to Dr. Watson's surgery as fast as the horses could dash through the streets of London. I went with Sherlock, of course, perched on his lap, and hoping he had truly forgiven me for the part I had played in his … let's call it an accident.

12 - A Storm in a Teacup

The carriage ride seemed long and Sherlock was inclined to drowse, not because he was sleepy, but because he was weak. He managed to give the cat on his lap a few feeble pats, and said, "Well done, Cat Watson. I could have done without being sliced by a broadsword, but it is preferable to being shot through the heart. The coachman carried a pistol, tucked into his belt, you know. I believe he intended to use it on me, whether or not I—we—had found the riches that dastardly pair were seeking."

Sherlock felt as frail as a woman when the police constable who had chauffeured him to Dr. Watson's surgery, assisted him from the carriage. It was early afternoon, and the sun was shining brightly as the young fellow walked him to the side door, a hand tucked firmly under his elbow so Sherlock wouldn't fall flat on his face.

He was aware of Cat Watson trailing rather morosely behind. It was true, the cat had been the cause of his latest and gravest wound, and possibly the previous day's four-time-stabbed-bottom debacle, but Sherlock truly didn't hold it against him. Cat Watson had been a big help in Wither Manor. He had located the riches, and led Sherlock unerringly to the hostages, when he was in no fit state to explore the entirety of the enormous mansion. And the cat's antics in the suit of armour had likely saved Sherlock from a much worse fate, at the hands of the murderess and her gun-toting companion. They had killed Lord Spoonwither, many times over after all, given the imposter's lively description of the man's death. And according to police, a number of other poor souls had met their end at the hands of the scoundrels.

The constable hammered on the door until Dr. Watson opened it. "Sherlock, you look terrible. What has happened now?" he cried. Surgeon or not, he couldn't fail to notice the blood that was dripping down Sherlock's arm to splat on his doorstep. The makeshift bandage was so sodden, it could no longer contain a single drop.

The young constable was the one to answer. "From all accounts, Mr. Holmes has been stabbed with a sword, by that there cat." He pointed down at Cat Watson, who cringed.

"Really?" John drawled. "And Gladstone nowhere in the vicinity at the time?"

Sherlock scowled. "If you intend to keep me standing on your doorstep, whilst I bleed to death, I shall take my leave and find a more amenable physician." He wobbled where he stood.

John immediately turned earnest. "Bring him in, quickly. Sherlock, sit there." He gestured to his treatment table. Sherlock found himself assisted inside, and he was happy to get off his feet, but not happy to plant his bottom on the hard treatment table. The constable immediately took his leave, to return to the more interesting crime scene at Wither Manor, no doubt.

John hollered for Mary to bring brandy, and he gathered together the necessary supplies. As he unwrapped the sodden kitchen towel, Mary hurried in, a full bottle clutched in her hand. "What has happened to Sherlock now?" she gasped.

"Stabbed with a sword, by the cat, apparently."

"I find that hard to believe," Mary said.

"As do I, but stranger things … pour him a generous amount of brandy. I think he is going into shock," John said.

"Don't be ridiculous. I am not going into shock. I am a man, not a swooning lady," Sherlock declared. He noticed Cat Watson, cowering on John's desk, ears down. Clearly, he was still sad and worried.

Mary tucked a blanket over Sherlock. He was shivering a bit, although it wasn't cold in the surgery. He extended his uninjured arm and crooked a finger at the cat. Cat Watson hopped down from the desk and up onto his lap. His little mewls sounded like cat cries. Mary handed Sherlock the glass of brandy and he drank it down. Warmth flooded him, from the brandy and the cat's small heat, and the larger wool blanket, of course.

He was feeling much steadier as John got to work, cleaning and stitching, and talking. "Once I've got you sorted, Sherlock, your payment for my services will be to tell me how a cat that can't weigh any more than a boot, was able to stab you with a sword."

Sherlock managed to say, through clenched teeth, "If I survive your heavy-handed ministrations, that is not a tale I will ever tell. And it wasn't Cat Watson's fault. He's the best companion a man could wish for. I think he saved my life, by stabbing me with that sword. A cat in armour, isn't that ridiculous." He chuckled weakly, which was not like him at all. Perhaps he was somewhat lightheaded from blood-loss.

"If you say so." John gave the thread an ungentle tug and Sherlock screamed, a bit.

"Is he delirious?" Mary asked, as if Sherlock had been struck deaf.

"He's something, all right." John's words were laced with frustration. "To turn up on my doorstep, bleeding like a stuck pig, and expect me to work a miracle. To say that scrap of fur is a better companion than me. Why, in all our years together, I never stabbed him with a sword, as much as I may have wished to, too many times to count." John gave a harrumph of disgust.

"I know it hurts your feelings, dearest." Mary stroked John's arm. "I'm sure he doesn't mean it."

"I fear he does. Well, I will stitch him up, bandage him, but after that, I am washing my hands of him, as he has washed his hands of me. Replaced me with a cat, for god's sake. Named the cat after me, adding insult to injury." John continued to grumble with gusto, occasionally spraying spittle on Sherlock's wound. The detective hoped the latest medical theory he had read, that infections were caused by germs transferred via contact, and not by a mysterious and evil miasma in the air, was wrong.

Mary said, "I will fetch tea, now. I think we could all do with a cuppa." She left them alone.

Sherlock was about to tell John that he did value their friendship tremendously, and did not, in truth, believe a cat, even a cat as special as Cat Watson, could replace him, but alas, he did not have a chance. Mary had not latched the door tight and Gladstone barreled into the room, baying rabidly. John shouted, "No, no, no, Gladstone," to no avail. The beast kept coming, straight at Sherlock, or the cat. Probably both.

There was a great deal of fresh pain, when the dangling thread stitching Sherlock's arm back together was yanked on hard by Gladstone's paw. Sherlock screamed. John shouted and tried to cut the thread free. Mary ran back into the room and tried to subdue Gladstone. Gladstone howled all the louder, and the cat hissed and spit and launched itself at the dog, in defense of Sherlock. It was sheer pandemonium on a scale usually reserved for a battlefield, not a doctor's surgery. Sherlock looked down at the thread yanking on his gaping wound, making it gape all the wider, and alas, he fainted like a woman.

When he returned to consciousness, the worst was over. The surgery was blessedly silent, except for the soothing and familiar sound of a quill scratching on paper. It was a sound he would have known anywhere—John's scribblings. Was he scripting another of Sherlock's adventures? Hopefully not this particular one. The world's greatest detective should never be stabbed by a cat, or made to faint by the stupidest dog in the land.

Gladstone was gone, thank heavens, and Sherlock's latest wound was neatly bandaged from elbow to armpit. The buzzing and dizziness in his head was no longer there. He was reclining on the treatment table, with Cat Watson curled up and purring on his chest. The sun was still high in the sky, so he hadn't been unawares for very long at all.

He sat up and adjusted his ruined shirt, attempting to restore his battered dignity. John, sitting at his desk, glanced up when he stirred. "How are you feeling, Sherlock?"

Sherlock nodded primly. "Perfectly well, no thanks to your horrible hound."

"Gladstone is not horrible, and you're one to talk. You have adopted a cat that stabs you with swords, although how that came about, I cannot fathom. How did it happen, Sherlock?" John was most curious, Sherlock could tell.

Cat Watson gave a little hiss in John's direction. Sherlock deigned not to answer the question, and said, "I do thank you for suturing my arm, although it is nothing that a woman with a handy needle and a bit of thread couldn't have done."

John glowered quite ferociously. "Such gratitude. Why don't I rip the stitches out then, and you can go off and find yourself a seamstress, and test your theory."

Sherlock rose, such a long way up. Without a doubt, he was a little unsteady on his feet. "No, thank you. Your dog has already ripped them out once. I'm sure that will suffice. I will take my leave now. You can send me a bill for your services." It was an insult to be sure. As friends, John had never billed Sherlock, nor would he.

Sherlock wasn't sure why he was being so nasty to John. It wasn't like him, at least he hoped not. Perhaps it was his wounded dignity, which needed some bolstering, or maybe he was embarrassed about all the screaming he had done. Or maybe it was the resentment he felt toward John for abandoning him, still buried deep within, leaching out.

He struggled awkwardly into his cloak, which had been draped over his shoulders when he arrived at John's surgery. He only inserted his undamaged arm, leaving the other sleeve dangling empty. John did not offer any assistance. Sherlock set his detecting hat on his head. It had miraculously come along with him, too.

He scooped his new crime-solving companion off the treatment table with his healthy arm. "Good afternoon, Dr. Watson," he said stonily, and departed through the side door. It was close at hand, and he had no desire to risk the house and suffer through a second encounter with Gladstone.

Sherlock hailed himself a cab, relieved one happened by so quickly. He definitely wasn't up to a long walk, or even a short stroll, or even standing for any prolonged period to await a cab. All he wanted was his bed, some proper sleep, and perhaps a gently purring cat.

13 - The Mystery of the One-eyed Jack

Once again, Sherlock was roused from sleep by a frantic knocking on his door. It was alarmingly reminiscent of the previous day. He sat up. Cat Watson was nowhere in sight. He rose and stretched stiffly. His bottom protested the movement, his arm more so. "Cat Watson?" he called, donning his robe over his pajamas. No little cat meowed in answer.

Sherlock limped through the sitting room and opened the door to find a familiar and scruffy lad without, shifting impatiently from one foot to the other. At least he wasn't accompanied by his entourage of little ruffians, as Sherlock was feeling less than hearty. Wiggins did not wait for an invitation. He tumbled inside as soon as the door swung wide.

Sherlock was surprised to see a familiar black cat trail in after him, almost like his shadow. How was the cat getting out? "Wiggins, what are you doing with Cat Watson?" Sherlock shut the door quickly, before Mrs. Hudson could sail in and do some robe adjusting.

Wiggins, the tousle-haired street urchin of about twelve, blinked up at him blankly. "Dr. Watson? He's a cat now? 'ow did he turn into a cat? Black magic, I'll bet! Least he came back, even if he is a cat, since you was so sad and lonely without him."

"I was not so sad and lonely without Dr. Watson. And Cat Watson in not Dr. Watson. Cat Watson is a cat, and my new companion." Sherlock gestured showily at the little scrap of fur.

Wiggins scrunched up his dirty, freckled nose. "I didn't see no cat following me, not 'til I came up the stairs. He's a sneaky one, that Cat Watson, but he's really a cat, you say? Not Dr. Watson in disguise, like when you wears one of them disguises, like that big moustache, so nobody knows who you is?"

Sherlock rubbed his temple. "My disguises are clever, admittedly, yet I do not think a disguise exists that could transform a five foot, and eight-inch-tall man like Dr. Watson, into a cat no larger than a loaf of bread."

"So that cat is really a cat?" Wiggins was not always quick to grasp certain concepts.

"He is truly a cat, and an uncommonly clever one at that," Sherlock attested. "Although I have no idea how he got out, again." All the windows had been closed and bolted. Unless it truly was Mrs. Hudson letting him out.

Wiggins was hopping from one foot to the other again. "Mr. Holmes, I've got a case for you. It's important. Real important, I tells you true." He yanked off his soiled cap to wring it between his equally soiled hands.

Sherlock sighed. "Wiggins, sit in the client's chair." He went to the door and opened it. Mrs. Hudson was standing without, as expected.

She smiled and licked her lips. "Good morning, Sherlock dearest."

"Tea, if you please, Mrs. Hudson." He shut the door. He opened it again. "Good morning, Mrs. Hudson." He closed it again.

He washed and dressed, and when he returned to the parlour, Wiggins was on the floor playing with Cat Watson, who was chasing a string being dragged along the carpet. Sherlock suspected the cat was merely humouring the boy.

Mrs. Hudson had impeccable timing, arriving with the tea tray. She set it on the table. Sherlock was not surprised to see two hefty sandwiches, for Wiggins. He was a skinny lad who never had enough to eat, and Mrs. Hudson was a kind-hearted soul. Sherlock nudged Wiggins with his toe. Wiggins blinked, and said, "Oh, I thanks you Mrs. Hudson, for the grand sandwiches. I'll gobble 'em right up, I will, every last bitty crumb."

Mrs. Hudson smiled down at the boy. "I am sure you will, and you are most welcome, Wiggins." She set a dish of fish on the floor for Cat Watson, taking her time about it and bending more that was necessary, presenting her bottom. Sherlock looked away. Duties taken care of, she departed, swinging her hips from side-to-side in an exaggerated manner.

Sherlock sat down gingerly and poured tea. He knew Wiggins never dropped by without good reason, well, not unless he was particularly starved. When the boy was finished wolfing down the sandwiches, and his mouth was no longer stuffed full of bread and meat and cheese and pickle, Sherlock said, "Tell me about the case, Wiggins."

Cat Watson, having licked his little dish clean, was hovering around the boy's chair, daintily nibbling fallen crumbs, cleaning the carpet. He was proving to be the most useful of companions.

The boy swiped his filthy sleeve across his mouth, and said, "I been waiting to. But I was being as polite as a lord, not talking with me mouth all stuffed full. I knows you don't like that."

"True. The case, Wiggins," Sherlock prompted.

Wiggins dug into his pocket and carelessly yanked out a pistol. Sherlock froze. Even Cat Watson sidled away. "Do have a care with that pistol, Wiggins." Sherlock's tone was calm, not wishing to alarm the boy. "Is it loaded? Perchance?"

Wiggins pulled a face and shrugged. "How's would I know? I ain't never laid so much as a finger on no pistol a'fore."

Sherlock slowly reached out to take the weapon. Wiggins handed it over, barrel aimed directly at Sherlock's chest. The detective did not breathe a sigh of relief, until he had possession of the pistol. He checked the cylinder. Three of the five chambers did indeed contain bullets, loaded and ready.

Wiggins had been very lucky not to have shot himself in the leg, or shot Sherlock dead. The gunpowder smell was strong. The weapon had been fired very recently. It looked to be the same model as Watson's old service weapon, an M1872 Mark III Adams revolver, issued to him when he was in the Second Afghan War. Watson had always carried it when they were investigating their more dangerous cases.

Sherlock removed the remaining three bullets and laid the pistol beside the tea tray. "Where did you come by this weapon, Wiggins?"

"I found it," the urchin declared with evasive eyes, and far too much bravado.

"Did you perchance find it in a gentleman's coat pocket?" Sherlock studied his nails, which did need a proper cleaning after all his latest trials.

"That fellow weren't dressed like no gentleman. His coat was torn and muddy, like he'd been in a brawl," Wiggins blurted, before he could hold his tongue.

"Where did you find the pistol, besides in the not-a-gentleman's pocket?"

58

"Not so far away. Just around the corner on Dorset, towards them little shops."

Cat Watson leapt onto Sherlock's lap, ears perked. "Describe the fellow in whose pocket you found this recently fired pistol," Sherlock said.

Wiggins scratched his nose, picking it a bit at the same time. "Well, he wasn't as tall as you."

"Few men are, and no women that I have ever met," Sherlock said.

"And he wasn't as skinny as a stick, like you is. Can I hold the cat?"

Sherlock handed Cat Watson over, saying, "I am not skinny. I am lean with muscle, and generally very fit." Although he could not lay claim to heartiness at that moment.

Wiggins stroked Cat Watson and said, "And his nose didn't stick out like a bird's beak, like yours does."

"My nose does not protrude that much!" Sherlock felt his nose, rather offended. It was his strongest feature, to be sure, but nowhere near as jutting as a hawk's beak, although sparrows did have smaller beaks. Perhaps it was akin to a sparrow's beak. No, it was proportionally larger than that. He stopped dwelling on his nose and asked. "Was this man's hair dark or fair?"

"Middling, brown like mud or dung. Not black and gray, like yours."

"My hair is black, only black." Sherlock was tempted to visit the bathroom mirror, to check for gray, but resisted the impulse. "Beard or moustache?" he asked next.

"Course he had both. Most manly fellas do, don't they? Guess you're not manly enough to grows hair on your face, and that's why you stick those fake beards and moustaches on sometimes. It's not just for disguises, is it?"

"My moustaches and beards are solely clever disguises, nothing more, certainly not an attempt at manliness. I am plenty manly. I could grow a beard and moustache if I wished, which I do not, especially after seeing that monstrosity on John's face. Have you seen Dr. Watson's new moustache?" Sherlock asked.

"I ain't seen Dr. Watson in a dog's age, since he don't come around here no more, so I ain't seen his moustache. The pistol chap's moustache and beard was real thick, so he was a right manly fella."

Sherlock sighed. He was getting a headache, to add to his numerous other aches and pains. "Approximately how old do you think he was?"

"Hard to tell, what with all that manly hair on his face, but I didn't see no wrinkles, not like those ones you's got 'round your eyes. He was maybe 30-ish. Not 50-ish like you."

"I am not 50!" Sherlock was surprised to find his volume almost a shout. "I was born on January the 6th, 1854. As this is the year of our Lord, 1890, that does not make me 50."

"You sure 'bout that?" Wiggins counted on his grubby fingers, then gave up and shrugged.

Sherlock rolled his eyes heavenward. "I am 36 years of age, Wiggins."

Wiggins leaned forward and squinted harder, then pulled a face. "If you says so, Mr. Holmes."

"I do says so—say so. My memory is infallible, and even if it wasn't, I would know my own age. Please describe the clothing the man was wearing, in detail."

"Not much to describe, he was dressed like most chaps, except for the ripped, torn coat. Not like a fancy fellow, like you. And he didn't wear no funny hat, and no coat with a cape, well he wasn't a detective, not that I knows of anyway, 'cause I don't knows him." Wiggins stroked Cat Watson some more and the cat purred like a steam engine. The little traitor.

Sherlock crossed his arms and leaned back in his chair. "Why are you here, Wiggins? I would have thought you would be delighted to have *found* a pistol. They do come in handy on the streets, and they can be sold for more than a few coins."

"I don't wants to keep that there pistol, or sells that there pistol!" Wiggin's eyes widened dramatically with alarm.

"Why ever not, Wiggins?"

"Oh, did I forgets to tell you that a beggar was shot dead last night, couple of blocks from here? Shot two times he was, leastwise, that's what I heard. I got my gang watching the coppers investigate, while I brought you that pistol I found in that fellow's pocket. I didn't want to be caught with it. If the coppers found it on me, why, they'd think I shot that beggar fella dead, they would. And they'd hangs me by my neck, and I don't wants that."

Sherlock was already on his feet. "You should have led with the murdered beggar, Wiggins." He gingerly donned his coat and detecting cap, not able to move as quickly as normal. As an afterthought, he shoved the pistol and bullets deep into his pocket. He headed for the door. Wiggins followed with Cat Watson in his arms.

Sherlock reclaimed his cat and hustled, as best he could in his delicate condition, to the scene of the crime. Wiggins was quicker on his feet and arrived well ahead of him. The detective was merely glad that the victim had been murdered so near to his rooms.

Wiggins had already consulted with his little gang of street ruffians, by the time Sherlock reached them. The gang, miniature in stature, not cleverness, totalled six that day, not including Wiggins. The number did vary from day-to-day, and all the lads and perhaps a girl or two, had a common enough appearance, clad in ragged, ill-fitting clothes, bone-thin, and desperately in need of a bath with stouthearted soap.

Beyond them, Sherlock could see the body. Thankfully, it hadn't yet been carted off. It was sprawled out under a discoloured, blood-stained sheet, near the entrance to an alleyway. "What have you observed?" he asked the group, who were all clustering close, trying to pet Cat Watson with their grubby hands. His cat would need a flea bath after such treatment, yet Cat Watson bore it without complaint.

Wiggins spoke for all of them. "Not much has happened. Coppers been walking all around, looking for clues, questioning all the lurkers and gawkers, and anybody hanging about. Nobody's told the coppers a thing."

Sherlock nodded. Those who inhabited the streets never did admit to seeing what was right under their noses, not unless coin was involved, and the coppers did not pay for information. Sherlock did, if it was useful information. "Did you see the body before the sheet was placed, contaminating any clues?" he asked. All the filthy little urchins shook their heads.

Sherlock surveyed the street. "I do not see Inspector Lestrade, or Gregson. I would like a look at the body before it is moved," he murmured, wondering how to accomplish it. Most of the police constabulary did not appreciate him *sticking his big nose into their business*, which is how they saw it, and put it, often expressed with great resentment, directly to his face.

Cat Watson squirmed to be free. Sherlock set him on the ground. The cat was quick to disappear in the direction of the body. Sherlock was intrigued to know what the cat was up to now.

"Where's Cat Watson gone off to?" Wiggins asked.

"Is Dr. Watson a cat now?" several of the urchins asked.

"No. The cat is a very clever cat that I have named Cat Watson," Sherlock explained, "and I do wish I knew what he was about." He edged closer to the body, scanning for clues with his eyes. Nothing caught his interest, or appeared out of place, well, except for the corpse.

As he watched, the body's hand began to rise, under the blood-stained sheet. Perhaps the victim was not as dead as everyone believed. The peelers had been known to make mistakes. They were not physicians, after all.

Sherlock was not the only one to notice the moving corpse. The constable standing guard by the body fell back and cried out, "He's a ghost!" The big fellow was shaking in his boots.

Everyone in the vicinity stopped what they were doing and stared at the victim. The hand raised again, a small movement, but enough to make many faces turn pale. Sherlock had his own suspicions. He stepped forth, right up to the body. No-one stopped him at that point. "Shall I have a look?" he asked the constable, who was unpleasantly familiar to him.

Constable Carron's white face nodded, the lip slightly curled. "I wouldn't stop you, Holmes. If you want to come face-to-face with a ghost, you have my blessing."

Sherlock crouched and immediately regretted it. His four-times-stabbed bottom and dog-bitten leg were making themselves felt most unpleasantly. His sword-slashed arm and cat-clawed head less so, but still, the aches and pains seemed to be everywhere. At least he had a case to take his mind off his physical maladies.

He peaked under the sheet, and was not at all surprised to find a small black cat pressed against the side of the body, beneath the hand, making it lift and lower. "You are the most extraordinary cat in the whole of London," he whispered, smiling, his face hidden behind the raised corner of the sheet. "But you had best make yourself scarce now."

Cat Watson gave a quiet little meow of agreement. As if they had orchestrated it, Sherlock folded the sheet away from the body, concealing the cat, until Cat Watson could slip away like a shadow. His nose was to the ground, as if tracking a scent.

"Just a rat, nibbling on the fingers," Sherlock announced, standing and biting back a groan. Making good use of the opportunity Cat Watson had gifted him, Sherlock studied the body, and the area all around it. With his infallible memory, it was as if he had taken a permanent photograph of all he saw, one he could carry around with him and examine, whenever the need arose.

The man had been shot twice in the chest, and stumbled about a bit, based on the blood spatter evidence. He had fallen, and died more or less where he lay. The largest pool of blood was beside him, so someone had turned him face up, most likely the killer or the coppers. The killer to make sure he was dead, or to check his pockets perhaps. The coppers to verify he was dead, or to identify him.

At first glance, the victim was a ragged beggar, with an eyepatch over one eye. At second glance, he was no such thing. The long, matted beard was strangely askew. Sherlock gave it a tug. The thing came right off the face. So, a false beard. A disguise perhaps, as Sherlock often employed? Or merely an attempt to look manly? Was the eyepatch also part of his disguise? Sherlock peeked beneath it. No, the fellow was missing one of his brown eyes, yet there were no disfiguring scars on his face to explain its absence.

There was a faint tan line around the eyepatch. The man had spent time under a hot sun. Beneath his worn, torn coat was a loudly patterned plaid shirt. His boots were of the Western American variety. He also had a tan line on his brow, where a Western hat would be worn. Clearly, the man was an American, or he had lived in America for some long time.

"Hey, what are you doing, messing around with that eyepatch, and yanking off the beggar's beard?" the constable snapped.

"It is a false beard. Beneath it, your victim is no beggar. Note the clear complexion, and the healthy muscles. This man is in disguise as a beggar. But why?" he mused. He spotted a corner of white peeking out from under the dead man's shoulder. He slid it out. It was a playing card, the Jack of Spades, also known as a one-eyed Jack. It had 'I.O.U.' scrawled across it.

Sherlock went through the pockets, ignoring the belligerent constable's grumbling protests. There was little in them, as if they had already been picked clean. The one item Sherlock did find was a card of a different sort—his own business card. It identified him as a consulting detective and provided his address.

Although it had been in the man's pocket, Sherlock knew he had never before seen or spoken to this one-eyed man disguised as a beggar, and he had certainly never handed him a card. Someone else must have provided him with it. Sherlock's cards were oft passed from person-to-person.

Was the victim so close to 221B Baker Street because he had been enroute to see Sherlock? To seek his aid? Had he been in fear for his life, and rightly so?

Constable Carron snapped both cards out of Sherlock's hand. "What's that you got there? Why, that's your card in his pocket. You know this man," he accused.

"No, I do not. I have no idea how he came to be in possession of my card."

"So you say. And here you are taking it off his body, trying to hide the evidence! You killed him, didn't you?" The constable was trying to sound like a detective himself, yet his conclusion, based on the flimsiest of evidence, was completely erroneous.

"Don't be a bloody fool, Carron. Of course I didn't kill him," Sherlock snapped.

The constable had already been of high colour, and flushed redder still. He shoved Sherlock against the nearest wall and proceeded to pat him down. He immediately felt the lump of metal in the coat pocket. He yanked it out. Sherlock was very glad he had removed the bullets.

"A gun!" the constable declared.

"No pulling the wool over your eyes," Sherlock drawled sarcastically.

"Proof that you killed the beggar!" Carron smiled with malicious satisfaction. Sherlock had to wonder what he had ever done to offend the constable, and earn his obvious enmity.

"He is no beggar, and a gun is not proof," Sherlock stated. "Why, if you searched this crowd of gawkers, you would find at least five more pistols, and we can't all be murderers, now can we? There is only one body here, not six, as even you can't have failed to notice. Unless you can't count as high as six." His scathing tone was perhaps overdone, but the constable was sorely trying his patience.

Carron turned even brighter red. "Oh, you're not going to wriggle your way out of this one. Messing about with the body, trying to conceal evidence, carrying the murder weapon. You are as guilty as sin, Holmes. You will hang for this. I am arresting you for the murder of this beggar." He motioned a couple of nearby constables over, to clap Sherlock in irons. They were not eager to join in the fray and hung back.

"Stop being an idiot," Sherlock said. "I am no more a criminal than you are. Or perhaps you murdered the man and are attempting to pin it on me. I may have to arrest you for this foul crime." He poked Carron in the chest, and noticed Cat Watson approaching. He was followed by a second cat, or kitten to be accurate. It was orange with a white face, quite tiny and half-starved. Cat Watson had something small clasped between his teeth.

"Assault! You've assaulted an officer of the law." Carron gave Sherlock a hard shove. He stumbled backwards, trying to avoid the body, and Cat Watson, and the tiny kitten, which would have been crushed flat underfoot. Carron shoved him again, for the sheer pleasure of it, no doubt.

Sherlock darted a glance over his shoulder. Cat Watson was directly behind him. He tried to sidestep and stumbled over the corpse's leg. Normally an agile man, he somehow fell backwards onto the body. At least the bloating stomach of the victim provided a cushiony soft landing for his sorely injured bottom, but alas, the force of that landing caused a great expelling of air from the posterior of the corpse. It was the longest, loudest fart Sherlock, or any man, had ever heard. Those who did not study the dead, which was almost everyone, had no idea that corpses could expel air in such a manner. All the gawkers, and there were many, pointed at Sherlock and began to laugh uproariously.

"It wasn't me! It was him, the dead man," he declared, pointing accusingly at the body. It only made them laugh all the heartier. Sherlock glowered and attempted to find his feet. The shifting of his weight caused another gusty, noisy rush of wind from the corpse's bottom.

Constable Carron was loving this development, laughing the loudest of all. Sherlock had rarely been the object of such blatant ridicule, and he did not like it at all. He could have used the support of a good friend, like John. He didn't have John by his side, but he did have Cat Watson. The cat dropped the object he had been carrying onto Sherlock's lap and gave a sympathetic meow. At the same moment, a hand extended down toward Sherlock. He looked up into the familiar, friendly face of Inspector Gregson.

"I find you are in the thick of things again," he said. Sherlock hoped it was not a bad pun in regards to the thickness of the air from the corpse's fervent farting. It proved to be just that when Gregson added, "And the butt of the joke."

"Yes, yes," Sherlock snapped. He stuffed the object Cat Watson had brought him into the pocket of his cloak, to examine at a more opportune time. He clasped Inspector Gregson's hand, and was pulled to his feet. "The corpse is the one expelling foul air, not me," he repeated, to be clear.

"I know the ways of the dead as well as you." Inspector Gregson gave a wink.

Sherlock was relieved to find this man in charge of the case. Of all Scotland Yard's inspectors, he was one of the ablest, Lestrade being the other. And he would welcome Sherlock's assistance. The detective often solved cases for the inspector, and preferred to let him take the credit. Being in the limelight made it hard for Sherlock to act covertly, so he remained in the background whenever possible.

Alas, John's stories appearing in The Strand had not helped the detective to stay incognito. Even now, a newshound had likely snapped a photograph of Sherlock sitting on the murder victim, as if that victim was a chesterfield. Or an artist was busily sketching a cartoon of him sitting on the corpse and farting up a wind storm, blowing away all the evidence. Something embarrassing, with Sherlock as the butt of the joke, would surely be printed in the next day's newspaper. Maybe even on the front page. He could imagine the headline now: *World's Greatest Detective Emits World's Greatest Fart*, or *Breaking Wind or a Break in the Case?* The possibilities were endless. John and Mary would no doubt read all about Sherlock's latest misfortune over their morning tea, and share a laugh or two at his expense. His cheeks heated at the thought.

"Are you just arriving at the scene?" Sherlock asked Gregson, focusing on the case. He did not believe so, given the lines of fatigue around the detective's eyes, unless he had been at another crime scene. Gregson was about ten years older than Sherlock and more often than not, had a careworn look, which was not surprising given his job. His brown hair was liberally threaded with gray, and his clothes were often rumpled from days of wear. Today was no different.

"No, I've been here since the wee hours. I just went to have a spot of tea, and returned to find you disrupting my crime scene, and upsetting good Constable Carron." Gregson shot Sherlock a reproving glance.

"The fool tried to arrest me. Me! For murder," Sherlock grumbled, but quietly.

"The only one who appears the fool at the moment is you, Holmes," Gregson said, every bit as quietly. "Now, let us all play nice together, so this foul crime can be solved without delay." It was an order. Sherlock had to cooperate, or he knew Gregson would have him evicted from the scene, or locked up, if Carron had his way.

"Oh fine, if I must," Sherlock agreed with a huff.

Constable Carron was not appeased. "But Holmes is the killer. He was carrying a pistol in his pocket, and he yanked the fellow's beard right off." Carron shook it around in the air. It looked like he was strangling a small dog. "And the dead man had Sherlock's card in his pocket." He held that up as well, along with the one-eyed Jack. He presented them as if they were damning proof, not merely two cards. "And the gun!" He waved that around carelessly, though Sherlock knew for a fact, he had not checked to see if the thing was loaded.

"All easily enough explained," Sherlock said. "The victim was in disguise, perhaps fearing for his life, hence the false beard. He was likely coming to see me, to engage my services, hence my card. And the pistol most likely does belong to the killer, though that is not me. It was delivered to my rooms this morning. I fear the person who brought it to me may be in danger, as he can identify the owner, and the likely killer." Sherlock glanced around and spotted Wiggins, still safely in the bosom of his little gang.

The Baker Street Irregulars, as Sherlock had nicknamed them, were standing as close as they could get. All of them were still laughing. Children will laugh much longer over a fart than adults, and it had been a fantastic fart.

Gregson took the beard from Carron and gave it a cursory glance, same for Sherlock's card and the playing card. He also claimed the gun. He did check to see if it was loaded.

"I removed the remaining bullets. Three," Sherlock stated. Gregson nodded and dropped all the items in an evidence carryall, motioning for Sherlock to add the bullets to the bag, which he did.

Gregson took a spoon out of his pocket, licked it, and dropped it into the bag, saying, "That was under the body."

"A spoon?"

"A spoon but no pudding." Gregson grinned. "I borrowed it to have my tea, since I forgot my spoon at home."

"Odd. I noted the body had been turned over. The victim was obviously killed here," Sherlock added.

"Obviously," Gregson agreed. "Have you noted anything less obvious?"

"I was too busy being manhandled, to have had a chance to assess the scene properly yet." Sherlock shot Carron a cutting glance, before he walked around the body. Cat Watson meowed stridently. Sherlock suddenly recalled the small object he had pocketed. He felt for it, hoping he hadn't given it away with the bullets.

"Are those cats with you?" Gregson gazed down at Cat Watson and the ginger kitten, in puzzlement.

"It would appear so, yes. The black one is Cat Watson, my new companion."

"So you and Watson haven't made up yet? That is too bad. I know you've been sad and lonely without him, but still, to have taken a cat as a companion, or two cats, that is, uh, strange, Holmes." Gregson frowned at him with evident concern.

Sherlock scowled back. "What is wrong with having a cat as a companion? Cat Watson is a remarkable partner. Perhaps even superior to Dr. Watson."

"Don't let the good doctor hear you say that," Gregson said, biting his lip, as if to contain laughter. Carron was laughing in a much unkinder way.

"Do control your mirth," Sherlock snapped and finally found the small object Cat Watson had brought him, in the very depths of his pocket. He took it out, glanced at it, then rather wished he was not holding it. Clearly, it was a significant clue. If it hadn't been, he would have flung it far far away. He dropped it back into his pocket for the time being. "Where did you find it?" he asked the cat.

Cat Watson meowed and padded back toward the nearest alleyway, trailed by the kitten. Sherlock followed the cats. Gregson followed him, no doubt curious. Carron came last. He probably couldn't wait to laugh at Sherlock some more. The detective did, in truth, feel a bit silly following the cats, but needs must. And this case did have to be solved quickly, so Wiggins would be safe, and so he himself wouldn't be arrested for murder.

14 - An Eye for an Eye

from The Observations of Cat Watson

I had tracked the dead man's scent back to the nearby alley. He had been lurking at its entrance for some long time before he was killed. Despite all the footsteps that had trodden over it, the victim's trail had been easy to follow. The man in the false beard had been acridly sweaty, perhaps because he had been in fear for his life. Humans do emit a very strong and pungent odour when they are highly distraught or feeling intense emotion. Not as bad as dogs or babies, but still entirely unpleasant.

The alley was as foul as expected, littered with trash and worse. A short way down it, I had come upon a most piteous kitten. I judged him to be less than three months old, and starved. He cringed in fear, as if I was a threat to him. I was no such thing, being a kind-hearted tom. I meowed a greeting. He mewled sadly back. I gave him a little lick, inviting him to accompany me. He did, with great eagerness. He was happy to have a friend.

A bit further down the alleyway, the kitten dashed behind a trashcan and batted something out to me, wishing to play. It rolled like a small ball, yet it was no such thing, or not exactly. It was an eyeball, human and rather dried out. It was a strange find, without a doubt. Logic dictated it had something to do with the man who had emerged from this alley, only to be shot dead. I batted the eyeball back to the kitten. It was an instinctive reaction, like chasing mice.

The kitten bounded after the rolling eyeball and pounced on it. Even starving kittens are playful. He gave it a lick and tried to bite it. Maybe he was so hungry, he wanted to eat it. I couldn't let him. It was a clue that Sherlock needed to examine. I meowed, telling him to follow me. He did not protest when I picked up the eyeball. Carrying it in my mouth, I hurried back to Sherlock. The kitten stuck close by my side.

The detective was clearly not having a very good time of it. A mean copper was bullying him. I was wondering if I should defend him, when he tripped and landed on the body, forcing a great deal of loud and smelly gas from the corpse. I backed off.

The crowd laughed heartily at his predicament. These people were not as kind-hearted as cats. I hurried forward and dropped the eyeball on his leg, trying to cheer him. He stuck it in his pocket without sparing it so much as a glance. Clearly, he was flustered by the situation he found himself in, sitting on a foul-smelling corpse, surrounded by people laughing at him. My poor Sherlock.

An inspector that Sherlock called Gregson helped him to his feet, and they discussed the case. Sherlock searched again for clues. I rubbed against his leg and meowed, to remind him of the clue I had presented to him. He smiled at me, stuck his hand in his pocket, and dug around for the eyeball. He removed it from his pocket and looked at it. It looked back at him. He gave a visible shudder.

I meowed insistently and headed back toward the alley, glancing over my shoulder to make sure he was following. He put the eyeball back in his pocket, made a sly hand signal to Wiggins, and came after me. The kitten and I led him to the place where the eyeball had been found. He, in turn, was followed by Inspector Gregson and the mean constable. Wiggins joined us soon after, discreetly, and out of sight of all the gawkers.

At his appearance, Sherlock said, "Wiggins, the man you saw with the gun, did he wear an eyepatch?" He made no mention of the pickpocketing.

Wiggins looked none too pleased to be in the company of coppers, and said, "He had two eyes, but one of them was red, and he had some scratches on his face. I would have told you if he was a one-eyed gent this morning. I told you all I knows already."

"You did not mention the scratches this morning, Wiggins. Is there anything else you have forgotten to tell me?" Sherlock asked.

"I wouldn't knows, now would I? If I's gone and forgotten it. Can I go now?" Wiggins was so twitchy around the coppers, he might have had ants in his underpants, or a mouse.

Carron snapped, "No."

Sherlock overruled him. "Yes, but stay with your mates, to be safe."

"We should haul him in for questioning," Carron argued.

Gregson also overruled him. "There is no need for that, Constable. The lad has shared what he knows, willingly. And turned the gun in, I presume."

Sherlock nodded in confirmation and said, "You go on, Wiggins, but remember, the man may well be the killer and we don't want him coming after you. Don't go anywhere alone."

"Yes sir, I means, no sir I won't, Mr. Holmes." Wiggins scurried away. He seemed to be a savvy lad. He did survive the mean streets of London after all. He would take the threat seriously.

I hadn't explored the area where the kitten had found the eyeball, but I did so now. I should have done so sooner. There were more clues to discover behind the trashcan, though no more eyeballs, I am happy to say. I dragged the small sack of halfpennies out to Sherlock. He picked it up and glanced inside. "Coins a beggar would collect," he mentioned to Gregson, a thoughtful expression on his face. "Perhaps our victim has been in the guise of beggar for some time, but to what purpose? Surely not for a handful of halfpennies, when he is not crippled or deformed."

"The bigger question is who shot him, and why?" Gregson took the pouch and glanced inside, too.

"Yes, why. We have a one-eyed man, most likely an American, disguised as a beggar, shot dead. My card and a Jack of Spades, with I.O.U. scribbled on it. A dried eyeball in the nearby alley. A spoon. A bag of coins. The likely killer with a wounded face and reddened eye. These are the clues." Sherlock's mind was already working to fit the pieces of the puzzle together. "I have seen all I need to here. I will do a bit more investigating elsewhere." Sherlock picked me up. I wasn't expecting it.

"Report back and tell me what you find, without delay. I'll be at the station, after I'm done here," Gregson said.

Sherlock gave him a salute and started to walk away. The little kitten mewled sadly from the ground. I meowed and squirmed to be free. Sherlock didn't have to be a detective to know what was going on here. He sighed. "Must I?" he asked me. I meowed and added a little purr. "Fine," he huffed, and scooped up the little kitten.

"Are you collecting cats now?" Gregson asked him, chuckling. "Will you name this one Watson as well?"

Sherlock did not deign to answer. Carrying us both, he left the alleyway. He avoided the crowd and headed for home. The little kitten purred happily all the way to 221B Baker Street. Upon entering the building, Sherlock shouted, "Mrs. Hudson!"

She was quick to fling wide her door, which opened into the foyer. "Yes, Sherlock?" She smiled and batted her eyelashes. "Oh, you have another wee kitty. A friend for Cat Watson. Isn't that delightful. Aren't you a wittle sweetie-pie, itsy-bitsy kitty-witty." She stepped very close, almost squashing both of us cats between her and Sherlock's bodies. Her perfume was so strong, it made me sneeze. The little kitten stopped purring.

Sherlock stepped back and handed her the kitten. "Can you take care of this one, feed it some fish. I can't stay, I am investigating a murder."

"Oh course I'll take care of the wee pusspuss, until you return." She stroked it and it began to purr again. "I'll feed it right up, poor wittle fluffy-wuffykins."

"Thank-you, Mrs. Hudson." Sherlock backed out the door, taking me with him. I was happy to be included in the investigation, but felt a bit guilty for abandoning the new addition to our household. And I was hungry for some fish myself. Hopefully we wouldn't be away too long.

Outside 221B Sherlock said, "If the victim is an American, he was most likely staying in a hotel or lodging house, probably nearby. A middling establishment, I should thing. We shall start asking our questions in such places. Normally I would send John to do this menial task." He gave a weary little sigh. "Alas, I shall have to do it myself."

On foot, since we would be making many stops, we began visiting various lodgings. Sherlock wisely started with those closest to home. Luck did seem to be favouring us. At the second hotel, a small one that Sherlock told me was called the Northumberland Arms, I gave an encouraging and significant meow. I had been in close contact with the dead American, when raising and lowering his hand, and this hotel smelled promising. The man had carried a trace of its scent on his coat, and person.

At the desk, Sherlock said to the clerk, "Do you have any one-eyed Americans residing here, at present?"

The man frowned at me and said, "No pets allowed. This is a respectable establishment."

I hissed at him in displeasure, as I was no pet. Sherlock felt the same. "This cat is no mere pet, nor am I booking a room, so it is neither here nor there. Do you or do you not have a one-eyed American, or any one-eyed gentleman, renting a room here?"

"Who wants to know?" the clerk countered.

"I am working with the police, investigating a foul murder that has taken place, not far from your door. Shall I round up some constables to search the premises for clues? I'm sure your guests would not appreciate being disturbed and having their rooms tossed. Or would you prefer to simply answer my questions." Sherlock delivered the barely veiled threat softly.

The clerk dabbed his forehead with his handkerchief, adjusted his spectacles, and slid the guestbook closer. He turned back a page. "I myself have seen two one-eyed gentlemen recently, but only one rents a room here. He is an American." He tapped a name.

Sherlock leaned in to read it. Of course I couldn't, and he spoke the name aloud for me. "Mr. Dillon Kid. Does that sound like a real name to you?" he asked me.

"Are you addressing me or your cat, sir?" the clerk asked.

"Merely myself." Sherlock gave me a little squeeze to let me know he had, in truth, been speaking to me, his trusty companion, and dare I say his friend. "This Dillon Kid, is he in his room now?"

"No, he didn't return last night. He's not the murdered chap, is he?" the clerk gasped out.

"He may well be. This second one-eyed fellow. Describe him for me."

The clerk pursed his lips. "Hmm … average-looking gentleman, except for the eyepatch, of course. Early in the week, perhaps three days ago, he stood right where you are now, and also inquired if there was a one-eyed American man in residence." The clerk hesitated at that point.

"What did you tell him?"

"I am not supposed to give out any information about our guests," the fellow said primly, smoothing a hand down the pocket of his waist coat.

"Yet you did, for coin," Sherlock stated. He too had noted the betraying gesture.

The clerk's face fell. "Yes, so I did. I confirmed such a man was lodging here. Oh, I do hope I did not cause the American's murder."

"Unless you pulled the trigger of the pistol that shot him, you did not. How did the man react to the news?"

73

"Why, he turned as pale as a ghost, he did. Or as pale as if he had seen a ghost. He left quickly, as soon as he knew the American was staying here. Oh dear, oh dear." The clerk had turned quite ashen himself.

Sherlock went on to quiz him about the other one-eyed gentleman. When he had learned all that he could, which was not much more than Wiggins had reported, he said, "I will examine the American man's room now."

The clerk hesitated for a heartbeat. "With the cat?"

"Yes, with the cat." Sherlock's tone was unyielding.

The clerk handed over the key and provided the room number. We went directly up to the second floor. The room was not large or fancy, yet neatly turned out. The bed was made, a clean blanket smooth atop it. A maid had been in since the man had last slept in the bed, or he was one excellent bed-maker.

Sherlock put me down immediately. I sniffed around while he looked around. We made a good team, if I do say so. The scent of the victim lingered in the room. It proved that he had stayed there. I meowed to Sherlock, confirming my findings.

"As expected, Cat Watson, as expected," he said.

I ventured under the bed to explore for clues, a task that would have been difficult for Sherlock, especially in his less-than-fit condition. The cleaning standard in the hotel was more than respectable. There was little dust on the floorboards beneath the mattress. There seemed nothing of interest at all, until I spotted a small notebook tucked between the bedframe and the mattress. At that moment the door creaked opened. From my floor-level view, I could see only the shoes of the newcomer.

He stopped just inside the door. "What are you doing in here?" He sounded both startled and displeased, and not American himself, as he had no harsh, grating, twangy drawl. He was an upper crust Englishman.

I peeked out from under the bed. Sherlock faced an average-looking man in his thirties, dressed in a brown coat. His hat was pulled low, so the top half of his face was cast in shadow. "This is my room," Sherlock lied. "What are you doing here? You do not appear to be the maid."

I started pawing at the little notebook, to dislodge it, while listening to their conversation.

74

"Your room? Oh, I do apologize. I thought it was my friend's room. I have obviously made a mistake. Excuse me." The stranger started to retreat.

"Wait. Perhaps I can help you find the right room. Who is your friend?" Sherlock asked. I think he was toying with the man.

"I'm sure you don't know him. He's not from around these parts." The man took another little step backward.

"Is your friend the one-eyed American?" Sherlock took a step closer.

At that moment, the little pocket-sized notebook dropped down to the wooden floor. The thud it made was faint, yet it was heard, as there was a lull in the conversation at that point. "What was that?" the man asked.

"My cat. I think he has discovered something under the bed, and I am not referring to a mouse," Sherlock alluded.

"Cat? Pets are not allowed in this hotel," the man said in a suspicious tone.

"This cat is no pet. I am a consulting detective, Sherlock Holmes at your service, and he is my companion. What is your name, sir?"

"My name is none of your bloody business. This isn't truly your room, is it? What has this so-called cat found under the bed?" The man stopped retreating. He closed the door, shutting himself in the room with us. There was a metallic click and I peeked out again, hoping he had not acquired another pistol, in the short time since Wiggins had pickpocketed his.

It was not a pistol, but an automatic knife. The blade had swung out and clicked into place in the handle. It was long, wickedly sharp, and pointed directly at Sherlock, who had suffered more than his fair share of injuries of late. We were in a pickle. Sherlock, as far as I knew, did not carry a weapon of his own.

"Sit in that chair," the man ordered, motioning to the only one in the room. It was situated in the very corner, furthest from the door. Sherlock cooperated and sat, gingerly, biding his time. At least the chair had a padded seat for his poor posterior.

Sherlock safely ensconced, and at a distance, the man crouched by the bed, saying, "There better not be anyone hiding under the bed, or I'll stab them where they lie."

Did that mean he would stab me? I clawed at the little notebook, dragging it as deep under the bed as it could go, which was the very center of the mattress, under the headboard, which was of course situated against the wall, as bed are normally positioned.

The man spotted me, and the notebook. I had put my paw atop it, claiming it. He could not reach it with ease now. If he crawled partway under the bed to nab it, I would claw his hand, and Sherlock could give him a boot in the behind. We would capture him then. Alas, I had miscalculated. I had overlooked the obvious.

The man didn't try to get the notebook himself. He stood up and said to Sherlock, "I see the cat, and he's got that damn book I've seen Dillon scribbling in. I need that notebook."

"Is Dillon Kid his real name?" Sherlock inquired.

"Yes, he's an American, isn't he," the man said, as if that was explanation enough, which I suppose it was. He continued, "Get the notebook for me, and I will leave you and the cat alive. I just want the book, that's all. Get it, now!"

"Why did you shoot him dead?" Sherlock asked, from the chair.

The stranger hissed through his teeth, like a snake. "You know too much for your own good. How do you know he's dead? How do you know I killed him?"

Sherlock probably rolled his eyes, though I could not see it from my position beneath the bed, guarding the notebook that was clearly important evidence. The detective replied, "You have red lines on your face from wearing an eyepatch, one you clearly do not need. You have scratches near your eye, as if someone has tried to claw it out. You are here in a murder victim's room, searching for something—the book, yes? I suspect it points a finger at you, as the most likely killer. Shall I tell you why you killed him?" Sherlock said.

The bed sagged over me when the man sat down on it. "How could you possibly know?"

"Did I not mention that I am a great detective?"

"You said detective, you didn't say great," the stranger said. "Tell me what you think happened, before I kill you, too. And I'm sorry to say, I'll have to kill you now that you know I killed Dillon."

Sherlock didn't react to that comment. He said, "You visited America. You still have faint tan lines on your brow, from wearing a Western hat. While there, you engaged in a card game with high stakes. Dillon Kid was one of the card players. He ran out of funds and believed he had a winning hand. He bet his eye on a one-eyed Jack, did he not?" Sherlock paused, waiting for an answer.

"Yes, the fool bet his eyeball, shouting about one-eyed Jacks. We were deep in our cups, drunk as lords, otherwise we wouldn't have been such fools, the both of us. So I agreed to the wager, an eye for a one-eyed Jack."

"He lost, did he not?" Sherlock made it a question, perhaps to encourage the killer to take up the tale.

"We showed our hands, and his was the losing hand. So you know what he does?" The fellow did not wait for an answer. "He picks up a spoon and ... and digs out his eyeball ... his own eyeball, with a spoon, just like that, sitting there at the table. I would never have asked him to honour the debt, never! But I had no chance to say so. Gods, it was hideous. He plunked his eyeball onto the table, in the middle of all the money and gold that had been bet. Blood running down his cheek. I was overset with revulsion. I fell away from the table. And that's when ... that's when ..."

The man was too overwrought to continue and Sherlock finished his sentence. "You had cheated at the hand."

"Yes, to my eternal shame, I had cheated. I had a one-eyed Jack up my sleeve and a couple of aces just in case, and in my haste, the cards fell out. Dillon still had one eye, and he wasn't so blind drunk he couldn't see the cards that fell out of my sleeve, right onto the floor by my boot. Oh, how he screamed and howled like a madman. He raged and ranted, and said I owed him. He points at my face, his hand all bloody, and he bellows, *An eye for an eye!*"

"But you were not about to dig your own eye out with a spoon, were you," Sherlock said, as calm as could be.

"What man would, other than Dillon Kid? Or perhaps Americans are another breed of crazy, as mad as hatters with bats in the belfry. They say only mad dogs and Englishmen go out in the noonday sun, but you can add Americans to that list. Why, they even go out and bask in it until their skin is as brown as dirt. As brown and tough as a turkey in the roaster. They even baste their skin with oil, to cook it under the hot sun. Oh, they're a mad breed, I tell you."

"Continue with the tale," Sherlock said, to get him back on track.

"Well, as luck would have it, I was leaving the next day, to return to London, so I ran. Drunk and stumbling and lurching, I ran. Dillon gave chase, but he wasn't used to having only one eye, and it was dark, and he was drunk. He bumped into a horse-trough and fell into the water. By the time he got out, I was long gone. I made it all the way home across the ocean, and tried to forget the horrible incident. I never dreamed the mad American would follow me here. He didn't even know my full name, as we only played cards by chance than one night, yet he tracked me down." He dragged in a deep shaky breath. "Several weeks ago, I spotted this chap with an eyepatch, and a big bushy beard, and I knew it was Dillon Kid. I didn't think he's seen me, and I managed to elude him. I took to wearing an eyepatch when out and about, in case he tracked me down again. I hoped he would believe I'd plucked out my own eye, and paid the debt. I hoped he would leave me in peace, go home to America where he belongs, with all the other mad Americans," he wailed.

"That was a faint hope indeed," Sherlock said.

"I know, but I was desperate. And he did find me again. I spotted him, scribbling in a little black notebook, keeping notes. I flagged down a carriage and eluded him again, but oh, it was all such a mess. I feared for my eye, if not my life. I bought a pistol, for my own safety. It's lucky I did, because he found me again, last night. He was disguised as a beggar. I didn't even notice him. Well, one doesn't notice beggars, does one? And I only had one eye to see with, since I was still wearing that eyepatch when out and about. Oh, a beggar! It was a clever disguise."

"I often disguise myself as a beggar, when I am investigating a case and do not wish to be noticed," Sherlock said, probably not wishing to be one-upped by the mad American.

"Yes, yes, and as a beggar, he could watch everyone pass by," the stranger agreed. He and Sherlock were getting so chatty, they should have ordered tea. The man shifted, as if leaning closer to Sherlock. "Why, I walked right by him, when I was alone, stumbling home in the wee hours, and a bit drunk to boot. I've taken to drink of late, given the terrible stress," he confided.

"Perfectly understandable," Sherlock commiserated.

"Dillon, he jumps up right in my face, demands to see under my eyepatch. He wants proof that I've plucked out my eye."

"It is reasonable that he would want proof," commented Sherlock.

"He grabs at the eyepatch, scratching my face. He sees I have two eyes, and he tries to claw one out. Can you believe it?" the man cried. Sherlock nodded once. "But then it gets even worse." The stranger was really getting into his tale now.

"How?" Sherlock asked.

"He screeches, *An eye for an eye!* He pulls a spoon out of his pocket, along with the card from our game. He had scribbled I.O.U. on that one-eyed Jack I had up my sleeve. I ask you, what else could I do but shoot him? So I did. I had to shoot him a second time, when he didn't fall down. Once he was dead, I felt for the notebook on him, but it wasn't there. I knew it would implicate me as the murderer, so I've been searching for it."

"And that is why you are here, now," Sherlock concluded. "It is quite a tale, to be sure."

"Yes, and I am sad to say it ends here. I have no choice but to silence you, and I don't want to. After I've burned that notebook, I can go on with my life. Forget this terrible ordeal. I'm not a bad man, you know. I just wanted to keep my eye, and I cheated at a card game. Those aren't terrible crimes, are they?" he appealed.

"No, but shooting a man in cold blood, and stabbing the world's greatest detective certainly are," Sherlock said.

"You never said you were the world's greatest detective," the man mentioned.

"Well, I am. Tell me your name. As I will be dead soon, it won't matter that I know it. I should know the name of the man who ends my life, should I not?" Sherlock said.

The bed shifted a bit. "Fair enough. I am Harry Crapper."

"Your father owns a toilet parts manufacturing company, and holds a patent on a key flush-toilet component. His company is doing very well," Sherlock stated.

"It is. That's why I was in America, to see if they wanted to import our flush-toilets, but that is neither here nor there. Get the notebook, now, or I'll have to stab you and get it myself," Harry ordered.

I had been mulling over how I could help Sherlock, and I had come up with an idea. I edged closer to the side of the bed where the man's ankles were. He stood up, but his ankles were still right there. Ankles are very sensitive. Cats' claws are very sharp, as sharp as cats' teeth. If I attacked his ankles, would it distract him enough for Sherlock to wrestle the knife away? No, Sherlock, with all his wounds, was not in fighting shape. I decided to bide my time a bit longer, in case a better opportunity presented itself.

Sherlock dropped to his knees and peered under the bed. I blinked at him, not sure if he wanted me to drag the notebook to within his reach. "If I toss you at his face, can you distract him?" Sherlock whispered, giving me a light stroke.

I purred in agreement, happy at the thought of helping my Sherlock in the life and death situation we found ourselves in. Sherlock rose from the bed, holding me instead of the notebook. Harry Crapper looked confused. "Where is the book?"

"Right here, under Cat Watson." Sherlock fumbled me a bit, as if he held the notebook, too. We were both black, after all, so my fur could have easily camouflaged the little pocket-sized book.

With a slight warning squeeze, Sherlock flung me at the villain's face. I was expecting it, yet still, it was alarming to be flying through the air. Sherlock's aim was dead to rights. I landed on Harry Crapper's face, each and every claw extended and at the ready. I sank not just the claws of my front paws into him, but my teeth as well. I bit him hard on the tip of his nose.

His hands flew to his face, to defend himself. He must have forgotten he was holding the knife, and he stabbed himself in the eye. He dropped where he stood, like a sack of wet sand. I leapt off him gracefully. Cats always land on their feet. I scampered back to Sherlock, my task successfully accomplished.

Sherlock was quick to remove the handle of the knife from the man's grip, and the tip of the blade from his eyeball. Harry Crapper groaned out, "I've stabbed my eye. Oh, my poor eye! Now I'm a one-eyed Harry." With that, he fainted dead away.

Sherlock picked me up and gave me a little hug. "Well done, Cat Watson. I do apologize for placing you in such peril, but it was the most expedient way to resolve the situation. You aren't harmed, are you?"

I meowed and purred at the same time, completely unharmed, and delighted to have helped my Sherlock out of a most sticky wicket.

To sum up the conclusion of this case, which Sherlock refers to as, *The Mystery of the One-eyed Jack*, Inspector Gregson was summoned. Harry Crapper was arrested, and treated by a doctor, who gifted him a new eyepatch. Because Harry's father was one of the richest and most influential toilet manufacturers in London, his son was not hanged for the murder of Dillon Kid, who wasn't even an Englishman, but a mad American. Harry's father did send him off to New South Wales in Australia. Although it hadn't been a penal colony for almost thirty years, it was still rough-living amongst dangerous criminal types. And there were no flush-toilets in Australia, only foul outhouses. It was deemed punishment enough for his crime.

Sherlock confided to me that the wealthy and connected are treated much differently for their crimes, when compared to the poor and desperate, who could be imprisoned for years over a stolen wheel of cheese. I already knew it was the truth, from my time growing up on the mean streets of London.

I was simply glad I was no longer a poor and desperate street tom, but a well-fed and well-connected detecting assistant to the world's greatest consulting detective, my Sherlock Holmes.

15 - Dr. Watson's Second Case

Sherlock was enjoying a nice lie-in for a change, when a knock sounded on his door. Cat Watson sprang up from atop the covers where he had been drowsing. The new addition to their household, the as-yet-unnamed marmalade kitten, rose too, and stretched. He had been cuddled up beside Cat Watson, purring ever so softly.

The cats darted out of the bedroom, before Sherlock had even slid his feet into his slippers. Alas, cats could not open doors, so that duty fell to Sherlock. He donned his robe, as he was again not wearing his pajamas. The restricting cotton cloth tended to chafe his many healing wounds in a most irritating fashion. He left the bedroom unhurriedly, despite the increasingly fervent knocking. Man's knuckles, not a smaller, more delicate woman's hand.

Cat Watson and the kitten were waiting, both seated politely by the door, as if eager to greet the guest or guests. The kitten was a quick study and keen to please. He had adopted the older cat's behaviour as his model, as if Cat Watson was his big brother. "You need a name," Sherlock said to the kitten, and he opened the door.

John tumbled in. He tripped over Cat Watson, and almost squashed the kitten underfoot. Cat Watson yowled and leapt into Sherlock's hands. So did the kitten, although he couldn't leap as high, and Sherlock had to bend down to catch him.

At least neither cat tried to go higher, because John was not accompanied by his dreadful dog. He was alone and in quite a state, his hair windblown, his cravat askew, and his hideous moustache in such spectacular disarray, it accomplished the great feat of looking even more offensive than usual.

"Sherlock, I need help," John cried, as soon as he crossed the threshold.

Sherlock rolled his eyes extravagantly. "You've woken me from a recuperative sleep, Dr. Watson. As my physician, you should know better than that." It was an untruth, yet Sherlock felt it was justified.

"I'm not a mind reader, Sherlock, nor can I see through solid walls. How on earth could I know you were still abed at this hour?" John wailed. He had a point. It was time for elevenses.

"This disturbance had better be a matter of life and death. Mrs. Hudson!" Sherlock bellowed.

The woman popped up on the landing, as though magically conjured. "Yes, Sherlock dearest?"

"Tea, strong and black and plentiful. Oh, and don't forget the cats' tea. Please, if it's not inconvenient." he added. He was not foolhardy enough to behave like a complete boor with the woman who boarded, fed, and occasionally groped him.

"Yes, Sherlock." Her eyes lingered on his robe, which, despite being tightly belted, was inclined to gape. He shifted the cats higher, protecting his chest from her eyes.

As soon as she disappeared down the stairs, John said, "You have two cats now, Sherlock?"

"You can count." Sherlock put the cats in the comfy basket that currently occupied John's former chair. It was Cat Watson's chair now, as the basket proclaimed, so John couldn't sit there. Sherlock sought his room to don his underpants, at the very least. Upon his return, he settled delicately onto the cushion he had placed atop his own armchair.

John regarded the two cats squatting in the big basket on his former chair, and huffily, with poor grace it must be noted, settled stiffly on the client's seat. "Why do you have two cats?" he asked.

"What is wrong with having two cats?" Sherlock asked coolly.

"Nothing, I suppose, as long as they aren't both named Watson."

"They are not," Sherlock declared. "You already know Cat Watson. Now I shall introduce you to John Marmalade. John Marmalade, I present John Watson. He is a doctor." The kitten's name had just popped out of his mouth without thought, but he liked it. It suited.

The newly christened John Marmalade blinked in confusion. Sherlock had noted that he was not nearly as clever at Cat Watson, but perhaps that was because he was a baby cat. Or Cat Watson truly was the cleverest cat in all of London. Sherlock hadn't met enough cats to know how clever cats should be, or how old they had to be to develop cleverness.

John groaned. "Why don't you get a girl cat, and name it Mary, and a fat cat, and name it Gladstone? Then you would have my whole family living here with you, as cats."

"No, two cats will suffice. Now, why have you come to call? What is today's calamity, John?" Sherlock asked with a long-suffering air. "Has a fork gone missing? A toast-rack, perhaps? Ye gads, do not say it is a soup pot!"

John pulled out his handkerchief and dabbed at his forehead, perhaps to conceal the fact that he was also dabbing at his teary eyes, as if he could have hoped to fool a great detective. "No, no, Sherlock. Nothing so mundane. It's Gladstone. Gladstone is missing, gone! Gone without a trace," John sputtered. "You are the only one I can turn to, to find him and bring him safely home. I know you don't think highly of Gladstone, Sherlock, but I care about him. If you have any regard for me, I beg of you, please help me to find my dog." John's voice actually broke and he could not continue.

Cat Watson gave a hiss. John Marmalade copied him with a smaller hiss. Sherlock said, "Oh no! No, no, no." He got no further. Mrs. Hudson bustled in the door, carrying a tray laden with tea and biscuits. She had not forgotten the small dishes of cream and fishy delectables for Cat Watson and John Marmalade.

John, ever the gentleman, rose to take the heavy tray from her hands. He set it on the nearest side-table and said, "Thank-you, Mrs. Hudson."

"Think nothing of it, Dr. Watson." She set the cat's tea on the floor below the table, saying, "Here, pusspuss and wee pusspuss. Some nice yummy num-nums for your wee wittle tum-tums." It looked to Sherlock like Cat Watson rolled his eyes, before he leapt down and began eating as if he hadn't been fed in days. He was quickly followed by John Marmalade.

Mrs. Hudson stroked both cats and Sherlock said, "The kitten now has a name. Mrs. Hudson, I present John Marmalade."

She gave the kitten an extra pat and looked up at Sherlock. Her eyes lingered on his bare legs. "Oh dear, Sherlock, why is your leg bandaged? Have you suffered an injury?" Her eyes moved over his bandage and traced up his thigh. From her crouched position, she could probably see more than she ought. Sherlock crossed his legs, very glad he had donned his underpants.

John got a gleam in his eye that Sherlock did not like, not one little bit. "As a matter of fact, Sherlock has suffered more than one injury of late," John hinted, his tone significant.

Sherlock narrowed his eyes to slits.

"But he is about to help me find my dog, so there is no time to discuss his other injury, which will need to be cleaned most thoroughly, and bandaged, daily. Perhaps twice a day, morning and night," John stressed, his eyes every bit as squinty as Sherlock's.

Before John could announce to all and sundry the exact location of the injury to Sherlock's bottom, Sherlock said, through gritted teeth, "Yes, as soon as we have enjoyed our tea, Dr. Watson and I shall set out to find his confounded dog. As the doctor is already in attendance, he will take care of bandaging any and all wounds."

The cats kept eating, and purring, oblivious to the goings-on. Mrs. Hudson, on the other hand, sighed out a sad little *Aw* of disappointment.

John picked up the teapot, saying, "Shall I be mother?"

"Please," Sherlock said, adding, "Thank-you, Mrs. Hudson." It was an obvious dismissal and she departed, possibly with tears in her eyes.

Tea was poured, then sipped, while John revealed the details of Gladstone's disappearance. He was even more distressed than he had been over the mystery of the missing and presumed stolen bicycle. He summed up the facts of the case in short, disjointed sentences, saying, "We went to bed, as usual. Mary and me, not me and Gladstone. Gladstone sleeps downstairs. You may recall, he does have a bit of gas in the evening. Not pleasant in a closed room."

"How could I forget?" Sherlock drawled.

"Mary prefers he sleep downstairs, in his basket by the kitchen. There's a backdoor there, so the servants can let him out if he needs out. When we came downstairs to breakfast this morning, Gladstone wasn't there to greet us, wagging his wee little tail, as he usually does." John pressed his napkin to his lips, as if he was dabbing at biscuit crumbs. There were plenty lurking in his moustache, making it even more distasteful than it already was, but he was obviously trying to contain his distress, and possibly a few sobs. He was so overwrought, he had a hard time talking at all at that point. At least he managed to dislodge the worst of the offensive crumbs.

Cat Watson returned to Sherlock's lap. John Marmalade kept licking dishes, every last scrap. Sherlock stroked Cat Watson almost absently and asked, "Did you question the servants? Did one of them let Gladstone out?"

John shook his head and took a shuddering breath. Sherlock sighed. "You are not being clear, John. No, you didn't question the servants, or no, they did not let Gladstone out?"

"Of course I questioned the servants. I'm not stupid. None of them let Gladstone out. He has simply disappeared into thin air." John tossed the hand not clutching his damp handkerchief into the air, to emphasize the point.

"That is not possible, John. There is no such thing as magic. Did you search the grounds thoroughly?" Sherlock asked next.

"Yes, the grounds were searched by everyone in my household. There wasn't a trace of Gladstone. Not so much as a fresh poop." John's voice caught in a sob.

"Praise be." Sherlock put down his teacup with a decisive little clink. "I will have to go and question the servants, and search the grounds myself, I suppose, since the alternative is to have Mrs. Hudson groping my bottom for the next week." He could not contain a shudder at the thought.

John sniffled. "But I questioned all the servants properly, Sherlock. And searched. I know how to do such things. I was your detecting companion for a number of years."

"I am aware, John." Sherlock sighed. "Yet, despite my brilliant tutelage, you do not possess my extraordinary observational skills and keen deductive reasoning, do you?"

"True enough," John admitted.

"And is that not why you have sought me out? To solve this mystery that you cannot? If one of the servants was lying to you, you may not have noticed, but I shall. If there is a clue on the grounds, or in the house, you might easily have overlooked what would be obvious to me." Facts were facts. And Sherlock found he was enjoying his morning tea with John, his former partner's distress notwithstanding. It was rather like the good old days. Silly sentiment.

Tea finished, Sherlock set Cat Watson on the ground and rose with a small groan. He truly did not care if the stupid dog was ever seen again, but for John's sake, and more importantly, to keep Mrs. Hudson's hands far away from his flesh, he would investigate, and solve, the case of the disappearing dog. He said, "As soon as I am presentable, we shall depart to track down your wretched beast."

John bobbed his head and stroked his moustache into place. Cat Watson gave a little hiss of displeasure, whether at John's moustache, or the fact that Sherlock had agreed to find Gladstone, was anyone's guess.

"Cat Watson, are you going to accompany us?" Sherlock asked. In answer, the cat slunk grudgingly toward the door, making his opinion crystal clear. He would come along, but most reluctantly. John Marmalade curled up near the low-burning fire in the grate. He would not come along. Young ones did need their naps.

"Can't you name the cat—both cats—something else? Anything else?" John said.

"I do believe it is much too late for that." Sherlock limped toward his bedroom, his bottom not looking forward to the carriage ride that was soon to come. His arm wound, as deep as it was, wasn't causing him nearly as much pain, perhaps because he did not keep sitting upon it.

"Cat Watson could be called Fluffy, or Whiskers, or Pusspuss, or how about Tippy, for that little bit of white on the tip of his tail? No? Blackie, or Midnight, or Shadow? That's a nice name for a black cat, don't you think? I like Shadow. Midnight is nice, too. Either would suit," John called.

Sherlock chuckled from the other room. "Ask Cat Watson what he thinks of those names."

John did not. "And the little marmalade kitten could be simply Marmalade, without the John. Or Ginger, without the John. Those are perfectly fitting names for a cat. And his nickname could be Marmy, or Gingy, or something." John trailed off lamely.

"Stupid," Sherlock said.

"But Midnight and Shadow are fine names, for Cat Watson," John insisted.

Sherlock did not deign to reply.

16 - The Case of the Disappearing Dog

🐱 from The Observations of Cat Watson

Dr. Watson gazed down at me, a deep furrow between his eyebrows. "I feel silly talking to a cat. It's not like you're a dog, is it?" I narrowed my eyes at him and stuck out my tongue. He looked quite taken aback. "Do you like the name Fluffy?" I pretended to cough up a hairball. "Whiskers?" I turned my back on him. "Pusspuss?" I did not bother to answer him. "Blackie?" I shook my head. He blinked.

"Well, I suppose Tippy is not worth mentioning. Do you know, if Sherlock was not alive in the next room, I might believe you to be a feline reincarnation of the great detective. You do seem to be an extraordinary cat. How about Midnight? That is a delightful name."

It truly wasn't a bad name. If I didn't already think of myself as Cat Watson, I might have considered it. I stretched, as if bored.

"Shadow then. I think that's the best name, after Midnight. Or if you prefer two names, you could be Midnight Shadow. Now that is an ideal name for a black cat," he declared with enthusiasm. It truly was a very impressive name. "And, given that Sherlock is your daddy, you should have his surname. Midnight Shadow Holmes, there could be no finer name than that." He was really on a roll with the naming business.

In truth, I did like the name Midnight Shadow Holmes, but alas, I had already been christened Cat Watson and the name had stuck, as tree sap will do, in fur. And Sherlock was certainly not my daddy. He was a human and I was a cat. Dr. Watson was being very silly indeed.

When Sherlock emerged from his room, neatly attired, Dr. Watson said, "I think your cat wants to be called Midnight Shadow Holmes."

Sherlock glanced at me. I gave a little hiss of disdain. "No, he does not. He is Cat Watson."

I chirruped happily. I was Cat Watson, and Cat Watson I would always be. Whether John Marmalade would keep his name, I was not

88

yet sure. The name was bigger than the kitten itself. Sherlock stepped toward the door, donned his coat and his detecting cap, and said, "Ready to find your dog, John?"

I dashed over to Sherlock's chair and pawed at the plump cushion he had been sitting upon. He pursed his lips, and said, "Yes, let's bring that along. A man with a four-times-stabbed bottom should carry a pillow about with him. I'm surprised you didn't think of it, John."

Dr. Watson snorted. "I did, yet doubted your dignity would allow for it. But I guess Midnight Shadow Holmes knows you better than I do, after being your companion for mere days." Was he jealous of my relationship with Sherlock, which was clearly warmer than his?

Sherlock tucked the pillow under his arm and opened the door. Mrs. Hudson was not without. She must have been busy elsewhere. On the street, a carriage was flagged down. The ride was not the ordeal of the previous day for Sherlock, thanks to the pillow, and some degree of healing. I enjoyed it thoroughly, my head out the window in the breeze.

As soon as we arrived at Dr. Watson's address, we entered the house proper to verify that Gladstone was still missing. Mary met us in the front parlour without delay, as if she had been watching for our arrival. She smiled at the detective. "How are you feeling today, Sherlock?"

Sherlock did not smile back. His face darkened with colour and he dropped his pillow on the nearest chair. If he was aiming for nonchalance, he did not manage it. "I am perfectly fine, Mary. And how are you?"

"Very well. I see you've brought Cat Watson along to help with the investigation." She crouched down and stroked my fur.

"He brought himself, but yes, he is here, obviously," Sherlock said.

"Sherlock has two cats now, and the other one is named John Marmalade, because it's a ginger," Dr. Watson declared with a scowl. "Mary, what do you think of the name Midnight Shadow Holmes for this cat? Don't you think it suits?" he said persuasively.

Mary considered me. "Oh, I don't know, John. He truly does look more like a Cat Watson, than a Midnight Shadow Holmes."

I purred loudly in agreement. I also appreciated that Mary did not resort to degrading baby talk when addressing me.

John surveyed the room, as if a big smelly dog might be hiding under a nearby piece of furniture. "Has there been any sign of Gladstone? Any at all?"

"There has not." Mary continued to stroke my fur. While she was close, I could not help but notice that the smell of foul dog was stronger on her than one might expect, given that she had reportedly not been in contact with Gladstone since the previous evening. There were also traces of dog fur on her skirt. Surely she had not worn the same skirt as on the previous day? Not without having a maid give it a thorough brushing and sponging. Or had the dog fur transferred from the upholstery, onto her clothing?

I strolled casually around her when she rose. There was a great deal of fur on the side of her ankle-length skirt, where Gladstone would rub against her if he walked close beside her, as I had seen him do when she ordered him to heel. There was very little dog fur on her backside, which is where one would expect to see it, if it had transferred from upholstery that had been sat upon.

I noticed Sherlock's keen gaze also fixed on Mary's skirt. He had noticed as well. I had to wonder if Mary had made the dog disappear, in the same manner as the bicycle, to reunite her husband and Sherlock on another case, after their recent wintery parting. If she had risen secretly in the night to spirit Gladstone away to places unknown, Dr. Watson could have slept through the devious deed, completely unawares. Maybe she had even drugged his evening drink with some of his own tablets, to make sure he slept undisturbed for the whole night.

I regarded Mary afresh. If she was a scheming sort, as I was beginning to suspect, and smarter than your average human, perhaps she had even done away with Gladstone permanently. I mean, who would want that smelly, saggy, gassy dog polluting their home. Just because she had married Dr. Watson, didn't mean she wanted to be stuck with Gladstone. She hadn't wedded the dog, only the doctor.

If she had poisoned Gladstone, or whacked him over the head with a stout walking stick, or shot him with a pistol—no that would make far too much noise in the dead of night—stabbing would be quieter, and poison quietest of all. Yes, a fast-acting poison would drop Gladstone in his tracks, to drool no more.

A few coins pressed into a lowlife's palm would see Gladstone's remains carted off to a meat-packing plant, or tossed into the foul water of the Thames, or buried in a nearby wooded area, or perhaps even a cemetery, or any such convenient locale. There are countless ways to dispose of corpses, be they dog or human, especially when one has an entire night to do so.

The more I thought about it, the more sense it made. Mary could kill two birds with one stone. I do love that expression. She could reunite Dr. Watson and Sherlock, and get rid of the horrible hound, in one fell swoop.

Deep in my ruminations, I hadn't been attending what the humans were discussing. I perked up my ears when Sherlock said, "Perhaps we should start our search at the former carriage house. Maybe the dog is napping where the bicycle was found."

"Of course we've looked there, Sherlock." Dr. Watson dashed a hand through his hair. "And if Gladstone was tied up nearby, he would be howling loud enough to be heard in Buckingham Palace, believe me."

Unless he is dead, I thought, trying not to smile, and yes, cats can smile. Humans just don't read the expression properly. In general, humans are quite clueless in regards to the nature and intelligence of cats.

17 – The Crucial Clue

Sherlock planned to begin his search for clues in the house, so he removed his detecting cap, which felt silly on his head when indoors. He also shed his coat, which was far too warm to wear with a fire burning in the parlour. John, as host, took his coat and draped it over the back of a nearby chair.

The detective rubbed his chin and said thoughtfully, "Gladstone must be far enough away that his howls cannot be heard, or he is dead, or so severely injured, he cannot howl."

John gasped at the plain speaking, but Cat Watson meowed in agreement. Clearly, the cat had been thinking along the same lines.

Mary tidied up some papers beside the chesterfield, folding them and tucking them under her arm. It was done rather too casually. "Is that today's morning newspaper?" Sherlock asked. He hadn't had a chance to buy one, due to having a lie-in and John's unexpected arrival.

John and Mary shared a look. Mary said, "No, it is yesterday's. I am putting it in the fire." She lied very smoothly. Anyone but Sherlock wouldn't have doubted her words. John's face was also a dead giveaway, that Mary was not holding yesterday's paper.

Sherlock held out a hand. "Oh, let me see it. I will soon enough, won't I? The Dillon Kid murder?"

John nodded and Mary handed it over. Sherlock was front page news, or an editorial cartoon of his antics at Dillon Kid's murder scene were. There he was, sketched sitting atop the corpse, puffing away on his pipe and farting. He had foreseen this, hadn't he? His nose was drawn as jutting and generously proportioned as a hawk's beak. The caption below the cartoon was not as clever as the ones he had imagined. It said, 'London's Greatest Detective? Or London's Greatest Windbag?' Cat Watson was even in the cartoon, a clothes' peg plugging his nose. John Marmalade had not been drawn in.

Sherlock did not bother to read the longer article on the murder, and its expedient solving by one Inspector Gregson. He could do that at his leisure at home. He tossed the paper back onto the table, saying, "You might want to frame that, John. Hang it in your office for a good laugh on dark days."

"There will be dark days to come, if I can't find Gladstone." John raised an eyebrow, in encouragement. He wanted Sherlock to get a move on, start the investigation.

Sherlock glanced down at Cat Watson, who was sniffing around Mary. "Cat Watson, can you track Gladstone's scent?" Cat Watson sat down and gave Sherlock a most affronted little glare. "Yes, I know you *can*. His odor is so pungent, I could probably track it, if I dropped to all fours and put my nose to the ground, but I have no desire to do any such thing. My true question is, will you track Gladstone's trail? I could investigate for clues, but that is a much lengthier process, isn't it?"

Cat Watson stood up with obvious grudging resignation. He half-heartedly made for the door which lead to the rear of the house, sniffing delicately as he went, his ears laid on his head with displeasure.

Mary and John shared another glance. "It's as if the cat truly understands Sherlock," Mary said in amazement.

"Yes, yes, let's all follow the clever cat," John said snippily. So they did, the three of them. Cat Watson led them straight out the backdoor. None of them bothered to don coats. The autumn day was crisp, but not overly chilly, and the sun was out for the moment. Clouds were wafting in from the west, but they had yet to arrive overhead.

Cat Watson bypassed the outbuildings and padded down the lane behind the house. At the end of the lane, where it intersected a more travelled road, he slowed. He went up the road a bit, sniffing, then down the road. Finally, he sat down and meowed in puzzlement.

"Ah, Gladstone's trail ends here, which means he was no longer waddling along. He must have been picked up by a conveyance. A wagon or cart," Sherlock proposed.

John gave a dramatic moan and wailed, "Gladstone has been dognapped! Oh, perhaps a ransom note has already been delivered."

Since there was no longer a trail for Cat Watson to follow, their small group returned to the house. John searched frantically for a ransom note in the mailbox, and around the front of the house, and in the entranceway. When he couldn't find one, he took calming breaths.

"It will be delivered soon, I'm sure. Let us have brandy while we wait."

They settled again in the parlour. Brandy was poured and sipped. Even Mary had one, after she fetched a little saucer of cream and a chicken wing for Cat Watson, who meowed a polite thank-you.

Sherlock relaxed on the chesterfield. It was a cozy sitting room with the fire burning low. He said, "Whoever made off with your foul dog will not deliver a ransom note. They will return the offensive beast, forthwith, I am sure. No-one, except you, would choose to keep Gladstone in their home." Sherlock tapped his nose. "I don't know how Mary puts up with the beast underfoot, and under-nose."

John sputtered a bit before he managed, "Mary loves Gladstone every bit as much as I do, don't you Mary?"

"Of course, John," Mary said dutifully. Sherlock knew it was a bald-faced lie, yet did not say so. John was upset enough, and Sherlock, despite their recent differences, did not wish to add to his distress.

"If no note is delivered and Gladstone is not returned this day, I will investigate in earnest on the morrow," Sherlock said.

John's moustache wilted, as did his face. "Can't you start investigating now? You are already here, and you're not working on any other cases at the moment, are you? Now that you have solved Dillon Kid's murder for Inspector Gregson."

"I have no other cases to engage my mind, at present," Sherlock admitted. "But I have not yet taken a meal today."

"Well, we'll feed you right up, won't we, Mary? We'll enjoy luncheon, not that I can eat a bite with my stomach a knot of worry over Gladstone, but still ... after luncheon, if no ransom note has been delivered, we will investigate Gladstone's disappearance. Together. The two of us, like the old days." It was decided, at least in John's mind.

Cat Watson gave a little hiss, because John had said two, not three, usurping Cat Watson's position as Sherlock's newest investigative companion. John didn't notice, or pretended not to. They relocated to the dining room. Luncheon was brought to the table and enjoyed by all, even John, who seemed to have found his appetite.

Directly after luncheon, the two men rose and went to smoke their after-luncheon pipes in the parlour, with yet more brandy. Sherlock noticed that John was pouring with a liberal hand, but he did not worry overly. The brandy numbed John's distress, and numbed the pain of Sherlock's many healing wounds, so drink they did. Not one to normally over-indulge in the mid-afternoon, Sherlock was surprised to find himself soon unsteady on his pins. And getting a bit silly.

"Dr. Watson, I presume?" he said with a chuckle, when John refilled his goblet for a fourth, or perhaps fifth, time. Sherlock's usually razor-sharp memory was a bit foggy on that point.

"John, if you please, but not Marmalade John or Johnny Marma'lady." John giggled and stumbled back to his seat on the chesterfield. "Shouldn't we commence with our 'vestigationing now?" John attempted to sip his brandy, missed his mouth, and dribbled down his shirtfront.

"Yes, let us commence with the investigationing forthwith," Sherlock drawled, trying to focus on John, who had gone all wiggly and out of focus, as if seen through a fast-rushing stream of fog. "Have to find your horrible beast. Do you know, I think your moustache is more horribler than your hound."

John puffed up like a pigeon and stroked his horrendous facial hair as if it was a cherished pet. "My moustache is the pride of my face," he declared. "Why, just ask my nose."

Sherlock squinted at John's foggy face and said, "John's nose, how can you put up with those ghastly whiskers lurking below you? Collecting crumbs and vermin? Why, I believe I see a caterpillar in there. John's nose, have you noticed a caterpillar in that moustache?"

John answered, as his nose. "There's not'a one caterpillar in the grand forest of hair below my nostrils. Why, if there was, I would feel it creepy crawling around. And Mary would have felt it too, when John kisses her all over her silky skin."

Sherlock clapped both hands over his ears and slammed his eyes shut. "I hear no evil. I see no evil, except that evil moustache where a caterpillar lurks. I'll prove there is a caterpillar in there, or a centipede at least." He hopped up and scanned the room. He stumbled off to the kitchen, and returned with a pair of scissors.

John waved a hand around, knocking over his almost empty glass. "Put those scissors down, Sherlock. You could poke someone's eye out with them, like that Killon Did ... Dillon Kid, or that other fellow, Harry Crapper'poo. They've both lost an eye, haven't they?"

"True enough, John, but scissors were not involved. It was a spoon and a knife, so scissors are perfectly safe, as long as you don't run with them. Let me trim that moustache of yours, just a bit, see if we can't find that caterpillar."

Sherlock stumbled closer, surprised that his feet were so unmanageable. He gripped one side of John's moustache, tugged it straight, and aimed for it with the scissors. "Cut, cut, cut, the hair right off your face," he sing-songed, and did just that. Half of John's moustache came away from John's face.

John cried out, "Ouch, you've cut my nose off."

"No, no, it's still there." Sherlock tweaked John's nose, proving the point. Although, there was indeed blood dripping down from a slice to one of John's nostrils, while his face had only half a ghastly moustache left to droop pathetically. "Just a little nick, I'm sure," said Sherlock, who was now seeing double: two Johns, two mangled moustaches, two rivulets of blood. Did he suddenly need spectacles? He managed to nab the other half of the uncooperative moustache, ignoring the blood trickling down John's face. He tugged it out from John's face and cut enthusiastically, as close to John's face as he could manage.

"Ouch," said John. "You've done it again. Wounded me."

True, another trickle of blood was now meandering down the other side of John's face, yet neither wound was life-threatening. Only ragged, short remnants of the moustache remained, so a few nicks were neither here nor there. But those ragged remnants had to go. "John, where is your straight razor? The scissors can only do so much. I need to shave you. Shall I play Sweeney Todd and be your barber?" Sherlock had never believed the tale of the murderous demon barber on Fleet Street himself, yet many did.

John used his handkerchief to mop at the blood on his face, which was taking its time to clot. Perhaps the nicks were deeper than either of them realized. John felt his nostril and said, "You've cut through my nostril, I'll have to stitch it closed, or I won't be able to blow my nose properly. I don't think I want you using a straight razor on my poor wounded face, when we've both had a bit too much brandy."

"It's fine, John. The rest of that moustache has to go. Now where is it? Your razor—not the rest of that moustache. Why, that is right there on your face." Sherlock poked at the moustache remnants. He accidentally poked John's eye instead.

"Ouch," John said. "Are you trying to make me a one-eyed Watson?"

"Don't be silly. I'll just go fetch your razor. I assume it is in your water closet?" He swung around to go and fetch it, and almost tripped over Cat Watson. The cat had been gone for some time and Sherlock hadn't noticed his return. Well, cats were the stealthiest of creatures. You would not know they were there, unless they wished you to.

"Sorry, Cat Watson," he apologized. He side-stepped the cat, and collided with Mary. He hadn't seen her enter, either. Was she as stealthy as a cat? Or had he truly had so much brandy, his normally sharp senses were as dull as John's?

"What is going on here?" Mary hands planted on her hips. "John, why are you bleeding?"

"Sherlock cut off my moustache." John dabbed more blood.

"Praise be," Mary muttered under her breath. Sherlock heard her, but John did not. So she didn't like John's insult to proper moustaches everywhere, not any more than she liked Gladstone, an insult to respectable hounds everywhere.

"I'm fetching John's straight razor, to do away with the scraggles of his hideous moustache. Did you know those razors are also called cut-throat razors?" he asked her.

"I have heard that name used for them." She looked from him to John, and back again. "I don't think this is the best time for you to use a cut-throat razor on John. You have already done enough damage to my husband's face with a pair of scissors. I shall trim off the rest of the moustache, properly, later. I do believe your cat has some news for you," she mentioned.

Sherlock forgot all about the razor. "Cat Watson, what news?" he asked, and half-expected the cat to answer in words. Cat Watson was looking disapproving and gave him a scolding meow. "Yes, perhaps I have drunk a bit too much brandy," he admitted. "But even in my cups, I am more astute than any man. I can find Gladstone, even though Mary has probably hidden him away much more cleverly than she hid her bicycle. Unless she killed him. Did you kill Gladstone, Mary?" he asked, as inspiration struck.

Mary's eyes widened in alarm. John gaped at Sherlock, then at Mary. It was if he didn't know who to gape at. He stopped gaping and sputtered, "You are way off the mark there, Sherlock. Too much brandy has befuddled your mind, addled your senses, and rendered you witless!"

"Even slightly inebriated, I can solve any case presented to me. Mary hid her own bicycle, and she is behind Gladstone's disappearance. Tell him, Mary," Sherlock ordered.

John cut in. "I know you resent the fact that I married Mary, and moved out of 221B, but you cannot make baseless accusations. My wife would never betray me. She loves me, and therefore she loves my dog. Why, the very idea of her dognapping Gladstone, or worse, is quite preposterous! Isn't it, Mary?"

"Quite preposterous," she agreed.

Sherlock grabbed Mary's skirt, and shook it. "Dog hair!" he declared. "It is all over her left side. If she has not been in close contact with Gladstone this very day, why are there copious amounts of dog hair on her skirt, where Gladstone walks beside her when he comes to heel?" Sherlock shook her skirt again, then gripped Mary by the shoulders and turned her around. He pointed at her posterior accusingly. "Look, there is minimal dog hair on her bottom. It is only on the side of her skirt where Gladstone walks beside her. She has not gotten dog hair on her skirt from sitting on an upholstered chair laden with dog hair." He pointed at her posterior again, emphatically, to reinforce his point. Perhaps because of the brandy, he misjudged the distance and gave Mary's bottom an enthusiastic poke.

She gasped and leapt around, her face the picture of shock.

John leapt to his feet. "Stop manhandling my wife! It is indecent. The height of boorishness! I know you do not always adhere to the strictures of decent behaviour, as do most gentlemen, but poking my wife's bottom! That is going too far. And accusing her of evil deeds, as if she is a common criminal! When she is the most upstanding and proper of wives. Sherlock, you have gone too far!"

"You have not even looked at her skirt, John, or acknowledged what I have said. This clue cannot be denied." Sherlock gave the skirt another shake.

As a waved cape will enrage a bull, the flapping skirt was too much for John. He let out an angry bellow and charged at Sherlock. Sherlock dropped into a fighter's stance, fists raised. He was a superior boxer, and could best any man. John might have been a soldier, but he was a doctor first, and no trained pugilist.

Cat Watson scurried out of the line of fire and cowered beneath an armchair, yowling in distress. Mary shouted, "Stop this uncivilized, idiotic, ungentlemanly behaviour, this instant!"

Neither man paid her any heed. John kept charging. Sherlock kept waving his fists about. The two men met in the middle of the parlour. The fight was short-lived, or one could say, non-existent. John ran into Sherlock's waving fist, and received a smart jab to the jaw. He dropped, out cold. John had always had a glass jaw.

Sherlock lowered his fists, dangerous weapons that they were, instantly filled with regret. Shocked sober, he looked down at John— his face bloody and cut with scissors, his hideous moustache mangled to scruffy remnants, his eyes closed and his face slack. Knocked out.

Cat Watson crept from beneath the chair and cast Sherlock a reproachful glance. "I didn't mean to knock him out." Sherlock bit his lip and turned to Mary. "You should have just told John you had done away with Gladstone."

"I did no such thing. Perhaps someone took him for a long walk, and decided to take him home for a day or two, because he was too tired to walk back. Gladstone is not the fittest of dogs." Mary shrugged. "Of course, that is merely a possibility. I am not saying that is what happened, nor am I confirming that I was involved in Gladstone's disappearance in any way."

"If you dislike Gladstone to such a degree that you cannot bear his presence in your home, you should have done away with him permanently. A day or two without the smelly hound does not solve your problem, does it?"

"Oh Sherlock, you can be quite clueless. I am not trying to solve my problem. No, there is another issue that needs addressing to ensure my husband's happiness, and that is what I am doing, to the best of my ability, although I do seem to be making a right hash of things." She brushed dog hair off her skirt. "I seem to be making matters worse, rather than better."

Cat Watson meowed sympathetically, as if he understood what was going on. "What issue?" Sherlock felt as clueless as she accused him of being, and not even as clever as a cat, albeit a most exceptional one.

Mary merely shook her head, in frustration. "I suggest you leave now. You have done enough damage to John." Mary crouched beside John and tapped his cheek lightly. "Dearest, wake up now. I'm going to get a cold cloth for your poor face."

John groaned and blinked. He squinted up. Sherlock and Mary were peering down at him. Cat Watson had taken a seat on his chest.

The cat was gazing down at John too, in the manner of a vulture eyeing prey.

"I seem to have fallen. I don't think I can get up," John mumbled hazily.

Sherlock nodded to John, donned his coat and hat, picked up his cat, and slunk from the house. He was shamed by his base behaviour. What had come over him? Brandy, that's what. He yearned to make amends, yet he wasn't sure how.

Cat Watson meowed stridently, and squirmed to be free. Sherlock set him down. The cat instantly padded around the side of the house, meowing plaintively and glancing over his shoulder.

"Yes, yes, I know you want me to follow you. But why are we going around the house, to the back?" he asked. Of course there was no worded answer, so he simply followed where the cat led, at that pointing trusting its judgement more than his own.

18 – Making Amends

🐱 *from The Observations of Cat Watson*

I felt so bad about the deteriorating situation between Sherlock and Dr. Watson, I had made up my mind to try again to find Gladstone. If Sherlock brought the dog home, both men would be happy. If he didn't, Dr. Watson might never speak to him again.

I will admit, my first attempt to track Gladstone had been a half-hearted effort. Suspecting that Mary had made him disappear, and given his offensive appearance, drooling affliction, and general gassiness, I wasn't convinced the dog should be found and returned home. Yet now, circumstances had caused me to alter my opinion. Gladstone must be restored to Dr. Watson, by none other than Sherlock Holmes. It would go a long way to mending fences, I was sure.

Nose near the ground, I again tracked Gladstone's distasteful scent. Sherlock followed me, sighing sadly every dozen or so steps, although I don't believe he was aware of doing so. When I again arrived at the spot where the back lane met the road, I sniffed about more thoroughly. Given the pungency of Gladstone's odor—I mean, had the dog never had a bath in his life? Cats wash themselves most meticulously, at least three times a day, to the point of fussiness. But dogs were useless. Unless a human plunked a dog into a tub of soapy water, the dog usually kicking and howling, a dog was a filthy creature. They were quite incapable of keeping themselves washed, and were prone to gamboling about in mud. I had even seen more than one dog roll around on manure, on purpose! Foul creatures, dogs, every last one.

As much as cats like being clean, they do not like being wet. If a human tries to plunk a cat into a tub of soapy water for a wash, there will be hell to pay. And you will never see a cat strolling happily about in the rain, playing in puddles, as dogs are inclined to do, foolish creatures that they are. But I digress.

Gladstone's scent, and therefore Gladstone, went to the right, along the larger road. He was clearly riding in some sort of conveyance, or his scent would have been far stronger. The road was not as busy as a main street, yet it was more travelled than a laneway. I trotted faster, until I noticed Sherlock flagging. I had forgotten how much brandy he had imbibed, on top to his accumulated injuries.

I slowed to a more manageable pace, turning now and then onto different roads. I soon knew the dog was riding in a farmer's cart, because his odor continued to co-mingle with the scent of cabbage, some on the verge of rotting. It was not a pleasant scent at all, yet it was still vastly preferable to Gladstone's own. Sherlock pointed out a consistent wheel mark to me, and we both had a trail to follow.

After almost an hour at a steady pace, Sherlock following the wheel marks and yours truly tracking the stench of Gladstone and cabbage, it began to drizzle. Fog rolled in. In concert with the sun lowering from the sky, it turned dark rather suddenly.

Like all cats, I had no trouble seeing in the night. If a cat has the tiniest speck of light to see by, it can see very well indeed. The same cannot be said for humans, not even exceptional ones like Sherlock Holmes. Luckily, we arrived at our destination then, before the drizzle increased to true rain, or the fog turned into a pea-souper so thick, a cat couldn't see his own tail, if he turned around to admire it.

Our destination presented as a generally rundown green grocer. We entered the shop. A man was attending the counter. As it was autumn, the counter was stocked mainly with root vegetables and whatever remained leftover from the late summer, that hadn't yet spoiled. In addition, there was a small selection of prepared meats, loaves of bread, a barrel of pickles, and some aged cheeses. I realized I was hungry.

I leapt onto an upturned crate, to have a higher view of the goings-on, not to help myself to a nibble of sausage or cheese. Sherlock let out a weary breath. "So the trail ends here," he said to me. I meowed in agreement.

At that moment, the grocer said, "Hey, get that moggy away from my foodstuffs!"

Sherlock laid a protective hand on me. "He is with me and he won't do any harm. I am here to retrieve Gladstone."

The man lowered his brow in a puzzled scowl. His skin had seen too much sun, and had weathered to a leathery texture. His wrinkles were as deeply ingrained as rivers, on the landscape of his face. He wiped a hand on his stained, work-worn apron, picked up a turnip, and said, "Gladstone? What's a Gladstone? I only got turnips, and cabbage and carrots, and squash and a bit of them meats and cheeses and breads - " He might have listed all the offerings in plain sight, if Sherlock hadn't held up a commanding hand.

"Gladstone is a dog, not a vegetable. Although, if I take a moment to reflect on it, he is about as intelligent as that turnip you are holding. Regardless, Gladstone is Dr. Watson's dog, as I am sure you know."

"I don't know nothing of the sort. I don't have nobody's dog, not even my own, as I don't have a dog." He picked up a butcher knife and stabbed a turnip as if he was intent on killing it. "Look how fresh these turnips are. I'm sure you want to buy a sack full of them. Cart them home to the missus."

"Perhaps I will purchase some turnips for my landlady, and potatoes and carrots and cabbage as well. If I purchase a large order, too much to carry, do you have a cart that can deliver it to my address?" Sherlock asked.

The man jerked a thumb toward the back of the shop. "Right out back it is. I can deliver tomorrow. What would you like?"

Sherlock said, "I will place my order, after the matter of the missing dog is settled."

"It's already settled. I don't know nothing about a dog."

At that moment, Gladstone's familiar woof sounded from somewhere in the bowels of the shop—the backroom area off-limits to customers. Gladstone must have heard Sherlock's voice, as he proceeded to growl with gusto.

"What was that I just heard?" Sherlock cupped a hand to his ear.

"Well, I guess the boss has a dog back there, but I didn't know it was there. I don't see what comes in through the back door. I don't know a thing about what goes on in the backroom," the man stressed, most emphatically.

"Be that as it may, I am going to go back there and see if that dog is the one I am seeking." Sherlock maintained a friendly tone and relaxed pose, adding, "I am not accusing anyone of dog thievery, or dognapping. Believe me, no-one would want Gladstone, well, except John. Gladstone is the foulest hound imaginable. He should be named

Sadstone or Badstone, as there is certainly nothing glad about him, or any gladness to be felt when around him. He smells like hell, gassy as a swamp, drools like a rainy day, sheds hair everywhere he waddles, and is about as intelligent as a turnip, as I have already stated, but perhaps I am doing the turnip an injustice to say so -" Sherlock might have kept maligning Gladstone, except Gladstone howled. Sherlock took a step toward the door that led into the backroom.

The grocer freed his sharp blade from the turnip with a jerk. He tossed it from one hand to the other. "The boss don't like to be interrupted when doing business."

Cats have a well-honed instinct for survival, and I was getting a very bad feeling about how this scene was unfolding.

"Finding Gladstone is a favour for a friend, and I must retrieve him." Almost like magic, a long stick appeared in Sherlock's hand. It had come from somewhere in his coat. I didn't think a stick was the best weapon to bring to a knife fight, and felt a distraction was in order. With no time to think of something truly clever, I simply leapt up onto the counter and sank my teeth into a sausage.

The grocer glanced at me, for just a split second. It was all the time Sherlock needed. As fast as a whip, his stick knocked the blade from the man's hand. The grocer howled in pain and clutched his fingers against his chest. His cries were heard.

The door to the backroom flew opened and an unsavory type filled it, barring the entrance. He was also holding a knife. At least it wasn't a pistol. Sherlock leapt forward with a strong agility that belied his healing injuries. The blade was dislodged from the thug's hand, by that amazing stick.

I did my part and darted into the backroom, right between the legs of the thug. Sherlock was close on my heels, knocking the thug down and out, with a brawler's punch, not his stick. He stood over the felled man and we surveyed the mysterious backroom.

It was bigger than one might expect, and much more lavish than the shoddy shop out front, which was apparently also *a front*. A round table in the center of the room was surrounded by four chairs. On that table was a wealth of banknotes, piles of coins, glinting jewelry, gold watches, valuable trinkets, etc. Ill-gotten goods if ever I had seen them.

Only two chairs were occupied, by a man and a woman. There was also a teapot and steaming cups on the table, to be enjoyed while counting the booty, no doubt. Gladstone was not in the room, but could be heard howling from behind another door to the side of the room.

Sherlock stood firm, poised in the threshold. He had one foot on the felled thug's neck, as he assessed the scene before him. "This is unexpected, but I haven't a care for your petty crimes," he began.

Before he had a chance to mention Gladstone, twin pistols were pointed at him. The man and woman each held one. The guns must have been on their laps, at the ready. "Take your foot off my son's neck," the woman ordered.

Sherlock was savvy enough to know that his stick was no match for two pistols. He removed his foot. When the woman motioned him in, with her gun, he entered. I stuck close to Sherlock's feet, afraid for both of us.

"My crimes are anything but petty." The woman narrowed her eyes on Sherlock. "How did you find our place of business?"

"I can assure you, I wasn't looking for it, madam. I was looking for something else entirely," Sherlock said.

"And what would that be?"

Before Sherlock could answer, her son found his feet. "Can I shoot him, Ma?" He shut the door to the shop, ensuring privacy, and pressed a pistol hard against the back of Sherlock's neck. This was a well-armed family, to be sure.

"Not here." His mother gestured around. "This is our headquarters. I keep it clean and proper. Presentable, not bloody. You know killing is done elsewhere."

"So I can shoot him elsewhere?" her son said.

"Yes." The woman definitely seemed to be in charge.

"Madam, I have only come to retrieve a dog by the name of Gladstone," Sherlock said.

The woman pulled a face. "Gladstone? Why would you want that beastie? He's awful."

"Hideous," her son said.

"The worst," the man added.

"Then you will be happy if I take him off your hands." Sherlock attempted a winning smile, I think. He wasn't very good at smiling, probably because he did it so rarely. It looked a bit like a snarl partnered with a wince.

The woman's eyes narrowed on Sherlock. Her gun did not lower. "Why do you want the hound?"

"Oh, *I* don't want it. Gladstone is a curse I can live without. I merely wish to return the dog to his owner, who is missing it. Almost impossible to believe, I know, but ..." Sherlock trailed off with a shrug.

"No, she wouldn't have sent you to pick him up, not here. You're lying." The woman glanced at her son. "Tie him up tight before you cart him down to the river. It's dark and foggy enough that you won't be seen. Slit his throat there and toss him in. And don't get any blood in the cart, like you did last time."

Sherlock chose to address something else, not his impending murder. "She? Who is she? Gladstone is owned by my former companion, Dr. John Watson."

The woman got a sucking lemons expression. "Oh, and who would you be then? You ain't been polite enough to introduce yourself."

The man seated opposite said, "He's that farting detective, Sherlock Holmes. Don't you recognize his nose, and that hat? And that cat?"

The woman squinted at Sherlock. She was clearly near-sighted. "Oh yes, now I see it. Well, it don't matter who he is. He's seen our place of business, our goings-on, heard talk of murder. He has to go into the river with the fishies now. Nothing else for it."

With two pistols trained on him, Sherlock had no choice but to stand unmoving while his hands were tied tightly behind his back. Things were not looking good for my Sherlock, and I didn't know how to help him. As clever and resourceful as I was, I was still only one small cat. His ankles were even hobbled, so he couldn't run, but merely take mincing steps. Lastly, a filthy rag was knotted around his mouth, making him gag, as it served as a gag.

At that point, the woman said, "The cart is still parked outside the backdoor, still hitched up to the nag. Isn't that handy. Make sure you cover him with that old blanket, so nobody sees him if they bump into the cart in the fog. Knock him out if he makes a fuss, but not so hard that you split his skull in two. No blood in the cart, remember."

The son prodded Sherlock in the back with his pistol, to start hobbling toward the backdoor. I hissed at the treatment, and the fellow tried to kick me. I eluded his big clumsy foot with ease. No-one had been paying me any attention, and perhaps I should have stayed in the shadows, yet my anger had gotten the better of me.

Sherlock was about to exit through the backdoor, when it was flung opened, bonking him on the forehead. It knocked him backward with force, and because his ankles were hobbled, he fell, landing hard on his wounded bottom. Even through the gag, he howled with pain. It cut off abruptly, when he saw who had entered.

I could not believe my eyes, but there she was, standing and towering over us. Mary Watson, of all people. And would her sudden appearance benefit Sherlock, or condemn him?

19 - Mary, Mary, Quite Contrary

Sherlock was gobsmacked as well as head-smacked, to see Mary rush into the backroom. Perhaps he should not have been, gobsmacked that is. Gladstone was present, after all. The head-smacked had been quite beyond his control, bound as he was. She took in the scene at a glance and wailed, "Ma, what are you doing?"

The woman, Mary's mother, and Dr. Watson's mother-in-law it would seem, put her pistol down on the table as nonchalantly as possible. She laid a napkin over it, as if hiding it from sight meant it had never been there at all. "Why nothing, Mary, only what needs doing. Your brother is taking care of the problem."

Mary scowled at her brother, who was hiding his pistol behind his back. "Robbie, you're going to shoot yourself in the butt. Put the gun down." Head ducked, Robbie set his gun on the table beside his mother's, sliding it beneath the napkin. Mary pointed a warning figure at the man, the only one still armed. "Uncle Theo, you as well," she ordered. He laid his gun down before him, reluctantly, with no attempt to hide it from view.

The guns all safely on the table, Mary shook her head at the three of them. Gladstone's howls had increased in volume. She took a paper-wrapped, string-tied little bundle out of her pocket. She slid an automatic knife from her boot, clicked it into position, and cut through both the string and butcher's paper with a deft flick of that razor sharp blade. Mary opened the side door in the room and tossed a big meaty bone to Gladstone, saying, "Now shut up." He immediately stopped howling and commenced chomping. She closed the door on Gladstone, leaned her back against it, arms crossed, and returned her attention to the occupants of the room, knife still in hand.

Sherlock grunted and jutted his chin out, reminding her of his plight. He wanted the disgusting rag out of his mouth, he wanted to be untied, and he was quite sure his bottom was bleeding again. At least, he hoped that was why it felt damp and a bit sticky. Worse possibilities did not bear thinking about. Cat Watson climbed onto his thighs and sat down, as if to guard him, now that the pistols had been set aside.

Mary smiled down at Sherlock on the ground. "Oh no, I am not taking the rag out of your mouth. I like you quiet. You are going to listen, not flap your lips, so the gag stays in." She pointed at him with her dangerous knife, her demeanor very different from when she was at home with John. It was much more aggressive and rather scary.

Sherlock huffed at her, all he could do in his present situation and degrading position on the floor. "So, you with your great detecting skills and keen intellect, have tracked down Gladstone. I didn't think you could, not to here, but alas you have. And now you know things you shouldn't."

Mary stepped over his long legs, and plunked down on one of the chairs. She laid her knife on the table before her, in hand's reach. Her brother joined them at the table, and the four sat together like a cozy little family. Sherlock was left on the floor, on his abused bottom, a bound prisoner at their mercy.

He grunted his displeasure and Mary said, "Do shut-up, Sherlock. I need to think." She reached for the teapot and poured herself a cup. Sherlock craved a cup of tea, but none was offered to him, nor could he drink one.

"Nothing to think about," Robbie declared. "I'm taking him to the river to slit his throat and toss him in. Fishies be hungry for fresh blood."

Mary's mother bobbed her head enthusiastically in agreement. "Problem solved. He's seen too much." She waved a hand over the clearly stolen valuables. "Heard too much. Knows our place of business. We ain't no penny mob, stealing pennies. We ain't no corner gang who can shift to another corner. We're well established here -"

Uncle Theo cut in, "Only thing for it, Mary."

Mary sighed. "But it will make John so sad, if Sherlock disappears without a trace. Or if his body washes ashore and John knows he is dead. I can't do that to my husband. And," she eyed each of her family members in turn, "I have told you that I don't want you murdering anyone any longer. Only stealing, and pickpocketing, and shoplifting and extortion. A bit of smash and grab, and a few beating if you have to, but no murder. Murder brings the coppers in swarms, like flies to dung."

Sherlock could not help but notice that Mary was the one in charge of this criminal gang. The rest of her family followed her lead. Did John suspect that his wife was a crime boss? Of course he didn't, which was not at all surprising given John's lack of observational skills. Mary probably could have run this whole criminal enterprise from their home, and John wouldn't have been any the wiser.

Mary finished her tea in gulps, rather than lady-like sips. She set her cup down with a thump. Her family waited in silence for her to speak, as if afraid of her wrath should they interrupt her ruminations. She picked up her knife and swivelled on her chair to face Sherlock directly. "I do not want to kill you," she began.

"Hey, I'm the one that gets to kill him. Ma said so," Robbie whined.

"He is not going to be killed at all, if he agrees to certain terms," Mary said. "Sherlock, John would be very upset, and his reputation ruined, if it became known that his wife is not only a working woman, but managing a … questionable business enterprise. How do you think we afford that nice big house John lives in? With all those servants to do our bidding?"

Sherlock rolled his eyes. He had presumed Mary came from *money*. As it turned out, she did, but not at all in the way he had supposed.

Mary continued, "I propose that you forget what you have seen here. Erase it from your mind. Pretend it never happened. John and I will continue to live happily, and you will be his friend. I can assure you, my associates and employees do little harm on the streets. We are no major gang, merely a minor player on the criminal stage. There are far worse criminal organizations out there."

Sherlock grudgingly nodded his head. Cat Watson meowed agreeably. There were very violent gangs on the streets, like the Peaky Blinders and the Backstabbers and the Kneecap Busters. Mary's gang did not seem to be of that ilk, although he wasn't sure about that brother of hers. And Sherlock didn't want John's life and reputation ruined. Gads, he had just cut up John's face and moustache, and knocked him out. The last thing he wanted to do was add insult to injury.

"Or we could just kill him," Robbie said.

Sherlock strained his eyeballs to peer down at his gag and grunted, indicating he wanted it removed so he could speak. Mary rose wearily and walked behind him. She sliced off the gag with an expert hand, spilling not a drop of his blood in the process. "Tea," he rasped. His mouth was sandy dry and tasted foul. Cat Watson gave a chirrupy little meow, wanting tea as well. Or cream without the tea.

Mary circled back into view and pursed her lips. "Do you agree to my terms, Sherlock?"

Sherlock sniffed. "Fine, for John's sake, I do. I don't want his life ruined. But no murdering. You'll have to control that bloodthirsty brother of yours."

"Robbie's not so bad. He's all talk," Mary said.

"I am not," Robbie whined.

"I don't think he is all talk, given how eager he was to slit my throat. If I discover that your gang is committing murder, I will not be able to keep silent. Nor would John wish me to. He is an honourable man."

"He is, and I love him. Fine, no murdering." Mary gave each of her family members a narrow, flinty glare. "You make sure everyone in the organization is made very aware of my command, or they'll feel the cut of my blade." They all bobbed their heads, even Robbie, though with sad regret rather than enthusiasm.

"Untie me now," Sherlock said. Mary raised one eyebrow at him. "Please. And some tea would not go amiss," he added.

"Don't push it." Mary used her handy blade to slice his wrists and ankles free, without inflicting a nick. She should have been the one to remove John's moustache. She would have done a much better job of it. Task complete, her automatic knife was closed. It disappeared from sight, back into her boot.

Cat Watson hopped off his legs and Sherlock rose stiffly from the floor. It felt a much longer way up that usual. Well, it was, because he was on the floor. He dusted off his cloak and said, "I had intended to return Gladstone to John, to put his mind at ease, but you can do it since you are here. I think I've torn the stitches out of my bottom, so I'm going to go home now." He adjusted his hat, and picked up Cat Watson. With as much dignity as he could muster, he limped toward the door that connected to the shop. He paused before opening it to ask, "What is the name of your gang?"

Mary smiled merrily. "Forty Flirty Thieves."

Sherlock had heard of the all-female gang of women who specialized in shoplifting and pickpocketing, hiding pilfered wallets and watches and jewelry in their specially sewn and secreted pockets. Women's fashions were so voluminous, they could hide a small pony on their person, if they were of a mind. Jewels and wallets and such, could easily disappear in the blink of an eye, never to be seen by their rightful owners again.

Truth be told, Sherlock found this new face of Mary quite intriguing. A woman at the helm of a crime organization was unusual, and fascinating. Maybe there was more to women that he had been raised to believe. He had recently encountered a female murderer, and now Mary had charge of a group of female thieves. Yes, John's Mary was becoming quite captivating to him.

Instead of turnips, potatoes and carrots, Sherlock purchased a selection of meats, cheeses and a loaf of bread. He also had to pay for the sausage Cat Watson had sampled.

A sandwich would be just the thing, when he finally got home, then he wouldn't have to disturb Mrs. Hudson for a meal. After the day he had endured, he did not feel energetic enough to fend off his landlady's advances. And if she spotted his bloody trousers, she might insist on bandaging his bottom. He quaked at the very possibility.

It was raining in earnest now. Sherlock hailed a carriage and settled into its dry interior with Cat Watson. He sat awkwardly on one cheek, the less punctured one, missing the plump cushion that was still on John's chesterfield.

Cat Watson licked the paper-wrapped package. "It's been quite a day, hasn't it? Do you like sandwiches, Cat Watson?" he asked, giving the cat a stroke. His little companion meowed agreeably and purred a bit. Sherlock opened the paper enough to remove some cheese. He enjoyed a few bites and fed Cat Watson nibbles, while they rode through the streets, discussing the unexpected discoveries of the day.

Sherlock had rarely felt so content to arrive home at 221B Baker Street. He slipped in through the outer door quietly, and tiptoed up the stairs, being sure to avoid the squeaky third step from the top. He shut himself in his rooms, and decided to take care of his battered body, before he made sandwiches. John Marmalade was not about. The little cat was probably keeping Mrs. Hudson company.

Only two of the stitches had torn out of his bottom, which he discovered by the strategic placement of his shaving mirror, and the striking of a most inelegant pose. Alas, his bottom would have to heal on its own, since John would not be in any fit state to act as his physician at the moment. Nor did Sherlock feel up to facing his friend, not with the newfound knowledge that Mary was a working woman, and in charge of a thriving criminal gang.

John had an almost sixth sense where Sherlock was concerned, perhaps because he knew him so well. John could always tell when Sherlock was lying to him. Even lying by omission to hide hard truths would raise John's suspicions. Sherlock would have to come to terms with what he had learned about Mary, and store it away in the deepest recesses of his mind, before he dared to face John again.

He lit the gas heater in the water closet, and indulged himself with a hot bath. A treat to be sure, but the cistern on the roof would contain a surplus of water as there had been plenty of rain. Well, there usually was in London.

Cat Watson slunk away when the hot water started flowing from the tap, and would not go near the tub. He seemed to cat-scowl from the doorway, when Sherlock lowered his long frame into the soothing water.

Sherlock was completely relaxed, enjoying a good soak, and drowsy enough to drift off to sleep right there in the bathing tub, when there was a light tap on his door. Mrs. Hudson's hand. He did not bid her to enter, yet he heard her key unlock the door. He had omitted to engage the sliding bolt lock, in case she had intended to return John Marmalade. Now he would pay the price. He sank lower in the water, wishing he had closed the bathroom door at least, but he hadn't wanted Cat Watson to think he was shunning him.

"Sherlock dearest?" Mrs. Hudson called.

"I am in the bath," he answered crisply. They were words that would ensure privacy when spoken to just about anyone in the land, excepting a most intimate acquaintance—and Mrs. Hudson, it seemed.

"I've just brought Johnny Marmalade home, and brewed you a fresh pot of tea. Wouldn't a cuppa be nice, in the tub?"

Sherlock opened his mouth to say, *No, it wouldn't*. He was not quick enough. Or Mrs. Hudson was too quick. She must have sprinted all the way to the bathroom like an Olympian. Sherlock barely had time to position his washcloth over his nether regions, before she darted right into the bathroom.

She was indeed carrying a tray. It held a teapot under a hand-knitted cozy, two cups, and a ginger kitten. John Marmalade was wearing a matching hand-knitted garment, which looked very much like the tea

113

cozy. "Good evening, Mrs. Hudson. John Marmalade looks very cozy, in that tea cozy." He willed his face not to redden.

"It is not a tea cozy, dearest Sherlock. It's a wee little sweater-vest. I knitted it for Johnny Marmalade." She balanced the tray on the sink and sat down on the toilet, intending to stay for a chat, it seemed. Hopefully not to do more than that, given where she had placed herself. Then again, it was the only seat in the room. "And don't you worry your fluffy wittle head, Cat Watson, I've almost finished knitting yours. It matches Johnny Marmalade's, so you can be two cutsy-wootsy widdle kitty-witty twinkins."

Cat Watson voiced a yowl of protest and glanced at Sherlock askance, from the safety of the doorway. Sherlock gave a helpless little shrug. He was in no position to save himself, let alone Cat Watson.

Mrs. Hudson lifted John Marmalade off the tea tray and set him on the floor, saying, "This wee pusspuss wouldn't stop meowing to come upstairs, once we heard you were home."

John Marmalade hurried over to Cat Watson, to rub against him and meow a greeting. Already the kitten was looking plumper and happier. He didn't seem to mind wearing the sweater-vest that resembled a tea cozy.

Mrs. Hudson proceeded to pour out two cups, clearly planning to stay and ogle Sherlock in the bath. "Thank-you, Mrs. Hudson. I do appreciate you looking after John Marmalade, when Cat Watson and I are out on a case. I will enjoy my tea now, and have an early night, after my bath," he said, in polite but firm dismissal.

She handed him his cup, not taking the hint. "Oh, Sherlock, it's no trouble at all. I enjoy his company. I do get lonely, downstairs, all alone, you know. Let me adjust that washcloth for you." Mrs. Hudson made to reach right into his bathwater.

"No," he cried out in alarm. "My washcloth is fine. It is exactly where I want it to be." He only wished it was larger, as large as a blanket.

"If you say so, Sherlock." She picked up her tea. "I have a problem and would like to engage your services," she said without preamble.

It was most unexpected. "You wish to be a client?"

"Yes, dearest. I have a serious problem, and I need help. You are the only one I trust to keep me out of jail. Although it wouldn't be jail, would it? It would surely be the hangman's noose." Mrs. Hudson tittered nervously.

Sherlock regarded Mrs. Hudson, and saw that she was in earnest. "My bathwater has cooled and I am turning quite pruney. I am going to dry and dress, and you will sit in the client's chair, while we discuss your case, out there, in the sitting room."

Mrs. Hudson nodded. "Yes, Sherlock dearest. Shall I hold your towel for you? Perhaps dry you off, a bit."

"No! I can manage perfectly well. Please take the tea tray out with you. And close the door," he added, in his most commanding tone.

Mrs. Hudson did so, emitting several heartfelt sighs. Sherlock breathed his own sigh, one of relief, to once again be alone in the privacy of his bathroom.

After drying off and bandaging his bottom as best he could, Sherlock donned his pajamas and his robe. He tossed his bloody trousers into the tub to soak in the water, before he drained it. He hoped they were not ruined. He would have no clothes left at the rate he was sullying them. And some of his clothes seemed to have gone missing of late. It was a mystery he hadn't yet tried to solve.

20 – A New and Unexpected Client

Sherlock hurried to join Mrs. Hudson in his parlour, truly curious about her case. She was waiting on the client's chair, as instructed. Cat Watson was already seated in his basket, in pride of place on John's former chair. Clever cat. John Marmalade was sharing the basket, but curled up and asleep.

Sherlock took his seat, most carefully. "Now, Mrs. Hudson, tell me what troubles you."

"You do know that I am a widow," she said.

"Yes, Mrs. Hudson."

"Have you ever wondered how my husband died?" she asked.

"No." In truth, he had never given it a thought. "I assumed it was in the war, which is how most men in their prime die."

"He wasn't in the war, and he certainly wasn't in his prime. He was a good deal older than me. He fell down and hit his head. We were fighting and I might have given him a little push," she said, eyes downcast.

"Did you really?" Sherlock was not often taken by surprise, yet he was now.

"And Mrs. Hudson isn't my real name," she added.

"Is it not?" Surprise number two.

"No, I was Mrs. Turner. After Mr. Turner died, I packed up all his banknotes and valuables and jewels. He had a lot of them. I moved to London, changed my name, and bought 221B Baker Street. I thought I had left my past behind me, well, except for bringing Mr. Turner along in one of my trunks. He's buried in the cellar now."

Surprise number three was the most shocking yet. "Why did you bring his body along?"

Mrs. Hudson, he could not think of her by any other name, frowned at Sherlock. "You are the detective. Isn't it obvious? I didn't want his body to be found. I didn't want to be accused of murder, even though it really was an accident. He was so old and frail, he was bound to fall

116

and hit his head sooner or later, and that's exactly what happened. I've kept his body safely hidden away these eight long years. I do admit, sometimes I go down there and talk to him, when I'm feeling particularly lonely. He never talks back, mind, but still, it's a comfort to know he's there. And he keeps Mr. Blakely company."

Cat Watson gave a questioning meow, as if he didn't understand what was going on. Sherlock was also feeling all in a fog, but before he asked who Mr. Blakely was, and he wasn't sure he wanted to know, he stuck to the topic at hand. "If the accident took place eight years ago, and his body has never been found, because it is buried in the cellar, why are you coming to me in regards to this matter now?"

"I've received an anonymous letter, Sherlock. Someone knows about the bodies in the cellar, or one of them anyway, and they demand to be paid to keep silent."

There was no avoiding the topic now. "Bodies?" He did not ask how many. He said, "Who is Mr. Blakely and why is his body in the cellar?"

"Oh, Mr. Blakely." Mrs. Hudson smiled mistily. "He was my beau for a time. I don't think you ever met him. You were away on a case when we had our affair. He did resemble you, you know, to some degree, being tall and slender, with thick dark locks, and gray eyes, and a prominent nose. I had a lot of money to spend and I liked to buy him presents. I bought him a lovely deerstalker cap, and one of those Inverness cloaks that you favour. He did look very attractive in them."

"Did he?"

"Oh yes. Mr. Turner was disgustingly wealthy, and old, when I married him, and of course, he was even older and richer when he died, by accident, mostly. So money really was no matter. Oh, Mr. Blakely and I did have our fun, until I found out he was gigolo."

"A gigolo?" Sherlock gasped out.

"He was some years younger than me, you see. He loved all those nice presents I bought him. I did like to spoil him, until I found out he was using me. I wasn't the only lady he was making happy. He had betrayed me. We had a bit of a squabble about it, and he fell down the cellar stairs. He landed on an axe, of all things. Can you believe it, Sherlock?"

He wasn't sure he could. He nodded his head anyway, his jaw rather slack.

117

"Such bad luck. What with the fall and the axe in his back, he ended up quite dead. How he died did look bad, even though it was an accident, mostly, so I felt it wise to simply bury him there, in the cellar. He was down there anyway, so it was convenient." Mrs. Hudson gave a helpless little shrug.

"I see. So there are two bodies down there?" Sherlock hoped it wasn't more, and in truth, he was rather terrified of his landlady at that moment.

"Yes, dearest. Only two, no more. And they both died by accident, mostly." She smiled reassuringly, as if only two bodies was nothing for him to worry his little head about. "I have come to you to discover who is set on blackmailing me, so let's forget about the deceased gentlemen in my cellar for the time being, shall we?"

"Uh … yes. I will focus on the case you have brought me, and that is the case I will solve. Do you have the letter?" Sherlock caught the quizzical glance Cat Watson cast him, complete with slightly tilted furry head. Sherlock gave a little shrug back. What could he do but take the case that his client, Mrs. Hudson, presented to him, and ignore the rest. At least for the moment.

Mrs. Hudson removed the letter from her cleavage and handed it over. It was warm and slightly damp. Sherlock read the short message aloud, to hear the words as well as see them. "If you want the body to stay buried, ha ha, pin that pretty blue carbuncle broach that Mr. Turner gave you, to your cardigan. Wear it to the corner market tomorrow morning. I'll take the jewel off your hands. You won't say a word and we'll be square. No coppers will come calling at your door, spades in hand, to dig up the body of your dearly departed husband." It was signed, *Your boss for now, ha ha.*

"Unusual wording, and disturbingly familiar." Sherlock examined the note down to the minutest detail. The paper was good quality, but readily available. The ink was an expensive true blue-black ink, not a substandard, watery sepia-black. There were no watermarks, or impressions of any other writing on the paper, perhaps left from writing on a sheet of paper atop it at some point. There was only the message itself. And one smear of grape jelly, with no discernable fingermark to indicate the size of the hand that had scripted the missive.

The penmanship was a bit of a puzzle. Some of the letters were well-formed, as if by a schooled hand, while others were hard to decipher, little more than a childish scribble. Normally, it was simple to determine if words were written by a man or woman, as they tended to form their letters differently. The blackmailer's script revealed no traits of either sex. And the wording—it was reminiscent of the letters purportedly sent by Jack the Ripper to the newspapers. Oh, how Sherlock would have liked to have solved that infamous case! Had someone imitated the tone of Jack the Ripper's letters, to write this blackmail note to Mrs. Hudson? Jack's letters had been printed in all the newspapers far and wide, repeatedly. Everyone in London, no, everyone in the Greater Britain, who could read, had read them.

Sherlock had a hard time believing that the never-caught Jack the Ripper was attempting to extort a broach from Mrs. Hudson. "This blue carbuncle broach, is it valuable? And was it gifted to you by Mr. Turner?" he asked.

"Yes to both. I wear it often, you must have noticed."

"I did. I notice most everything. I assumed it was costume jewelry, as I did not know that you were once, and perhaps still are, a wealthy woman," Sherlock said.

"Oh, I still am a very wealthy woman," Mrs. Hudson said proudly.

Sherlock tapped the page. "Who would know that the broach was given to you by Mr. Turner, your late husband?" Cat Watson leapt onto Sherlock's lap to sniff at the note. He even licked the little smear of grape jelly. Sherlock gave the missive a sniff, as well, but did not lick the grape jelly. It smelled like paper and ink, and Mrs. Hudson's perfume. She had been handling it and carrying it about on her person, rather intimately.

Mrs. Hudson said, "I do keep my past hush-hush, for obvious reasons. I've never mentioned my private affairs to anyone, except Mr. Blakely, and he's dead in the cellar. Has been for almost a year now. He can't be the blackmailer, now can he?"

"No," Sherlock agreed. "So, whoever saw you wearing the broach, recognized it, and possibly you as well. This blackmailer must have known you, or Mr. Turner, in the past. Perhaps they once lived where you did, and spotted you by chance in London. Or they followed you here, though that is unlikely. It has been eight years." He stroked Cat Watson. "It is also possible Mr. Blakely mentioned your circumstances and past history to someone else, before he had his … accident. At least the blackmailer has suggested a meeting in a public place, so you will not be in any danger."

Mrs. Hudson's face fell. "Do you think I should go to the market and let him take my beautiful blue carbuncle broach?"

"The alternative is worse. If the police were to find corpses in your cellar, it would be your ruin, and see you swinging," he said plainly.

"Oh, you make it sound so bad, Sherlock." Mrs. Hudson pouted. "It's not like I'm Jack the Ripper."

"It is bad, Mrs. Hudson. Alas, the trouble with blackmailers is that they are rarely satisfied with one payment. They tend to repeat their demands, getting ever greedier. So, I propose you go to the market, wearing your broach." Sherlock held up a hand for silence when she began to protest. "I will be there, close at hand, and in disguise." Sherlock could not help but smile. He did love to don a disguise and move about unseen, like a shadow.

"You'll stop him?" Mrs. Hudson said.

"Not initially. Let him take the broach. I will be watching and see it happen. I will follow him away from the market. Then, I will deal with him, and retrieve your broach." Sherlock left it at that. He could not predict how events would unfold after the blackmailer got his hands on the broach. Sherlock would have to react according to the situation, once he learned the identity of the blackmailer. As to the bodies in the cellar ... well, that was not his case. And he preferred not to dwell on it at all.

"Well, if you're sure, Sherlock." Mrs. Hudson finished her tea, a deep furrow of worry between her eyebrows.

"I will not let you come to harm, Mrs. Hudson. Trust me."

"Oh I do, Sherlock dearest." She fluttered her eyelashes.

He cleared his throat. "The blackmailer has not stated a time, merely morning, so I suggest you go to the market later, around eleven. That will give me time to observe all the comings and goings, whilst in disguise. It will also be less crowded at eleven, so it will be easier for me to spot and follow our villain." He rose, indicating that their meeting was over.

Mrs. Hudson stood, too. "You do think of everything, Sherlock. Such a clever detective." She adjusted his robe, ironing it smooth on his chest.

Sherlock stepped back. "I will bid you a goodnight now, Mrs. Hudson. I must prepare my disguise. Do as I have instructed and know that I will be watching you at the market, even though you won't be able to see me. Do not look for me, as that would alert your blackmailer to my presence."

"Yes, Sherlock. I do like the thought of you watching me, and watching over me." With a little titter, she departed with the tea tray.

Sherlock closed the door and made sure to slide the security lock into place, not only because Mrs. Hudson could be entirely too familiar with his person, but because she had corpses in her cellar. At least two. Hopefully not more.

"Now for some sandwiches," he said to Cat Watson. He was hungry and long overdue to eat. He fetched the package of food and noticed something was amiss. The paper was torn opened and a great deal of the meat and cheese was missing, or had bites out of it. The impression of sharp little teeth was a blatant clue as to the culprit, or culprits.

Sherlock turned to frown at Cat Watson. "I was going to make us sandwiches. This is very rude behaviour. I would expect it of a dog, not you, Cat Watson, or John Marmalade," he scolded.

John Marmalade blinked sleepily, while Cat Watson hunched and mewled, ears at half-mast. Sherlock sighed and gave the cat a stroke. He had a hard time staying angry with him. "Don't do it again. I will always feed both of you, and Mrs. Hudson will always feed both you. You will never go hungry here, under my care."

Sherlock made sandwiches with the less chewed meats and cheeses, and fed the cats the mangled bits. He ate his cold supper before bedding down. He fell asleep mulling over what disguise he would don on the morrow. Catching a blackmailer, especially one who was threatening Mrs. Hudson, was a worthy case indeed. He did not want her imprisoned or dangling on the end of a noose. He liked living at 221B Baker Street. The rooms and location suited him to a tee. Add to that, the upheaval of moving residences was always a terrible inconvenience.

Cat Watson and John Marmalade purred him to sleep. If he had any dreams of Mrs. Hudson standing over him, axe in hand, he did not remember them when he awoke. No-one was knocking urgently on his door, which was a nice change. He yawned and stretched and wondered about the time. The cats were not abed, so were already up and about. He limped out to the sitting room to check the clock.

"Eight-thirty, oh dear," he said. He would have to hurry to apply his disguise and get to the market. He had wanted to arrive well ahead of Mrs. Hudson, to observe the lay of the land. Now, he would be lucky to have an hour of surveillance before she arrived. An hour and a half at best, if he rushed his preparations.

"Cat Watson?" he called. There was no answering meow. "John Marmalade?" he said. The kitten appeared from near the fire, yawning and stretching, still wearing his tea cozy sweater-vest. Sherlock picked him up and stroked his head. "Has your friend left you behind? I have no idea how he is getting out. It is a mystery for the time being." He set the little cat in the basket on John's chair, decided he liked cats very much, and got busy.

Sherlock brewed a pot of tea, adding a saucer of milk for John Marmalade. He did not concern himself with breakfast. He rarely felt hunger when he was on a case. He had been torn between disguising himself as a common loafer or an elderly book collector. Neither would attract notice at the market. He opened his disguise kit, and surveyed the contents. A common loafer would be a quicker disguise to enact, and allow him to move about more freely. As an elderly book collector, he had to stoop and hobble, and cart about at least a dozen weighty tomes, to be believable.

A layer of make-up on his cheeks made his complexion less robust. He added a scar, the illusion of stubble to his jaw, and some shadows beneath his eyes, as if he had been sleeping rough. That done, he affixed a dark bushy moustache to his face. It helped to camouflage his nose, which was reputedly his most distinctive feature. He also applied caterpillar-like eyebrows atop his own, to conceal his steely gaze. A shaggy wig and a suit of work-worn, soiled clothing were next. Lastly, he plopped a battered hat on his bewigged head and dangled a soiled handkerchief sloppily from his pocket.

He posed before the full-length mirror in his bedroom, adjusting his posture to a slight hunch, as if he had an aching lower back. It also reduced his measure by two to three inches. His lofty height, over six feet, was a characteristic that he could not disguise, short of cutting off his feet, or his head, and that was not a practical solution. Sherlock barely recognized his reflection in the mirror. He was ready to go adventuring.

Cat Watson was not there to accompany him, and although he missed the cat's company, it was a good thing. The cat might have given Sherlock away, especially since he had been sketched with Sherlock in the embarrassing editorial cartoon, on the front page of the newspaper, there for everyone and their maiden aunt to ogle. One didn't even have to buy a paper, but glance at another's in passing. One didn't even have to be able to read, to see the funny picture and have a good laugh at Sherlock's expense.

"I shouldn't be too long, John Marmalade," he told the kitten, who showed no sign of wanting to follow him. "And do use the box with sand, by the door, if you have the need." Mrs. Hudson had thoughtfully provided it for the cats, to do their business when they couldn't go outside.

With a slight limp, Sherlock descended the stairs. He exited through the backdoor, in case the blackmailer was spying on Mrs. Hudson and the Baker Street residence.

The sky was more gray than blue, with a light layer of cloud blocking the sun. There was no threat of rain, and perhaps even the promise of sun. He moved through the back alley, poking into trashcans as a common loafer might do. He made sure to smear dirt on his hands, though he was loath to do so.

The outdoor market was only five blocks from the house. He arrived in no time and strolled from one end to the other, taking everything in—each shopper and vendor and stall. Some of the structures were very shoddy indeed, while other stall owners took pride in their presentation, putting flowers about, clearing away trash, and displaying their wares in artistic arrangements.

Sherlock eventually bought himself a meat pie, after the seller assured Sherlock that there was no cat meat in his pies, only mutton. He didn't buy the meal because he felt hunger, but to help him to blend into the background. He sat on a low bench in the shadows, hiding his height entirely. He ate slowly, pleased to discover the vendor had spoken truth. The pie held only mutton, not cat or any other mysterious, unidentifiable meat.

Sherlock was almost invisible, shrinking into his worn, gray coat, manly hair obscuring his face, and sitting very still while he nibbled small bites. Grease and crumbs collected in his large moustache, despite his best efforts to keep them out. And stray hairs kept tickling his nose in a most irritating manner. How did men abide such facial hair?

He observed the ebb and flow of the market: women buying food for the day, vendors hawking their wares, children dashing about with the surplus of energy children are gifted with. He caught sight of

Wiggins with one of the Baker Street Irregulars. He had been hoping to encounter the boy, who often frequented the market to pick some pockets.

Wiggins and his mate didn't notice Sherlock, not until he coughed four times followed by one sneeze. It was a prearranged signal between them. Wiggins stilled for a fraction of a second, then glanced surreptitiously around. Sherlock blew his nose into his soiled kerchief, the code to approach. Wiggins and a smaller boy followed a zigzag path toward Sherlock, as if ending up before him quite by chance.

"You got a ha'penny to spare, mister?" Wiggins said. "We's awful hungry."

No-one was paying them any attention so Sherlock said, in as few words as possible, "Mrs. Hudson will be here at eleven. She is being blackmailed for her broach. Follow anyone who approaches her, without being spotted." He slipped some coins out of his pocket as if with great reluctance, and tossed them to Wiggins, saying, "The blue stall has meat pies made with mutton. Quite tasty."

Wiggins bobbed his head, and he and the smaller boy melted away. Wiggins knew to keep their exchange as brief and muted as possible. Sherlock continued to watch the scene before him, slipping into something of a light trance, wherein movement became a pattern that was a dance of sorts. The market dance. The steps predictable, based on how people moved, and avoided other bodies in motion, their purpose, and the physical world itself. Every single person's movements were logical and therefore predictable, except for those who were not going about their business as normal, having a nefarious purpose perhaps.

When Mrs. Hudson appeared, her shopping basket over her arm, Sherlock had not yet spotted a single soul who presented as the blackmailer, lurking in the shadows, awaiting his target. His landlady was wearing her blue carbuncle broach on her thick woolen cardigan, and she was carrying John Marmalade in the basket. Dressed in his sweater-vest, he was kept warm on the nippy autumn day. Sherlock belatedly noticed that the chill had seeped into his bones, and made his slashed arm throb and his sore bottom ache. Alas, he had had to forego his soft cushion. It was not something a common loafer would cart about with him. Plus, it was still at the Watson residence.

Sherlock rose and wandered past stalls selling sheep's trotters and hot eels and pickled oysters. Keeping one eye on Mrs. Hudson, he stopped before a man selling ginger beer from a cart. He was feeling thirsty after his meat pie, and ginger beer was only mildly alcoholic, being made by boiling ginger and sugar together, adding yeast and a bit of flavouring like cloves. This ginger beer was served warm, which would help dispel his chill.

"You don't brew your beer in the same washtub where your missus boils the babe's nappies, do you?" he asked the younger man, who had betraying spittle stains on his shoulder, and bags under his eyes, from too many sleepless nights.

The fellow shook his head. "Nah, I got my own washtub for brewing, just for brewing. I always have a batch of quality ginger beer on the go," he assured Sherlock.

His gaze was forthright, and he showed pride in his brew, so Sherlock judged he was telling the truth. "I'll take one bottle for now," he said. "I'll bring you back your bottle and buy another, if the ginger beer is as good as it looks." Complimenting vendors never went amiss.

The man smiled and they completed their transaction. Sherlock sipped from the bottle as he meandered in the same direction Mrs. Hudson had taken. The beer proved tasty, fresh and warm. Sherlock was surprised to find himself enjoying the common street beverage immensely.

Mrs. Hudson visited several stalls. She purchased some food and stowed it in her basket with John Marmalade. She was acting as instructed, as if it was any ordinary market day. Wiggins had waited to buy his meat pie until Mrs. Hudson appeared, so he could stroll near her, eating it. Smart lad. The smaller boy was nowhere in sight. He would be watching from a different vantage point. Street lads were so much cleverer than their so-called betters, in the ways of survival anyway.

With still no sign of the blackmailer, Sherlock wandered back to his low bench to sit down, and wait, and watch.

21 - An Exciting Chase

🐱 *from The Observations of Cat Watson*

I shadowed Sherlock to the market. He had no idea, because I was so stealthy. I had suspected, rightly, that he would not take me with him on this case. I knew I would have compromised his disguise, if we were seen working a case together. Yet, I didn't want him to be without backup, so I decided to tail him, pun intended.

The detective almost got away from me, by exiting through the backdoor. I hadn't anticipated that, and couldn't watch two doors at once. It was by chance that I caught a whiff of his scent carried on the light breeze, and clued in that he was on the move.

I hurried in the direction of the market and found him. His disguise could not fool my nose. And I would have recognized his nose regardless. His height also gave him away. No matter how clever his costumes, they could only do so much to conceal his jutting beak and looming height. I do believe it was his austere leanness that made him appear even taller than he truly was.

From a hidden nook, I observed Sherlock make contact with Wiggins. It was a comfort to know he had additional support. There was only so much a small cat could do, if events turned truly dangerous, and I was starting to fear they might.

I was sensing a malevolent presence, watching Sherlock as he was watching others. He was both the hunted and the hunter. Cat senses are so highly honed for survival, they might almost be called a sixth sense. And mine was telling me that all was not well. Was it the blackmailer, plotting violence on Sherlock, as well as extorting Mrs. Hudson? Or was it someone else, entirely unrelated to this case?

Mrs. Hudson made her appearance then, strolling through the market and purchasing food from the green grocer as well as the butcher. I was happy to see John Marmalade in her basket, enjoying an outing. He looked ridiculous in the knitted garment, as if cats needed clothes when they had perfectly good fur, yet he did not seem to mind. He was smiling joyfully at everyone he passed.

I hoped Mrs. Hudson might buy some nice fresh fish from the fish monger. I was quite hungry as I had missed my breakfast, and I hadn't found anything worth eating on the ground, during my travels that morning. Perhaps my palette was already becoming finicky from living the high life. Sherlock and Mrs. Hudson did pamper me.

I slunk closer to Sherlock, hoping to spot or smell whoever I sensed, and alert him to the impending danger. Before I could get within spitting distance of him, I smelled something else, something foul and disgusting, and horribly familiar. Gladstone! Was he the danger I had sensed closing in? Or was the deplorable dog a secondary menace?

The dog wasn't alone. Dr. and Mrs. Watson were out for a stroll at the market. Dr. Watson sported several bandages and bruises on his face, and alas, he still had his moustache, though it was much smaller, and properly trimmed to look neat. It wasn't half as hideous as it had been.

The couple had brought their hellish hound along. Perhaps Dr. Watson did not want to let him out of his sight, after his suspected dognapping. I don't know how Mary had explained his reappearance, as I had not been there to witness it. She had probably said something vague like, *Oh, he just waddled on home, all by himself.* Gladstone was waddling nearer now, on the end of his leash. I noted Sherlock stiffen ever so slightly, when he too spotted the trio.

Dr. Watson would have sauntered right by Sherlock, if not for Gladstone. A dog's nose is not nearly as keen as a cat's, but it is still far superior to a human's. Gladstone stopped dead. Dr. Watson almost fell over him, and stumbled to keep his footing. "What's caught your interest?" he asked his dog, as if the dim-witted thing could speak, or understand him.

Mary glanced around and her eyes narrowed on Sherlock. Clearly, she was far more observant than her husband. Given her previous encounter with Sherlock, did she suspect him of spying on her now?

That's when Dr. Watson spotted someone he did know, who was not in disguise. "Mrs. Hudson!" he hailed loudly. She froze, and glanced at Sherlock as if for guidance. If anyone was watching her, she had just betrayed his position. Then again, Gladstone had already done a stellar job of that, straining on the end of his leash and snarling directly at Sherlock. The detective's surveillance was going pear-shaped.

"Good day, Dr. Watson," Mrs. Hudson said, and with a brisk nod, hurried on her way. Her broach was still pinned to her sweater, glinting brilliantly under the sun like the diamonds and gemstones it was.

"Not very friendly today," Dr. Watson commented to Mary, straining to keep his hound under control. "What has Gladstone in such a tizzy?" He was still unaware of Sherlock's presence. Given the number of years they had worked together on various cases, Dr. Watson really should have spotted his friend in disguise.

"Heaven knows," Mary said, tongue-in-cheek.

Gladstone began to howl and tug harder, ensuring every eye in the market was turned their way. "Gladstone, heel," Mary commanded. The hound cast her a despairing look, as if he really wanted to obey, but couldn't control his impulse to attack Sherlock. I wondered if I should fill the role of decoy, and draw Gladstone to chase me.

Before I could act, Gladstone gave an enthusiastic lunge. Pulled off-balance, Dr. Watson tripped and lost his grip on the leash. Mary made a grab for it. She wasn't quick enough. Gladstone bayed and barrelled toward Sherlock, who was still doing his utmost to appear as a common loafer.

With an angry hiss, I darted in front of Gladstone, trying to entice him to chase me. I wasn't worried about him catching me. At his sluggish pace, I could have run circles around him, backwards, on two paws, with my eyes closed. Alas, he ignored me completely. He was intent on savaging Sherlock. I skidded around and made a beeline for Sherlock's bench.

Dr. Watson chased Gladstone, and Mary followed him. Sherlock abandoned his bench and vaulted athletically over the stone wall at his back. He ducked low and disappeared. "Why, it's Sherlock!" Dr. Watson cried. He had recognized Sherlock's way of moving, and possibly his height. "That's who Gladstone is chasing, Mary. He's chasing Sherlock," he called over his shoulder.

Everyone in the market who was not both deaf and blind, now knew Sherlock Holmes was there. But I didn't think anyone had spotted me. I crouched, low and unmoving, in the shadows under the bench, where weeds grew defiantly tall and trash had amassed in shabby piles.

Gladstone was stopped by the wall. He certainly couldn't jump over it. With his stubby legs and bloated belly, I doubted he could jump over his own shadow. Dr. Watson caught the leash as Mary reached him. "Hush, John. He is on a case," she said quietly, for his ears alone.

"Oh, yes. He was in disguise as a common loafer. I should have realized. Now Gladstone has given him away. I didn't help either, by calling out his name."

"Twice," Mary mentioned.

"Yes, twice." Dr. Watson grimaced.

At that moment, a woman screamed on the other side of the outdoor market. "That sounds like Mrs. Hudson," John said. It certainly did. My ears knew her voice.

Everyone in earshot hurried that way, including the Watson trio. I leapt up onto the bench and looked around for Sherlock. I spotted him, but unlike the majority of humans, he was heading away from where Mrs. Hudson had screamed. I realized why when I caught a fleeting glimpse of a cloaked figure, running with speed, to the west and slightly ahead of Sherlock. Was it our blackmailer? With the broach already in-hand after Gladstone sabotaged Sherlock's stakeout?

I leapt from the bench onto the stone wall, then hopped down on the other side. I raced after Sherlock, and spotted Wiggins also giving chase. The smaller boy was slightly behind, trying his utmost to keep up with them.

Soon, heavy panting could be heard at my rear, and it wasn't the boys. They were off to my side. I darted a glance behind and couldn't believe my eyes. Gladstone had escaped, again. He was gambolling after me, still in pursuit of either Sherlock or myself. He must have found an opening through the wall. He was some ways back, of course, being chased by Dr. Watson.

The mysterious cloaked figure was leading quite the parade. Unfortunately, we were nearing a busy thoroughfare. It was chock-full of horse-drawn carriages and bicycles, and as many humans as ants around honey. Our quarry could disappear into the bustling river of humanity and we would lose him.

Sherlock had realized the same. He put on an extra burst of speed, his long legs pumping. He could certainly run when he set his mind to it. As fast as I was, I lost sight of him.

22 - The Case of the Burgled Broach

Sherlock ran like the wind, his heart and legs pumping. He had given Mrs. Hudson his promise, and he would not fail. He would catch the blackmailer red-handed, or his name wasn't William Sherlock Scott Holmes.

Alas, they were nearing the main thoroughfare of Oxford Street. If the villain had any sense, he would shed his dark cloak and lose himself in the crowds. And the man was displaying a great deal of intelligent forethought in his criminal planning and execution.

Sherlock hated to fail, almost as much as he hated to be bested. He ran faster still, wondering if Cat Watson was managing to keep pace. He hadn't been surprised to see the cat at the market. And acting as a decoy to entice Gladstone from chasing Sherlock—well, the cat never ceased to amaze him. If only the whole of mankind was as clever as his new feline companion, the world would be a far more interesting and tolerable place.

Sherlock reached Oxford Street and scanned for any sign of the dark-coated figure. He didn't see him, per se, but many heads were turned, looking fixedly to the northeast. His quarry had run in that direction, and people had taken notice. Sherlock lunged to the left and moved as fast as he could, weaving through the crowds. He was forced to slow his pace to a trot, then a fast walk. Traversing the crowds was akin to swimming upstream. He finally stopped, admitting defeat. The villain had gotten away.

He stood still, sweaty, aching, and dragging in great lungfuls of London's foul air. Cat Watson was quick to catch up. He meowed at Sherlock's feet, which were throbbing from pounding the pavement in his ill-fitting, common loafer's footwear.

"We have been bested." Sherlock scooped up the little cat. Wiggins was the next to appear, panting like he was going to expire. "Did you get a look at the man?" Sherlock asked, as soon as Wiggins had enough air to speak, by which time, the smaller lad had also joined their number.

"A better look than you, but not clear enough to knows his face." Wiggins gasped in several more breaths. "Arnold, what about you? You was closer."

Before Arnold, the smaller boy, could answer, Gladstone caught up. Thank heavens John had a good grip on his leash at that point. Add to that, Gladstone was exhausted from his exercise. Being fat and unfit, he could barely stay upright. He gave a half-hearted growl and flopped to the ground.

"I see your hound found his way home," Sherlock said, by way of a greeting. "You should run him more often. He would be easier to control, and not so fat."

John panted hard and waved a hand in front of his face, as though surrounded by gnats. He had not enough breath to defend his dog.

At that moment, Mary trotted up. Sherlock shared an awkward glance with her, both recalling their last encounter. But Sherlock had other things to occupy his mind, so he didn't dwell on it. He said to John, "Gladstone ruined my covert surveillance. And you called me by name, twice. Mrs. Hudson is my client and I promised to protect her from a blackmailer. Thanks to you and your beastly hound, the villain has stolen a most valuable possession from her, and eluded capture." Sherlock raised a finger when John opened his mouth to speak, or perhaps he was merely dragging in more air. "And that means he will blackmail her again. Blackmailers always do. They are never satisfied with one payment, as we both know too well." The pair had taken on a number of cases involving extortionists, so they did know their nature firsthand.

"I am sorry, Sherlock." John pulled out his kerchief and dabbed his sweaty brow.

Sherlock chose to change the subject. "Did you get a look at the villain, at least?"

John shook his head. Mary said, "Someone in a dark cloak, wearing a hat. Average in all ways, at least from a distance."

"*You* didn't get a look at him?" John asked, emphasis on the *you*.

Sherlock should have. He was normally the most observant of men. In his defense, he had been rather distracted, "No, and it's all your stupid dog's fault," he snapped and turned to the smaller boy. "Arnold, you may have had the best look at our culprit. Describe him and leave out no detail."

Arnold flushed, to be the center of attention with so many eyes upon him. "I did get a fair look-see at the thief who took Mrs. Hudson's pin," he said, "but you's wrong, Mr. Sherlock. It wasn't no man what nabbed it, it was a lady. Well, maybe not a lady, seeing as she was wearing trousers, but she wasn't no man."

Sherlock shook his head. "No, that can't be right. No woman could outrun me."

Mary snorted most inelegantly, yet did not comment other than that.

Arnold flushed even redder. "Well, I hates to say you's is wrong, Mr. Sherlock, I really does. But she had … you know …" Arnold cupped his hands and held them in front of his small, thin chest, as if he had breasts.

"Boobies," Wiggins chimed in helpfully.

Sherlock mulled that over for a moment and came to a conclusion. "He was in disguise, as was I. He must have stuffed his shirt to look like breasts, to confuse us and hide his identity."

Arnold swiped at his nose, which was running snottily. "It wasn't no stuffing. No sir, Mr. Sherlock. When she was running hard, they was moving, bouncing, swaying, jiggling. All two of 'em." He mimed the described motion with helpful hand gestures. Mary clapped a hand over her mouth to stifle laughter.

"No stuffing I knows can bounce and jiggle like that," Wiggins said. "They must have been real lady boobies, which means she wasn't no man."

Sherlock heaved a sigh of frustration. He looked down at Cat Watson and said, "What do you think?" The cat might have shrugged. Sherlock refocused his attention on Arnold. "What else did you observe, besides what appeared to be flopping, jiggling breasts?"

Arnold said, "Well, she wasn't so tall or short, or skinny or fat. She was kind of middling, like the doc's missus said. Her hat hid her hair, but I thinks it was dark-ish. I didn't see much of her face. She could run real fast, especially for a woman who wasn't a man, or a man who was a woman."

Sherlock glanced at Wiggins. "Did you notice anything else?"

"Not so's much. No more'n you." Wiggins lifted his cap to brush sweaty hair back off his forehead. "Mr. Sherlock, all that running made me and Arnold real thirsty and hungry."

"I'm sure it did. And you performed most admirably." Sherlock reached into his pocket and handed over some more coins. The boys grabbed them with hot, grubby hands and made a quick departure, skipping happily, already recovered from their hard running.

Together with the Watsons, and the now docile Gladstone, Sherlock walked back toward the market. He continued to carry Cat Watson, who had run a long way for such a small cat. He wanted to verify Mrs. Hudson's wellbeing, even though he was ashamed to face her, after failing to apprehend the blackmailer.

They located her easily, as she was still surrounded by concerned market-goers. She was seated on a bench, a bottle of restorative ginger beer in hand. Her broach was gone. Her basket was on her lap, with John Marmalade nestled safely inside it, amid her food purchases. He was being fussed over. Everyone seemed to find him the most adorable kitten they had ever laid eyes on, in his ridiculous tea cozy sweater-vest.

Sherlock dragged off his hat and wig, still quite warm from the wild running. He shooed the small crowd away, laid the wig on the hard bench beside Mrs. Hudson, and sat on it. His bottom was throbbing from all the exercise. Cat Watson settled on his lap, and the Watsons and Gladstone hovered. The hound was drooling liberally, his bloodshot eyes fixed on the ginger beer. "I regret to inform you that the thief escaped capture when Gladstone tried to attack me," he said. He was content to blame John's beastly dog. It had been wholly Gladstone's fault that things went awry, after all.

John harrumphed. "Well, we didn't know you were here on a case, in disguise. How could we? It was a chance encounter, nothing more. I wanted to take the air. Since you knocked me out yesterday, my head's been all woozy."

Mrs. Hudson latched onto Sherlock's hand and squeezed it so tightly, he couldn't disengage it, short of yanking it free forcefully. She also stroked his palm with her thumb, which tickled a bit. "Well, you didn't catch him today, Sherlock, but I'm sure you will very soon. I have complete faith in you." She fluttered her eyelashes at him.

"Did you get a look at the culprit?" Sherlock asked.

"Not even a peek. He dashed up behind me and grabbed the broach right off my sweater, tore a hole in it. Look Sherlock, look at the hole in my sweater." Mrs. Hudson jutted out her bosom and rubbed it with her free hand, where there was a small hole. Mary coughed and choked, as if she had swallowed a spider.

"Yes, I see it. Your sweater is quite ruined," Sherlock said. Cat Watson leaned close to sniff at Mrs. Hudson's sweater, or perhaps her breast. Sherlock hoped it was the former. He said, "Wiggins and Arnold were also keeping watch. Arnold claims the person who stole your broach was a woman. Is that possible?"

He didn't think so himself, unless the woman was an Amazon who could run like the north wind, but how else could the jiggling breasts be explained? Water-filled balloons strapped to a man's chest? Or perhaps held in place in one of those new-fangled garments that had recently been invented to contain women's breasts?

The device was called the corselet gorge, or 'le bien-être', which translated to 'the well-being', although how strapping down women's breasts resulted in any sort of well-being was a mystery to Sherlock. Never having had breasts, the things themselves were a bit of a mystery to him. Yet, water-filled balloons to mimic breasts was an inspired idea, if a man wished to disguise himself as a woman. Perhaps Sherlock would give it a try, if he ever needed to disguise himself as a woman. Then again, his height would probably give him away as a man, even if he strapped gigantic water-filled balloons to his chest.

He stopped pondering the nature of breasts and attended Mrs. Hudson's answer to his question. "I have no idea if the blackmailer is a woman, Sherlock. I didn't see the person. Although it is hard to believe a woman could commit such a crime."

Sherlock made a noncommittal murmur. Of the two women nearest him at the moment, one was the head of an organized crime gang of women, and the other had at least two corpses, who may or may not have died accidentally, buried in her cellar. It suddenly seemed very plausible indeed, that a woman might be blackmailing Mrs. Hudson, and stealing the broach off her chest in broad daylight.

"At least I am unharmed, and wee Johnny Marmalade is as safe as houses in my basket." Mrs. Hudson finally released Sherlock's hand, only to give his thigh a squeeze.

He rose with alacrity. "If you are well enough to see yourself home, I will resume the investigation, before the trail gets too cold. I am sure you are eager to have your broach restored to you, Mrs. Hudson."

Mary gave John a little shove in Sherlock's direction. "Why don't you assist Sherlock, for Mrs. Hudson's sake," she said. "I will see her safely home, and take Gladstone with me. He's quite calm now."

"Yes, of course, for Mrs. Hudson's sake," John said, "if Sherlock will have me, after I made a right hash of things today."

"I suppose more help would not go amiss," Sherlock said grudgingly, and he picked up Cat Watson.

John's face fell. "Are you bringing the cat, then? I thought it would be you and me, investigating like old times. Mrs. Hudson could take the cat home. Put him in the basket with the other cat."

"Are you jealous of a cat, John?" Sherlock asked. Cat Watson hissed at John, making his opinion on the matter crystal clear.

"No! Of course not. The very idea." He gave a little harrumph.

"I would not sentence Cat Watson to endure another moment of Gladstone's company," Sherlock said implacably.

John pouted and Mary said, "You boys go on now, have fun." She shot Sherlock a threatening glare, before the two women strolled off, Gladstone waddling between them.

"I just want to help, because I care about Mrs. Hudson. She has always been so kind to me. But if you want the cat to come too, well, I suppose that's alright." John had not noticed Mary's threatening glare, as he didn't notice so many things.

Sherlock carrying Cat Watson in the crook of his elbow, the two men headed out of the market. They were not fully at ease with each other, but not at odds either. "How shall we proceed?" John asked.

"I am not yet sure. I am considering the matter." Sherlock turned in the direction he had taken to chase down the villain.

"What are the details of the case?" John asked.

"Peculiar and disturbing. And you are the only person in the world to whom I can reveal them." Sherlock knew John would keep Mrs. Hudson's secrets, so while they retraced their chase path, he told his friend the tale, more or less as Mrs. Hudson had told it to him.

John was shocked to learn there were at least two corpses buried in the cellar of the place he had called home for a number of years. "But that is not our concern," Sherlock stressed. "Mrs. Hudson has asked me to apprehend the blackmailer. That is the case, and that is what I shall do."

John pulled a face, then winced. Clearly his skin was still sore from the drunken moustache-trimming debacle. "I do wish I could write this adventure for The Strand," he mused. "Once it is solved, perhaps I can change the names and -"

"No," Sherlock cut in. "We cannot risk Mrs. Hudson, or my home. This is one tale you may not write about."

"Oh, fine. So, what is the next step?"

Before Sherlock could answer, Cat Watson gave an excited meow and squirmed to be free. Sherlock set him on his paws. They were near the spot where he had lost track of his quarry. Cat Watson sniffed around where they stood.

"He's like a wee hound dog, isn't he?" John said lightly.

Cat Watson stopped sniffing and bared his teeth at John, rather as a dog would snarl. "Cat Watson does not like to be compared to dogs in any way, so do not do so," Sherlock told John. Cat Watson hissed threateningly at John, emphasizing the point.

"Have you discovered something of import?" Sherlock asked the cat.

Cat Watson meowed and began padding along the sidewalk. Sherlock stayed close, so the cat would not get stepped on or kicked. Not everyone was kind to cats, especially black ones. Some felt they were a nuisance or bad luck. Clearly, they had never met this particular cat.

Cat Watson turned left at the next cross street. They followed. He kept going straight for a bit, then turned left again. They kept following. After twenty or so minutes, and several more turns, Sherlock found himself standing before 221B Baker Street, his own domicile.

John laughed. "He wasn't tracking the thief. He just wanted to go home, probably hungry for some fish and cream."

"I don't think so, John." Sherlock pointed at the door. An envelope was tacked to it. The little white square emanated an ominous presence, for all its diminutive size and pristine condition. "I do believe our thief has already delivered a second missive." He snapped the envelope off the door, and asked the cat, "Can you track where the villain went from here?"

Cat Watson sniffed around, then started back the way they had come. "Our adversary has doubled back over their own path. Very clever." Sherlock said. "Well, no point in tracking a dead-end trail. Let us go read this note. Nor would a cup of tea go amiss."

They entered the Baker Street residence. Sherlock paused in the foyer and listened for sound or movement from Mrs. Hudson's portion of the house. There was nothing. The women either hadn't arrived yet, or Mrs. Hudson had returned, and was taking a nap to recover from the distressing events of the morning. Or she had returned, and being something of a drinker, had imbibed a few too many glasses of sherry, and passed out.

As soon as they reached his rooms, Sherlock stoked the fire and put the kettle on to boil. John Marmalade had not yet been returned, suggesting Mrs. Hudson was still out and about with Mary. Perhaps the two women were discussing the most efficient methods to get away with murder. Sherlock smiled at the fanciful notion. He stopped smiling and frowned, when it struck him that the notion might not be so fanciful at all.

Sherlock was so anticipating reading the note, it was rather like his best Christmas present. He did not want to rush the opening of it, so tea preparations came first. Once an improvised and rather haphazard meal was ready, from what could be scavenged in his small, almost bare pantry, they took their places. Sherlock eased into his chair, stifling a groan of pain.

With a defiant air, John shifted Cat Watson's basket to the client's chair and claimed his former spot. Cat Watson was on the floor for the moment, lapping at cream and sardines, and if he noticed, he let it go.

Teacups in hand and luncheon platters at their elbows, Sherlock studied John, across from him. "Why don't you just shave off the rest of that moustache and be done with it?"

"I like my moustache. It will grow back to its former glory in no time." John gave it an affectionate stroke.

Sherlock snorted. "Your moustache was never glorious, John. It was an insult to proper moustaches everywhere. Mary doesn't like it, you know." Perhaps he shouldn't have brought up John's wife, but it had slipped out.

"Mary loves my moustache." John glared.

"Mary hates your moustache." Sherlock glared back.

"How would you know that?" John challenged.

Sherlock rolled his eyes. "I am the world's greatest detective and an expert at reading people's emotions and thoughts, as you well know."

"Not women's emotions and thoughts, Sherlock. You've never been an expert at women. Quite the opposite. Why, I am more of an expert than you, in regards to the female sex." John sipped his tea.

"Clearly not, or you would know Mary loathes your moustache almost as much as she loathes Gladstone." Sherlock sipped his tea right back at John. Before their disagreement could escalate, he added, "Perhaps neither of us is terribly canny about women, so let us agree to disagree." Sherlock eyed a bottle of brandy, then rejected the thought of opening it. John's face was a testament to the folly of indulging in drink, and he had an intriguing case to occupy his mind.

"Will you open the blasted note now?" John asked, as he had five times already. His tone had grown increasingly plaintive. He often had trouble controlling his curiosity.

"Yes, John. It is time. Far better to open the note than look at or discuss your appalling moustache." Sherlock set down his cup, and fingered the so-anticipated envelope. He unsealed it carefully, preserving any evidence. He found himself smiling, to be confronting a worthy adversary.

There was a single page inside. He unfolded it, and read aloud, "I thank you for the pretty blue and pointy, stabby pin, but we're not square yet. I will be the one digging up Mr. Turner's body, to plant a fresh one in its place, unless you gift me another pretty. Better yet, I'll take it off your man upstairs. That way I'll know where he is, and he can't catch me by my coattails. Ha ha. Send your servant with the beryl and pearl necklace your dead as a doornail husband gave you on your last anniversary together. I do hope he keeps well in your cellar. The Regent's Park, tonight. Ten o'clock sharp. I'll meet your man upstairs where forty ghosts moan and roam, and I might just keep him. He does remind me of someone I once knew. Your boss for now."

Sherlock found himself smiling more widely. "Oh, John, the game is truly afoot, and I am now an invited player. Be our opponent a man or a woman, they are proving to be a most intriguing foe."

"It's dangerous, Sherlock, to meet by that cursed lake in the dark of night, as it is obvious that is the location. Many believe the lake is haunted by the forty poor souls who drowned in it, when the ice collapsed, on a winter night not so long ago that it can be forgotten," John said. Cat Watson meowed in agreement.

"Poppycock and superstition. Of course I will keep our meeting by the lake. I will retrieve Mrs. Hudson's broach, and catch the villain in the act." He studied the note, observing the same bizarre scripting style as on the previous missive. Proper penmanship interspersed with childish scribbles, and still generic in that it did not look either masculine or feminine in nature. And the writer knew of Mr. Turner dead in the cellar, so Mr. Blakely had broken Mrs. Hudson's confidence with at least one person. The author of the missive had even made note of Sherlock's similarity in appearance to Mr. Blakely, but did not seem aware that the fellow was deceased, and now occupied the same final resting place. Clearly, the author of the note only knew of one body.

"I'm not letting you go alone, Sherlock. I'll have your back, tonight. Do not doubt it," John declared.

Cat Watson shot John a dirty look, perhaps for usurping his position as Sherlock's companion. He left his bowl of cream unfinished and leapt up to perch on Sherlock's lap, as if claiming ownership. Sherlock knew the loyal little cat would also be accompanying him on the evening's adventure. The parkland was the perfect terrain for him to slink about and track their opponent. Sherlock was content to have both companions by his side.

"We had best ask Mrs. Hudson for this beryl and pearl necklace, if she has such a thing," John said, still frowning.

"No. I will not risk another of Mrs. Hudson's treasures. I will go without the requested item. I will package up a fake, as a hoax, and present the wrapped decoy in its place." Sherlock absently stroked the soft cat, his mind already formulating a plan. "In fact, I will not even mention this second note to Mrs. Hudson. There is no need to distress her further."

John nodded in agreement. He had always been rather protective of Mrs. Hudson when she was his landlady, and apparently he still was, even though she no longer brought him his tea and toast. "So, how will we catch the culprit?" John knew to leave the planning to Sherlock, who did feel satisfaction at hearing the *we*. Maybe he had been a tinge sad and lonely, without John to share his adventures.

Sherlock ruminated for a few minutes longer, brow furrowed. "Why has the blackmailer chosen the park as a location for the exchange? It does not work in his, or her, favour. There are no crowds to lose one's self in, no labyrinth of alleyways to disappear down, no plethora of doorways to duck into. It is almost as if our adversary wishes to be caught, especially by meeting with me, an athletic man, rather than Mrs. Hudson. Me! In a fairly open parkland. As much as the chosen location is to my advantage, I do not like this development." Sherlock steepled his fingers. "Why? Why would an intelligent adversary place himself, or herself, in such a vulnerable and exposed location to make the exchange?"

John pulled a face, which again made him wince a bit in pain. "I don't know. It doesn't make sense, does it?"

"It does not, and I do not like the illogic. Regardless, I have no choice but to attend this meeting, otherwise Mrs. Hudson may hang."

"We don't want that, do we?" John said, stating the obvious, as he was oft inclined to do.

"I am going to give this puzzle some concentrated thought." Sherlock picked up his violin, which was always near at hand.

John jumped to his feet. "And I'm going to go see my wife, and let her know I will be out with you this evening. I shall return well before ten."

"Make it eight, John. I wish to survey the park thoroughly before the rendezvous." Sherlock positioned his bow. Cat Watson relocated to the chair John had just vacated, when the bow came within a whisker of his whiskers.

John left hurriedly, yanking the door closed behind him. As exceptional as Sherlock's playing, John was not appreciative of violin music. He claimed it reminded him of tomcats in heat. When they had shared 221B, John tended to make himself scarce whenever Sherlock picked up his violin. And if the weather was inclement, or he had nowhere to go, he would stuff his ears with cotton wool and sulk in his bedroom, pillow over his head.

Playing the instrument always helped Sherlock to puzzle out problems. It had been some long time since he had played. Come to think of it, he hadn't touched his violin since he had brought Cat Watson home.

As soon as the first note filled the air, Cat Watson gave a yowl. He sprang up, back arched and fur standing on end, as if Gladstone had invaded the room. Sherlock kept playing, hoping the cat would settle down, and appreciate the music. Alas, he did not. He kept yowling, then dashed away. He disappeared in the direction of the two bedrooms and bathroom, as if he was the fox in a fox hunt.

So, another roommate who did not appreciate his excellent musical talent. Sherlock kept playing, and thinking. Cat Watson did not show his furry face again.

23 - The Boudoir & the Sweater-Vest

🐱 from The Observations of Cat Watson

My ears aching, I fled my new home through the small gap I had discovered beside the pipe that carried water down to the bathroom, from the roof. Once again, I was happy to be a small cat. A larger cat would not have been able to squeeze out. A larger cat would have been trapped and destined to suffer the torturous caterwauling racket Sherlock was making. Did he think it was music? If so, he was sadly mistaken. It was enough to make a cat's ears bleed. How had Dr. Watson endured the sound when he had shared the rooms with Sherlock? How did Mrs. Hudson endure the screeching, as she could not help but hear it in her rooms below?

With sudden concern for little John Marmalade, I made my way down the stairs. In addition to finding an exodus from Sherlock's lodgings, I had also discovered an entrance to Mrs. Hudson's domain. It was through an ill-fitted baseboard beneath the stairs, in the entrance foyer. I squeezed through the small gap. It was a tight fit, and I realized I would have to limit my intake of cream, if I was going to keep slipping in and out of the rooms in Baker Street.

All was quiet. Mrs. Hudson and John Marmalade had not yet returned, so perhaps Mary had taken them to her home to keep them safe. Despite heading a criminal organization, she seemed a caring sort. And yes, I could still hear the horrible noise coming from above. Thank goodness its volume was greatly reduced.

I had never explored Mrs. Hudson's home, and decided to do so now. It had the same basic layout as Sherlock's, with two bedrooms at the back, the adjacent water closet, and a spacious parlour. Her kitchen was twice as large as Sherlock's, and much better equipped for cooking. After a good sniff around that room, and a bit of nibbling on crumbs, I checked out the bedrooms. The door to the first bedroom was fully ajar, so I padded right in. It was minimally furnished with a small bed and empty dresser. Perhaps it was a guestroom, if Mrs. Hudson ever had guests to stay, ones that she did not kill and bury in her cellar.

The door to the second bedroom was pulled closed, but not latched. A little push was all it took for it to swing inward. This room's décor was feminine and frilly. The air smelled cloyingly of Mrs. Hudson's perfumes and lotions and potions. There was a row of such bottles, jars, and vials, lined up on the dresser as if they were standing in a queue. Clearly, this was the landlady's boudoir.

I sneezed and paced around the space. I had a bit of a fright when it appeared that someone was sleeping in the bed, unmoving beneath the coverlet. After all Mrs. Hudson's talk of corpses in her cellar, I half-expected yet another body. But no, there was no scent of death, or life, for that matter. The distant screeching of the violin was not helping my nerves. I felt quite skittish when I leapt soundlessly onto the mattress to get a look at who, or what, was in the bed.

A head was on the pillow, capped with dark, slightly curly locks, like Sherlock's. Even so close, there was no sound or movement, or smells of the living or dead. I bravely pawed back the blanket and couldn't quite believe my eyes. A dummy that wore my Sherlock's face was tucked in the bed. The stuffed body was wearing pajamas, and I knew they were Sherlock's. His lingering scent proved that.

The face was an excellent likeness, sculpted from wax. I had heard talk in the streets, after humans had visited a museum filled with wax figures—of people, not cats. They enthused about how life-like the wax sculptures truly were. Had Mrs. Hudson's paid one of the wax artists to sculpt a likeness of Sherlock? To keep her company? She claimed to be a very wealthy woman, so she could surely afford it.

Despite the excellent likeness of Sherlock's face, it was a most creepy find indeed. I took note of other things in the room. Sherlock's pants and one of his shirts sat folded on the corner chair, ready for the stuffed dummy to wear, as if it would truly awaken, stand up, and dress. Did Mrs. Hudson prop the thing up in a chair, to take dinner with her? Did she converse with this likeness of Sherlock? Did she sleep in the bed, cuddled up with it, as if they were a married couple? Humans were such odd creatures, and Mrs. Hudson, for all the delicious meals she set before me, was proving odder than most. Or perhaps all humans were equally peculiar and I was simply unaware, because I had never before resided with them.

I belatedly noticed pictures of Sherlock, tacked on the walls. There were both photographs and editorial cartoons cut from the newspapers. Even the one of Sherlock farting on a corpse was there. Sherlock would not like that, nor would he be pleased to know a wax twin of himself resided in Mrs. Hudson's home, and bed.

I was about to slink from the bedroom when I heard a sound outside the window. Mrs. Hudson's rooms were on the ground floor, but no-one should have been lurking outside, in the small and private back garden.

A shadowy face peered through the glass pane, hands cupped around the eyes. I flattened myself on the bed, in a fold of cloth, to remain unseen. The figure had a hood pulled low over the head, so I could see no details of the face, not through the glass. It was grimy and needed a good cleaning. Then again, given what was in her bed, Mrs. Hudson wouldn't want voyeurs peering into her boudoir. Perhaps she even soaped the glass, to cloud it and make it impossible to see through.

The hands lowered and the glass rattled a bit, as if the intruder was trying to raise the window. It was either not latched, or the latch was faulty, for it began to creak up slowly. I held my position, hidden in the blanket, eager to see the face of the villain.

So fixated was I, spying on the mysterious figure, I failed to notice the sound of Mrs. Hudson's front door opening. Some of that can be blamed on the violin not-music, I suppose, which went a long way to drowning out other, better sounds. Like birdsong. As much as I liked to catch and eat birds, I did enjoy listening to their musical songs.

The intruder must have heard Mrs. Hudson as well, through the partially raised window. They slid it back down, and disappeared from sight. Alas, I had seen nothing to identify them. And I was about to be caught, an intruder myself, in Mrs. Hudson's most private of sanctums.

I dashed out of that disturbing bedroom in the nick of time, right before she came bustling into the parlour with her basket. I could have slipped out unseen, the same way I had slipped in, except John Marmalade scented my presence. He was a cat, after all. He meowed an enthusiastic greeting and almost fell out of the basket, so eager to greet me was he. Being a kind-hearted tom, I stayed and greeted him in turn, rubbing against him with a purr.

Mrs. Hudson cried out in delight. "Oh, Cat Watson, you have come to call on Johnny Marmalade. How nice! And I have fresh yum-yums for both your wee tum-tums, my sweetie-pie pusspusses."

What could I do but stay to eat some delectables with John Marmalade? And though I wasn't overly hungry, I could always eat more, especially if the more was fresh plaice. Mrs. Hudson fed us well, and we ate well. It made me sleepy.

Before I could curl up for a nap on her chesterfield, as the violin not-music was still playing upstairs, Mrs. Hudson picked me up. She stroked my fur and lisped, "I finished knitting your wee sweater-vest, so you and Johnny can be the cutsy-est wittle twin-kin kitty-witties in the whole world."

Before I could meow, *Help me, Sherlock!* not that he would have heard me, I found myself trussed up tight in a tea cozy sweater-vest. It was just like John Marmalade's, only slightly larger. Alas, there was no escaping it, as it had buttons I couldn't reach to bite off, and ribbons that tied around my neck and behind my back.

I had seen a madman carted off in a straightjacket once, destined for the insane asylum. My sweater-vest felt exactly like such a straightjacket to me, although it was a kinder version, since it did not restrain any of my limbs.

John Marmalade smiled at me and purred happily. He liked us to look like twins. Or perhaps he truly liked sweater-vests, and wearing sweater-vests.

I settled down, not wanting to upset him, or Mrs. Hudson, who truly was a great provider of the very best food I had ever enjoyed. I knew Sherlock would rescue me from my sweater-vest, as soon as he stopped torturing my ears, and he laid his eyes on me and observed my plight. But alas, my outfit did not stop at the sweater-vest. There was far worse still to come.

24 - Prelude to the Evening's Exchange

Sherlock set his violin down with gentle care. Dusk was falling. Dark shadows crept across the carpet like ink on wet paper. Sherlock did not bestir himself to light even one gaslamp. John would be arriving soon, and he could do it. John was a dab hand at lamp lighting. He had never once blown them up.

The same could not be said for Sherlock, though it had only happened a singular time, and it had been a minor explosion with a quickly doused fire. His mind had been fully engaged on an interesting case at the time, which is why it had happened. He had learned his lesson, though. One should never light one's pipe at the same time as one is lighting a gaslamp, when one's mind is fully engrossed on other matters. And Sherlock's mind was certainly otherwise occupied at the moment, on things other than lighting gaslamps.

He believed he had considered every possibility as to how the night's encounter might unfold. He still wasn't at ease with the blackmailer's illogical choice of location, yet he could not change it. He would cope admirably, he was sure, the morning's failure notwithstanding. And he would have reinforcements, both John and Cat Watson. He believed the blackmailer was working alone. Such villains did tend to be loners. Therefore, it would be three against one. No, more like five against one. Sherlock was worth at least three men, perhaps more.

After hours of beautiful music, the silence itself seemed overloud. More so because of the gathering darkness and creeping shadows. Everything tended to sound louder in the dark, as if one's ears sharpened to compensate for the lack of sight.

When it was fully dark and John had still not appeared, Sherlock roused himself and carefully lit two gaslamps. He intended to smoke a pipe while waiting. He did not try to light it at the same time as the gaslamps.

He was seated in his chair, puffing away, when he heard quick footsteps on the stairs. Lighter and faster than both John's and Mrs. Hudson's. The rap on the door was quick and light too. "Enter," he called.

A lad of about fourteen stepped in. Sherlock had seen him at John's house. "Message for Mr. Sherlock Holmes," he proclaimed, his chest puffed out proudly, as if he was addressing a large group, not one detective lounging in a chair. He trotted over and extended an envelope. Sherlock tipped him with a coin and sent him on his way, before he glanced at it. His name and address were written on the envelope in a female hand. He sniffed it. Mary's perfume.

He opened it without delay. The note inside was brief. *John will not be able to accompany you to The Regent's Park this evening. He sends his regrets. But you should not feel alone there. Many flirty girls enjoy the park at night and may wish to keep you company.* Mary had signed the note with a fancy *M*. She did have a beautiful script.

He sniffed her perfume on the note again, absently. Why was John unable to attend Sherlock? And why hadn't he written the note himself? Was it Mary's will? Did she simply wish to keep John out of danger? Safe by her side? If so, Sherlock could not fault her actions. And were some of her female thieves going to watch his back in the park, instead of John? The note alluded to that. Then again, the words could also be interpreted as a threat. They were criminals after all.

Sherlock was still sitting thus, note in hand, lost in thought and sniffing Mary's perfume, when he heard another set of footsteps coming up the stairs. Mrs. Hudson's, a bit heavier than usual. Hopefully she was carrying a tea tray. He could do with a cup, before setting out on his evening's adventure.

He rose and opened the door for her. She entered with a smile, saying, "Why thank-you, Sherlock dearest." He did not respond. He truly could not. He was dumbstruck by what he saw.

His landlady was carrying a tea tray, with John Marmalade sitting beside the pot in his sweater-vest, as on the previous day. That is not what had left Sherlock speechless. Mrs. Hudson was also carrying Cat Watson. Poor Cat Watson was restrained in some sort of pouch, which was strapped to her chest. Sherlock had seen lower caste women carrying their babies in similar sacks or wrapped scarves, as they went about their work.

This sack was knitted and baby-blue in colour. It tied at the cat's neck, and Cat Watson was quite trapped. He was also highly offended and thoroughly miserable. Sherlock could see it in his eyes. Add to that, Mrs. Hudson had knitted two little deerstalker caps, one for each cat. They were quite like Sherlock's own detecting cap, except for being knitted and baby blue and very small. His deerstalker was none of those things. If it had been, he wouldn't have been caught dead wearing it. The little caps were tied onto both cats' heads, under their chins, with ribbons.

Mrs. Hudson set the tray down and struck a fashion model's pose. "Look Sherlock, I've knitted you a present, a carrier for Cat Watson, for when you are on a case. And I've made him a matching detecting cap, just like yours, so he can look like a proper detective. And one for wee Johnny Marmalade, so he wouldn't feel left out." Cat Watson gave a miserable little yowl.

"Yes, I do see." Sherlock realized his eyes were wide and possibly bulging. He blinked several times, restoring them to their normal state.

"And look at this," Mrs. Hudson cried excitedly. She untied the cord at Cat Watson's neck and lifted him out of the carrier. He too was wearing a tea cozy sweater-vest. Sherlock should have expected it. Of course he should have. "Doesn't he look a treat? Have you ever seen a handsomer kitty-witty than Cat Watson, in his wee little detecting cap and sweater-vest?"

"No, I can't that say I have," Sherlock managed.

"Except for Johnny Marmalade. He's every bit as adorable," she said, in case the kitten's feelings were hurt, which they clearly were not. He was purring happily, leaning sleepily against the warm teapot.

Mrs. Hudson set Cat Watson down. He made a beeline for Sherlock, mewling in distress. Sherlock finally found acceptable words. "That was very thoughtful of you, Mrs. Hudson. I thank you for the present. I'm sure Cat Watson and John Marmalade do as well."

"They've already had their tea, and I've brought you a fresh pot. Do you have any news on my case?" Mrs. Hudson began to untie the straps of the carrier pouch, and remove it from her chest. She made quite a performance of it, it must be said, almost as if she was an exotic dancer shedding her clothing to musical accompaniment.

"I am working on it. No updates as yet," Sherlock said, in brief. "Hopefully I will have good news tomorrow. And now I will enjoy my tea."

Mrs. Hudson finished stripping off the cat-carrier and approached Sherlock. "Let me show you how to wear this," she said, as if he lacked the intelligence to figure it out for himself. Yet, there was no escaping her.

Mrs. Hudson wrapped her arms tight around Sherlock, pressing her chest against his, to wind the straps behind his back. She adjusted them just so, tying them snuggly around both his neck and back, taking her time to ensure that they were in exactly the right spot. She adjusted the front as well, draping the pouch over his chest and smoothing his shirt beneath it. "There, a perfect fit for when you have to carry Cat Watson about on a case." She smiled up at Sherlock, eyelashes fluttering like butterfly wings.

Cat Watson slunk beneath a chair, ears flat under his little detecting cap.

"Yes, a perfect fit." Sherlock stepped back. "Again, the cats and I thank you." He tucked a hand under her elbow and urged her toward the door.

"Let me take the carrier off before I go." She tried to dig in her heels.

"No need, I am going to keep it on. Get used to wearing it," Sherlock lied, and did his best to smile. They reached the door and if he did shove her outside, it was done politely. He closed the door quickly, not quite in her face. He leaned against it and exhaled in relief, twice, before he attempted to struggle out of the cat-carrier. He contorted, trying to reach the sturdy strap behind his back. He was flexible, yet the thing eluded him, and Mrs. Hudson seemed to have knotted the additional ties many times over. Just how many straps were there on the cat-carrier? Perhaps he should have let her release him from it, as he seemed to be stuck fast.

Cat Watson gave a loud meow, reminding Sherlock of his plight. "Ah, yes, let's take care of you first." He untied the cap and unbuttoned and untied the sweater-vest. Cat Watson gave his fur a good shake as soon as he was free, and began to groom himself.

"I wish you could free me from this cat-carrier." Sherlock reached for John Marmalade. The kitten scurried away, eluding him. Clearly, he liked his little outfit and wanted to keep wearing it. "There's no accounting for taste, is there," he whispered to Cat Watson, who meowed his agreement.

Sherlock sat down to sip the fresh tea, still stuck wearing the cat-carrier. He was not pleased to be meeting the blackmailer without John, yet he was not overly concerned. He had dealt with, and bested, far more nefarious criminals. This blackmailer treated their exchanges like a game. Still, best to get to the park well ahead of time.

He read Mary's message aloud Cat Watson, so he would be completely informed, then he readied his pistol. Next, he wrapped a length of jewelry chain and a walnut in butcher paper, to act as a decoy necklace. He chose his outerwear with care, wrapping his longest, darkest scarf around his neck to hide his pale skin. He donned his long, caped coat, which was dark enough to blend into the shadows. Alas, he was still wearing the cat-carrier. He hadn't wanted to cut the thing off, for fear of offending his possibly murderous landlady, but it was well hidden by his coat. The thing would even add a bit of warmth in the chill night. Lastly, he plunked his deerstalker on his head, both for added warmth and because he was on a case.

He could never be a shadow like Cat Watson. He was much too large and pale-skinned for that, yet he did his best to mimic one. He examined himself in the mirror to verify his shadowiness. He approved of what he saw, and was ready for the evening's adventure.

It was almost nine o'clock when Sherlock tip-toed down the stairs, avoiding the squeaky third step from the top. He did not wish to alert Mrs. Hudson to his activities on her behalf. Cat Watson followed on his heels, moving as stealthily as always. John Marmalade opted to stay curled up by the fire. Perhaps he was the wisest of them, or he was merely tired.

Out on the street, Sherlock did not hail a cab. The Regent's Park was not so far from 221B and Sherlock felt like stretching his legs after sitting for hours, playing his violin. He scooped up Cat Watson and carried him warm under his cape, as it was a long walk for a small cat. He did not once consider stuffing Cat Watson into the cat-carrier. The cat would never have forgiven him. Add to that, how very foolish he would look, a man strolling along, carrying a cat strapped to his chest as if it was a babe. Ridiculous!

If a newshound witnessed that, it would make front page news. Sherlock could see the editorial cartoon in his mind's eye, himself once again the object of ridicule. And what would the caption be? *London's Greatest Detective Moonlights as Cat-minder,* or perhaps, *Is London's Greatest Detective Also a Cat-burglar?* He liked the word play of that one, as if he burgled cats. And who would do such a thing, anyway? Burgle a cat when they were as plentiful as pickpockets in the back alleys of London.

When Sherlock neared the park, he lightened his step. He pulled his cap lower and his scarf higher, hiding most of his white skin. He set Cat Watson on the grass with a whispered, "Remain close."

Cat Watson gave an affirmative meow and disappeared into the darkness. One second he was there, the next he had vanished completely. Midnight Shadow Holmes would have been an apt name, if he wasn't already Cat Watson.

Sherlock was as shadowy and invisible as he could make himself, when he crossed into the park. It was unlit and coal black. He paused for twenty heartbeats, silent and still, both listening and granting his eyes time to adjust to the blackness. Sherlock had no desire to carry a lantern and place a spotlight, and target, on himself. Nor was he foolish enough to do so.

The park at night was not a friendly place. Honest folk avoided it. Bloodthirsty lowlifes did not. If you encountered someone in the park in the dark, they would not be there to wish you well and give you a hearty handshake. They would be there to wish you ill and give you a hearty knife-stab.

Garroting had also become fashionable since the Second Afghan war. Strangling was such a quick and quiet way to dispatch someone, whether it be an enemy soldier or a hapless victim. Any handy, everyday item could be employed. One had no need of a pistol or automatic knife, not when a scrap of rope could do the job. Even one's own scarf could be used as a ligature, in a pinch. A coil of fishing line or a piano string in a pocket could be employed to deadly effect, and wouldn't get you arrested if the coppers found such a mundane object in your pocket.

Senses on high alert, Sherlock moved forward, making his way across the park to the meeting place by the lake of ghosts.

25- A Shameful Performance

🐱 *from The Observations of Cat Watson*

At a distance, I tailed Sherlock across the huge park. I did not want to get too close, as he was making so much noise, he might as well have trumpeted his approach. Humans are such loud creatures. They breathe loudly, and step loudly, and their clothing rubs loudly with each stride of their legs and swing of their monkey-long arms. They even pass wind loudly, not that Sherlock was doing so now. He was trying to be quiet, after all. Perhaps he even believed he was succeeding.

I could hear other humans, lurking and rustling about in the dark of the park, yet none approached. They were up to their own nefarious, or sometimes amorous, affairs. I smelled the lake before we reached it. How could I not? Lakes have a strong vegetative odor, not to mention the fish that swim in them. Fish have a delicious fragrance, unless they are dead and rotting on the shore, which some clearly were. I could also hear the ripples licking wetly at the water's edge.

Sherlock was probably carrying his handy-dandy stick somewhere on his person, in addition to the pistol he had put in his pocket. And he had me. I liked to think of myself as his secret weapon—his eyes and ears in the dark. His Midnight Shadow. Maybe it was a good nickname for me after all, when I was on a case with him in the night. It could be my crime fighting persona.

I prowled along the shore, following Sherlock. I stopped when I heard breathing from a thick patch of shrubbery that bordered the lake. Again, the human probably thought they were silent, when they weren't. Was it our blackmailer, lying in wait? Or merely a common criminal skulking about? Or one of the Forty Flirty Thieves watching over Sherlock at Mary's behest?

I moved closer, sniffing. I knew the blackmailer's scent from both Mrs. Hudson's sweater and the note left at our door. Alas, I was upwind of the person, and as light as the breeze was, it carried their scent away from me. Nor had they trodden the ground around me. I had to get closer, if I was going to be of any help to my Sherlock.

As quiet as a cat, I crept nearer and nearer. Before I could identify the person in the bushes, a tremendous explosion lit up the sky. I yowled in fear, I am embarrassed to admit. But I had never seen anything like it. I was only eight months old, you may recall, and had yet to see all the wonders and evils a year of living in the world holds. I had never before seen explosions in the sky, with trails of lights rocketing about in patterns. Night turned to brilliant day. Was it the end of the world? Or had cats come down from the heavenly stars, to eliminate humanity, so cats could rule the planet? Clearly, I was letting my imagination run away with me, and yes, cats can have an imagination. At least the clever ones like me.

Alas, I was so thoroughly distracted, I was caught by surprise when the figure in the bushes rose up and darted out. Before I could yowl again, in warning, I was nabbed by the scruff of my neck. I squirmed with abandon. Sadly, I was in no position to do any damage with my claws or teeth.

Dangling me on the end of an extended arm, my captor strode toward Sherlock. And to state the obvious, there was no hiding in the dark for him now, not when the world was revealed in flashes of such brilliant light, it was as if the sun was flickering on and off, on and off. The strobing effect was most discombobulating.

I managed a glance behind and saw my captor. The figure closing in on Sherlock had a strange face under a dark hood. I had seen the occasional mask-wearing human stumbling their way home in the dark, after leaving a masquerade ball. Clearly, Sherlock was not the only human who liked to wear a disguise.

The mask my captor wore was as white as snow, with a nose even more prominent than Sherlock's. Beneath it, a long thin black moustache curled upward, echoing an exaggerated smile. Sherlock turned to face the approaching figure, a hand already in his pocket. He stilled when he saw me, captured. Oh, the humiliation. I, the stealthiest of creatures, had let myself be caught by a lumbering, bumbling human. If I survived, it was a shame I would never live down, not in nine lifetimes.

"A trade," the villain said in an irritating screechy voice. "Your kitty-cat for that pretty necklace."

Sherlock raised the decoy package into view. "I agree to the trade." His tone was so cold, I felt chilled. It was a tone of voice I had never heard him use.

"Open the package. Show me the pretty," cried the screechy voice.

Sherlock proceeded to do so slowly, perhaps granting time for a few flirty thieves to intervene. I did not hear anybody else approaching, though it was hard to hear a thing, other than the explosions in the sky overhead.

"I had not realized it was Guy Fawkes Night. How remiss of me," Sherlock said in the same cold tone, laced with self-disgust.

"And how clever of me!" I was shaken roughly and I yowled. "Hurry your hands or it will be the end of your pretty kitty." The villain yanked a sack from a coat pocket and held it up.

Sherlock stilled again. "Do not harm the cat, or there is nowhere on this earth you will be safe." His voice had turned even colder, if that was possible. Ice should have formed on the lake beside us.

My captor gave a showy bow, doffing an imaginary cap in salute. It was still impossible to tell if our foe was male or female, what with the costume and absurd voice. It would have better suited a Punch and Judy puppet performance. I had seen one of those once, on the street.

In one quick motion, I was dropped into the sack and the top was knotted tight. It was even worse than the offensive cat-carrier Mrs. Hudson had tied me into. At least my head had been in the air then. Now, I was completely in the dark. I couldn't see a thing inside the sack, save the cloth that trapped me. I yowled and thrashed, to no avail.

I, in the sack, was swung back and forth, back and forth, as I had seen children do on rope swings. It was most disconcerting. Why did children think it was fun? I certainly didn't find it at all enjoyable, but perhaps that was because I was trapped in a sack by a villain.

The next thing I knew, I was swung over a shoulder to dangle behind and against my captor's back, yet he or she still seemed to be swinging a sack and taunting Sherlock. I did not understand what was happening outside my cloth prison. My captor's muscles bunched and released as he or she cackled. I heard the splash of something landing in the lake. Sherlock cried out in great distress, and then I clued in. The detective had been tricked by sleight of hand, the old switcheroo. He believed I had been tossed into the lake to drown, like a sack of kittens. Sherlock had brought a decoy necklace, and the villain had brought a decoy sack. They were thinking alike.

My captor started running, me bumping against the hard back most jarringly. Meanwhile, I heard a great deal of splashing and knew Sherlock had rushed into the icy water. He was trying to save me, while letting the villain get away, with me in their evil clutches.

26 - The Mystery of the Baker Street Blackmailer

The ensuing drama would give Sherlock nightmares in the days and weeks to come. The costumed villain swung the sack vigorously back and forth, cackling in a most offensive high pitch. Sherlock did not have the jeweled necklace needed to save Cat Watson's life. He had made a grave error in judgement by not bringing it, and silently castigated himself.

As excellent a marksman as he was, he could not risk firing on the villain, for fear of hitting the cat. With the world around them strobing between black night and blinding bright, and the villain gambolling left and right, swinging the cat around in the sack, he might easily miss his target. Even a graze could well be fatal to a small cat. With Cat Watson's life endangered, he suddenly realized how deeply he had come to care for the little scrap of fur. Ridiculous sentiment, yet undeniable.

And to be beaten twice by the same opponent, it had never happened before, yet it seemed about to now. Was this villain cleverer than him? At least in the carrying out of criminal activities?

"This has been such fun. Now show me the pretty sparkly!" the villain screeched, swinging the cat more enthusiastically back and forth. Sherlock pretended to fumble the package, and drop it to the ground. He shrugged and kicked it toward the villain, hoping to gift himself an opportunity to act.

"Oh, man upstairs. That will not do." And with that, the villain flung the sack enthusiastically into the air. It flew a long way and landed with a splash, surprisingly far out in the lake. When the villain scooped up the decoy parcel and ran, Sherlock did not even consider giving chase. He tossed off his cloak and hat as he sprinted toward the lake. He was able to see a bit of the floating sack when a firework

156

flared overhead. But could he save Cat Watson without freezing to death? He suspected it would be a close-run thing.

The water was like ice. Well, it was November 5th in less than sunny Britain. How could he have neglected to realize the significance of the date? It was Guy Fawkes Day, otherwise known as Gunpowder Treason Day. There were always fireworks over London and The Regent Park on that night, to commemorate the fact that King James I had survived the attempt to blow him up, almost 300 years earlier.

Moving fast, Sherlock surged through the water. Moments earlier, he had been cursing the fireworks display, now he was praying it would continue for as long as possible, to light his path to Cat Watson. He was a smart cat. Surely he would be holding his breath, nose plugged. No, cats didn't have hands. Could cats' noses even plug? Perhaps not. They were not as malleable and putty-like as human noses. Sherlock was not thinking clearly. Was he becoming hysterical? Like an overwrought woman?

Running through water was not the fastest way to move. He dove in and tried swimming. Alas, his sodden clothes weighed him down. And he was getting tangled in the weeds that grew so thickly around the shore of the lake. He tried wading again, but the water was now over his head. He thrashed as much as he swam. Another flash of fireworks illuminated the scene, turning black water into a beautiful display of dancing coloured lights, as it reflected the fireworks in the sky.

The world went black again as Sherlock reached the approximate spot where the sack had landed. He groped around. Nothing. He ducked under and swished his hands through the water more frantically. He surfaced for air and did so again, and a third time. Finally, his frozen fingers brushed something. He managed to grip what felt like wet cloth. Hopefully not some random drowned body. He hauled it closer. It was small and light. Yes, the sack!

He immediately started swimming for shore, so cold he could barely move his limbs at that point. He certainly couldn't open the sack with fingers he could no long feel. He sank below the surface. Even without his cloak, his drenched clothes were so heavy, they were pulling him down like an anchor. Nor was there any movement in the sack, which he was struggling to hold up and out of the water, as he himself sank to a greater depth. His feet touched bottom. He launched up and forward and hauled in air. Alas, he could not remain afloat and sank again. He was too cold to even shiver. He launched off the bottom of the lake again, seeking the air.

Another firework explosion illuminated the night. He saw a figure splashing toward him. Was it the villain? Making sure he drowned? No, a hand reached out and yank him up. He kicked, trying to help. A second person was there, tugging him closer to shore. He was mostly a dead weight, and almost dead to boot.

He was dragged from the water onto the frozen ground. He thought he heard Mary's voice. When the next burst of fireworks provided more prolonged light, probably the climax of the fireworks display, Sherlock squinted through frozen eyeballs and did see Mary. Good lord, she was wearing trousers! Was she dressed as a chimney sweep? He expected the figure at her side to be John. Sadly, it wasn't. It was her brother Robbie, who had wanted to feed him to the fishies. Now, he was saving Sherlock from the fishies. He laughed at the irony of it, and spewed up a gush of water.

Barely conscious, he thrust the sack at Mary and rasped, "Open it. Cat Watson."

She yanked her automatic blade from her boot, clicking it opened in the same motion. She sliced the sack's tie and pulled out a ragdoll. "There is no cat in here, Sherlock. Only this." Mary held the thing up for his perusal.

Had Sherlock retrieved the wrong sack from the water and left Cat Watson to drown. He squinted at it. No, it was the same cloth sack. His brain might be half-frozen, yet it still functioned well enough to deduce what had happened. He groaned loudly. He had been played for a fool, by a decoy sack holding a Raggedy Ann doll with a vacant smile.

"Did you almost drown to save your cat? And it wasn't even your cat?" Robbie crowed with laughter. "World's greatest detective, my Aunt Fanny's arse."

Sherlock wished to defend himself, yet his teeth were chattering so hard, he could not speak. Nor was he feeling very clever, or even slightly great at the moment. And where was Cat Watson now?

Mary tossed the sack and ragdoll into the lake, before he could indicate it should be kept, and examined as evidence. She said, "Get him on his feet, Robbie. Wrap his cloak around him. It's dry. Don't forget his hat. If we don't get him home and warmed, he will die from the cold."

"Do I have to?" Robbie whined.

Apparently, he did. Sherlock was wrestled to his frozen legs and his cloak tossed over his shoulders. He was half-carried, half-dragged to a waiting cart. Likely the same one Robbie had wanted to toss him in, to take him to the Thames to end his life, that first time they met.

Sherlock was driven home as fast as the nag could trot, which did not seem fast at all, to his frozen flesh. He was hauled up the stairs and a hot bath was run. He was stripped and dumped into it, by Robbie, not Mary, thank heavens. Hot tea and a hot toddy were provided. He drank them down. It was all something of a blur, until he must have passed out.

Sherlock awoke in his own bed, feeling surprisingly well, and toasty warm. A number of hot-water bottles hemmed him in. Someone must have tended him through the night, ensuring he did not succumb to hypothermia, a condition he had read about only recently. The sun was barely up and someone was hammering on his door. That's what had woken him. Sherlock mumbled, "Can you get that, Cat Watson?" And then he remembered, with a stab of pain like a knife to his heart. Cat Watson had been cat-napped by a fiendish villain. Not that the little cat could open doors, even if he had been there.

Sherlock fell out of bed. He was clad in underpants, nothing more. He yanked on his robe and rushed to fling open the door. Illogically, he was hoping it was Cat Watson being brought safely home, or at least some news of him.

John raced in and almost felled Sherlock, who only managed to save himself by catching the back of an armchair. "Sherlock, Mary is missing!" John wailed. "Gone all night long, I tell you. She has been abducted. You must help me find her. Oh, this is even worse than when Gladstone went missing."

"Well, I should hope so. She is your wife John, not your hound. And finding Mary will not be difficult," Sherlock drawled. Mary's wet gloves and scarf had been left to dry by the fire, as had the knitted cat carrier. His rescuers must have had a good laugh to find him wearing such a ludicrous garment.

John could have reached out and touched Mary's accessories, but he was blind to them. He didn't even notice the cat carrier. If John was any less observant, he would walk around on his hands and think the world had turned upside-down. Why, he had probably passed right by Mary on her way home, and not even noticed. Maybe he had tipped his hat at her and ogled her, not recognizing her as his wife. That is how unobservant John could be, on any given day.

Mrs. Hudson appeared like clockwork. Sherlock didn't know if she was aware of what had transpired the previous night, though she didn't seem to be. Drinker that she was, maybe she had gotten sloshed, passed out, and slept through his less-than-triumphant return to his rooms.

"Tea please, Mrs. Hudson," he said.

"Of course, Sherlock dearest. I won't be a tick." She swished back down the stairs.

John dropped onto his chair as if his legs had been chopped off. It was lucky John Marmalade hadn't been curled up there, or he would have been squashed flat. "First Gladstone, now Mary," he wailed. "Where can she be?" He dropped his head into his hands in despair.

"I suspect she is home by now," Sherlock said. "You probably missed her return by scant minutes." He did not want to reveal more. If he explained how Mary had rescued him the previous night, it would raise too many questions, ones he could not answer, not without exposing her position as boss of an organized criminal gang. Or doing a great deal of lying, and John would spot that.

"But where would she have spent the night? Do you think she is having an affair?" John sobbed.

"No, I do not. John, why did you fail to return last night? Why were you unable to accompany me to the park?" he asked, to change the subject.

John got a foggy look about him. "Oh, I don't know. I was supposed to return, wasn't I?" Sherlock nodded once. "Huh, I went home, had tea with Mary, told her I would be assisting you on a case. She brought me a brandy, I drank it and … I must have fallen asleep, right there in my chair. I am so sorry, Sherlock. When I awoke this morning, still in my chair, she was nowhere to be found. So she must have been kidnapped. What other explanation can there be? Unless she is having an affair." He gazed piteously at Sherlock.

At that moment, Mrs. Hudson arrived with the tea, and John Marmalade. As always, he was clad in his sweater-vest, now paired with his little detecting cap. John rubbed his eyes as if he was seeing things. At least the sight jarred John from his misery.

"Here you go, boys." She set the tray down and scanned the room. "Where is Cat Watson? I've brought his tea, too." John Marmalade

160

prowled around, sniffing, searching for his friend. He gave a sad little mewl when he couldn't find him.

"I am not sure where Cat Watson is." Sherlock felt every bit as sad as the kitten. He picked up John Marmalade and cuddled him on his lap.

"Have there been any developments in my case?" his landlady asked, eyeing the client's chair as if she should settle there and stay for a cuppa.

"I'm afraid not. Things did not go as planned with my investigation last evening, and there are no developments to discuss as yet." Sherlock left it at that. Bad enough to fail twice, worse yet to speak about it and relive the shame.

They were a morose lot: John with his missing wife, Sherlock with his missing cat, John Marmalade missing his best friend, Mrs. Hudson missing her broach. Add to that, a blackmailer threatening her very life. Into the silence came the sound of running water, from the water closet. Sherlock glanced at Mary's damp gloves and scarf. Perhaps she had not left yet, after all. This could be difficult to explain.

"Ah, John, I think we have located your missing wife," he declared.

Mary emerged from around the corner, dressed again as a chimney sweep, perhaps to sneak home unnoticed. People did not notice chimney sweeps any more than they noticed beggars. She was in the process of buttoning up her sooty blouse.

John's jaw dropped. If he had been sitting on the carpet, rather than his chair, it would have hit the floor. He quickly recovered his wits and sputtered, "Mary? Is that you dressed as a chimney sweep?" He did not wait for an answer. "You spent the night with Sherlock? In costume? Were you playing dress-up is his bedroom? Or perhaps I should say dress-down, or dress-out, or undress? Yes, that's it. Were you playing undress with Sherlock?" His eyes bulged, until they were in danger of popping right out of his skull, and he would have been a no-eyed John. He looked back and forth between them with those rather crazed and bulging eyes, twice, before he found his tongue again. "Mary, you and Sherlock? Sherlock, you and Mary?"

"Of course not," they said in unison.

Sherlock added, "Don't be an idiot, John."

Mary added, "Let us discuss this over tea."

Alas, John was having none of it. He roared in rage and surged to his feet. Sherlock sensed an eminent attack and tossed John

161

Marmalade to Mrs. Hudson. She caught the kitten and ran from the room, sobbing so loudly and despairingly, it was as if her heart had broken in two.

John tackled Sherlock, the fact that he was still seated in his chair notwithstanding. The chair went over backwards and Sherlock's head hit the floor, hard enough to crack the wood, as well as his skull. He was quite dazed when John punched him in the nose, then he was even more dazed.

"Oh John, please stop. You must know you are being ridiculous," Mary said.

"You are an idiot, John," Sherlock repeated. Perhaps he should have kept his mouth shut. John punched it. Oddly, it brought Sherlock back to his senses. He said, "Do stop, John, or I shall be obliged to punch you back."

For some reason, that made John punch him again. Sherlock punched him back, in the nose. From there, they tumbled about the room in a flurry of fists, and a great deal of thrown items, breaking furniture, smashed crockery, and cursing. By the time they had worn themselves out, they were both in very sorry shape indeed, as was Sherlock's home.

In the meantime, Mary had rescued the teapot by relocating it to the small kitchen. She had even poured herself a cup, in one of the surviving cups. Sherlock knew she was cool-headed, and she was proving it, in spades.

"Have you two quite finished?" she asked, when they lay on the floor, panting and groaning and bleeding.

In answer, John tried to punch Sherlock. He was too beaten and exhausted to manage more than a light slap, not even worthy of a woman whose honour had been insulted. "Yes," John moaned.

"Then do sit down, John, and have tea. We need to talk." Mary settled pointedly on the client's chair.

John dragged himself into his own chair, and with teary eyes, said, "You're leaving me for Sherlock, aren't you?"

Sherlock burst out laughing, which made him groan in pain. "John, if you were any less observant, you would walk off a peer, thinking it was a road, and drown to death, as I almost did last night."

"So it is just an affair then? Or a one-night stand?" John's voice broke and he mopped at his streaming eyes with his handkerchief. He was cleaning off a lot of blood at the same time—the result of all the punching.

Sherlock helped himself to a napkin to do the same, and said, "Don't be an idiot, John." He raised an eyebrow at Mary. It was her tale. It was up to her to decide how to tell it. Would it be truth or lies? Admittedly, he was curious to hear what she would come up with.

Mary worried her lip, clearly undecided. After another sip of tea, she said, "It is more complicated than that, John, and has not a thing to do with affairs of the heart, or lust. There are some things you don't know about me."

John sniffled loudly. "Like what? That you work nights as a chimney sweep?"

"There is no need for sarcasm, husband. It does not become you," Mary said evenly.

"Well, playing dress-up as a chimney sweep in Sherlock's bedroom does not become you," he snapped back.

She crossed her arms. "I am referring to my family business, John. We aren't in manufacturing."

"What does this have to do with you spending the night with Sherlock?" he cried.

Sherlock was losing patience, and he had a cat to find. He said, "Last night, Mary and her brother Robbie, a cut-throat killer if ever I've met one, saved me from drowning. The rendezvous with Mrs. Hudson's blackmailer did not go well for me, and I ended up in that cursed, ice-cold lake. I suspect Mary drugged you, again, so you would not be fit to accompany me. She and her brother saved me from drowning, which is the only reason she is here now, and I am here now."

John blinked twice. "You drugged me, Mary? And what does he mean by 'again'? How many times have you drugged me?"

Mary frowned quite ferociously at Sherlock. "You're explaining it all wrong. Be quiet."

"Well, you're doing no better. Get to the point."

"I will get to the point, if you would bloody shut up!"

"Mary, your language!" John said, shocked.

"When will you get to the crux of the matter? When Christmas has come and gone? When the New Year is upon us?" Sherlock said, with biting sarcasm.

"Keep this up, Sherlock, and I'm going to gag you again, and maybe I will let Robbie slit your throat and feed you to the fishies," she snarled.

"You gagged Sherlock?" John gaped at his wife. "I've been tempted to do so myself, too many times to count, but you gagged him? And why would Robbie kill him? I've been sorely tempted to do so myself, more than once, let me tell you, but why would Robbie do such a thing? One of you tell me what is going on!" John had clearly reached his breaking point.

"Mary is the head of a criminal gang of thieves and cutthroats," Sherlock blurted out, deeply offended to hear that his supposedly best friend wanted to gag him and slit his throat, to kill him off.

"Not cutthroats, John, or hardly ever. Just thieves. Mostly thieves." Mary trailed off, avoiding John's gaze.

"Mary? Can it be true?" John said.

"I just said so, didn't I? Don't look at me like that, John, as if I had suddenly sprouted two horns and a forked tail, and turned into a devil. I am Mary, your loving wife, born into a crime family, and having something of a knack for organization. I was voted head of the organization, so I am the boss. I don't steal, myself, or slit throats. Or, not very often. The stealing, not the slitting of throats. I never do that. I am merely a business woman," she stressed.

"You being Sherlock's lover would have been easier to swallow than this bitter pill. And you've been drugging me! You did dognap Gladstone, didn't you? And you don't like my moustache, do you?" John's dander was up now.

So was Mary's. "If you most know, it's a horrible, hideous, ghastly excuse of a moustache. I have had to resist the impulse to drug you and shave it off, every single night we bed down together."

John gasped and clapped a protective hand over his reduced moustache.

"And don't get me started on that dog of yours -"

Sherlock cleared his throat loudly, a prelude to speech. The conversation between John and Mary was not productive, and was turning injurious. He felt he should intervene before worse things were shouted—things that could not be taken back. "John, Mary, this is a private conversation between husband and wife. You should go home and clear the air between you."

"Shut up, Sherlock," they said in unison.

Mary added, "And there is no clearing the air in that house, not with Gladstone fouling it. Every time I light a candle, I'm afraid the whole house will explode, from all his gas."

John added, "I can no longer call that house my home, as it is financed with ill-gotten gains. I am moving back to Baker Street, with Gladstone."

Sherlock grimaced. "I don't think that's a good idea. Gladstone I mean. The cats, you know." He gestured around the room, which was in a deplorable state after their brawl. It might be handy to have John move back in. He would have the place tidied and tickety-boo in no time. John did not like a mess. But there was no longer a place for Gladstone.

"What cats?" John snapped. "Mrs. Hudson has clearly adopted John Marmalade, and you've lost Cat Watson, haven't you?"

"Cat Watson has been cat-napped," Mary said.

John glared at his wife. "By you? If you dog-nap dogs, you probably cat-nap cats as well."

Mary gasped, rose, and stomped to the door. She donned her still damp coat, which had been hanging behind Sherlock's on the coat-tree. "If you wish to leave me, it is your choice, John. I do not agree with your decision, as I love you dearly, but I cannot force you to come home with me."

"I bet you could, if you drugged me and dragged me back there. You could shave my moustache off at the same time." John's jaw jutted pugnaciously.

Mary sighed. "I hope to see you at home, John, once you have settled down and come to your senses. We shall discuss the matter there." She left, almost bumping into Mrs. Hudson on her way out.

The landlady scuttled in, John Marmalade tucked in the crook of her elbow. "So you're not having an affair with Dr. Watson's wife?" she asked.

"I am not," Sherlock declared. "The very idea. John is moving back in."

Mrs. Hudson passed John Marmalade to Sherlock. "Then you'll be needing this wee kitty, until Cat Watson comes home. I'm going to make you both a lovely feast, to celebrate Dr. Watson's return. We all know how Dr. Watson enjoys his meals, likes his three squares, not like you, Sherlock. I swear you would live on tea and toast if I didn't feed you." She clapped her hands happily, and blew Sherlock a kiss on her way out the door.

"This place could really do with a cleaning, John. I'm going to dress now." Sherlock set John Marmalade on his chair and left the room. He took his time over his toilette, leaving John to put the place to rights. The shambles of the room was John's fault, after all, since he had initiated the brawl.

Sherlock found himself most content to have John back, and at the same time, sad that Cat Watson was missing and possibly in grave peril. He could not bear to think that Cat Watson might have been killed, so he did not. To rescue Cat Watson, he would have to quickly solve, *The Mystery of the Baker Street Blackmailer*, as he had come to think of the case. Maybe he would even permit John to write up the adventure as a tale for The Strand, names and key details changed of course. John might well need the distraction, now that he had left his wife and returned to Sherlock.

27 - The Cat is out of the Bag

from The Observations of Cat Watson

I was unceremoniously dumped from the sack into a rusty, metal-barred cage. The door on the side of the prison was shut and latched, before I had gathered my wits enough to attempt an escape. My abductor scurried away, still masked. One low-burning lantern was left to light the place where I found myself.

The new accommodation was far from luxurious, nor did I find myself alone. There was another cat already inside the cage, a female. She was as petite and black-furred as me. We could have been twins, except she did not have a little white tip on her tail. Had my abductor nabbed other cats? And if so, why?

We meowed a greeting. From the smells in the cage, I knew she had not been imprisoned for long, maybe only a day or two. Although an assortment of animals had been imprisoned in there before us. That was obvious to my nose.

She was underfed, but not emaciated, so she was no worse off than a cat living on the street. Perhaps she had been a back-alley cat, before being cat-napped. There was a bowl of water in the cage. That was important. All living creatures will die far faster from dehydration than starvation.

Clearly, I would not be going home to Sherlock yet, if ever. Would I and the other cat be cooked into a meat pie? As small as we both were, I doubted the scraps of meat on our bones would be worth the effort required to skin us and carve us up. Even combined, we would make for a skimpy meal indeed.

When the other cat concluded I was not a threat, she curled up close. I gave her a reassuring lick and paced about, surveying where I had ended up.

The cage was set on a rickety table in a shack with a dirt floor. Very probably an outbuilding. One small and dirty glass window let in enough light for even a human to see by. There was little of note in the shack: a stool, wall shelves holding rusty old cans and assorted jars, mysterious bits and bobs, old stacked crates, a worn straw broom propped in the corner. Most of the stuff appeared abandoned and forgotten, except for the axe and butcher knife. They lay on the edge of the table, close beside the cage. They looked sharp and lovingly polished. I did not judge it to be a good sign.

I tried to strike up a conversation with the other cat, to learn what I could, but she was not very bright or forthcoming. I imagine my communication with other cats was much like Sherlock's communication with the majority of humans, simply not on the same intellectual level.

After observing all that I could, with my eyes, ears and nose, I curled up beside the other cat and slept, exhausted from the trauma of my ordeal.

I awoke to brighter light. Cracks between the boards of the ill-constructed shed's walls let in almost as much sunlight as the filthy little window. I was still alone with the other black cat. No humans had made an appearance, and my stomach was starving. The other cat meowed hungrily, telling me not to expect any regular feedings. She had no name, as I had once had no name, when living on the streets.

She pawed at the bars. She did not like being caged any more than I did. Well, she was a cat and it was our nature. Much more alert after my recuperative sleep, I examined the latch that closed the cage door. There was no lock on it. It was merely a manual eye and hook clasp. It did not appear overly difficult to open, if you were a clever cat, which I was.

I was pawing at it when I heard footsteps. I stopped what I was doing. The door to the shack opened. I cringed beside the other cat, eager to learn what I could about my cat-napper—not to be confused with someone who naps with cats, which is what most people who have cats do, to enjoy their soothing purrs.

The human who entered was no longer wearing a mask or hood, seeing no need to hide her face from cats. The young woman wasn't one I recognized, nor I had expected to. She was pretty enough for a human, not that they can ever be considered attractive, with their bald skin and round ears jutting from on the side of their heads, and lack of tail. How can anyone or anything be attractive if they don't have a tail? But I digress.

She was wearing quality clothing of a modest nature. Her dark gown and cloak were unadorned, no lace or ribbon. Her long hair was also dark and shiny clean. She smelled of soap, and that scent was familiar to me, having tracked it from the market when Sherlock was pursuing her.

She looked perfectly respectable, until one gazed into her eyes. There was something deeply unsettling in their depths that gave me a shiver. She smiled at us in our cage. The smile was even more disturbing than her eyes, it being malicious and utterly unhinged.

Her madness was further revealed when she spoke in a sing-song voice. "A-tisket, a-tasket, two kitties in a basket, or better yet a cage, a cage is all the rage." She pulled a dead mouse out of her pocket by the tail, kissed it on the nose, and dropped it into the cage. Was it to be our breakfast?

She resumed her little song. "I sent a letter to my lover, on the way I dropped it. I dropped it, I dropped it. Yes, on the way I dropped it. My rich old daddy picked it up and put it in his pocket. He took it, he took it, and he wouldn't give it back. Now he'll have to pay, my lover's gone away, seduced by an old prune, her face like a baboon." She pulled a second dead mouse from her pocket. It also got a farewell kiss before it was dropped into the cage. One for each of us then. I did not meow a thank-you. She did not deserve politeness.

And she wasn't finished her song. "A-tisket, a-tasket, my lover's gone away, my lover's gone astray, now Daddy has to pay. He'll go in a casket, sardines in a basket, with the old prune, and her man upstairs." Her song lost its musicality toward the end. Regardless, the words were alarming. I hissed a protest. She stuck her tongue out at me, like a rebellious child.

With a little girl's giggle, she dragged the stool closer and perched on it. She ran her thumb along the sharp blade of the nearby axe and chanted, "A-tisket, a-tasket, three bodies in a casket, or better yet a cage, a cage is all the rage." She doffed an imaginary hat, as if on stage, her little show over. At least she did not pick up the axe, or produce a third mouse. As hungry as I was, I couldn't stomach more than one. Her words had sorely dampened my appetite.

She leaned closer. "I could have just killed prune-face and Daddy, you know. Daddy for driving my love away, and her for stealing him, but where would the fun be in that?"

I gathered my courage and meowed inquiringly.

"That prune-faced wretch must suffer as I suffer. My lover told me all about the dead husband in her cellar, and all about her jewels, and how much they mean to her. Oh, boohoo. I'll take every last sparkly, when I end her, and her man upstairs. I'll even take his doppelganger from her bed. She'll have no comfort at all. I'll end her man upstairs first and she'll have no protection. Won't she cry buckets of tears? He'll come for you, you know. You should have seen how he almost froze to death in the lake, trying to save your furry little hide. Why would a man care so for a cat?"

I meowed indignantly. What was wrong with caring for a cat? Cats were worthy creatures, especially yours truly, if I did say so myself. Her words had also confirmed that she had been the hooded figure at Mrs. Hudson's bedroom window, as I had already suspected.

The girl snorted. Her eyes gleamed with malicious intent. "A-tisket, a-tasket, a green and yellow basket, to catch the river of tears she'll cry, when I end her man upstairs, to catch the river of blood he'll bleed, when I stick him like a pig." She picked up the butcher knife and thrust it about, willy-nilly, as if stabbing ten men, not merely one. She laughed the entire time, and it was no longer the little girl giggle, but a maniacal cackle that would have done an evil witch proud.

She stopped stabbing and jabbing the air, and leaned her face close to the cage. "Now enjoy your mousies, my wee kitties. For one of you, it will be your final meal. I'll use your twin's carcass to make him sooo sad, when he thinks you are the dead kitty." She pointed the knife tip directly at me.

Clearly, she had no idea how clever my Sherlock was, if she believed she could hoodwink him into believing the other black cat was me, his trusted companion. She was a female, and she had no little white tuft on the end of her tail or her chest. Unless the girl planned to chop or burn the fur and body, to a degree where it would not be identifiable. The thought made me feel ill.

She still wasn't finished. "I have another note to send. An invitation. I've already decided where to meet with her man upstairs. It's sooo clever. He'll come for you, and all he'll find is a-tisket, a-tasket, a dead cat in a basket, and his own bones in a casket." She grinned madly and poked at me with the knife, through the cage bars. "I'm going to keep you forever to be my pussy cat." I cringed back. "Now be a good kitty-kitty and eat your breakfast yummies." She dropped the knife and shook a scolding finger at me, before skipping from the shed, chanting a new rhyme. "Pussy cat, pussy cat, where have you been? I've been to London, and guess what I've seen? Pussy cat, pussy cat, what did you see? Why only the bars of the cage that kept me. Pussy cat, pussy cat, what did you there?"

Her voice faded away and I did not hear the rest. I was merely relieved to see the back of her. Madness is a most unsettling condition to be around.

Clearly, we had to escape before she killed the female cat, just like she had killed the two little mice. I would not be used as a pawn to torment and doom my Sherlock, nor did I wish to be the mad girl's plaything in a cage for the rest of my days.

While my companion enjoyed one of the mice, I attempted to open the latch again. My paw wasn't slim enough to fit through the bars. I rooted around in the debris on the bottom of the cage and located a sturdy chicken bone. Perfect. Gripped between my teeth, I stuck it through the bars and tried to lift the clasp. It was tighter, or perhaps heavier, than I had expected. It didn't budge. I put down the bone and paced around the door, examining the latch with my eyes, as best I could from inside my prison.

Yes, it was merely a simple cabinet hook, where the hook dropped into the eye, holding the door closed. All I had to do was raise the hook out of the eye and push the door opened. We would be free from our prison—as free as two birds, or two cats who were chasing two birds. The chicken bone should do the job.

The other cat meowed at me. She had devoured the tastier bits of her mouse, and was asking if I wanted mine. I had eaten well for many days, and she had not. I pushed the mouse closer to her and meowed encouragingly. She purred an appreciative little thank-you, before she dug in.

I returned to the lock. With the chicken bone gripped tight between my teeth, I stood up, my paws braced on the bars. I maneuvered the bone as far as I could through the gap in the bars, and shoved it upward with a bit of a flick, like taking a running start at prey one is stalking. And voila, the hook lifted out of the eye and dropped, to swing against the side of the cage. The door was unlocked. I had done it! I wished Sherlock was there to see how clever and resourceful I had been.

With a shove of my head, the door creaked opened. I meowed at the other cat to follow me. She frowned in puzzlement. Yes, cats can frown as well as smile. I had even seen a strange cat once, a pampered pet, with a face in a permanent and exaggerated grumpy pout. It was most unnerving. I felt bad for the poor thing, to be born with such a disfigured face.

I meowed encouragingly. She returned to eating her mouse. She didn't want to leave it. Silly really, a mouse is so small it can be carried about by its tail, as a snack. Why, five mice could be carried around as five snacks, and a cat would barely notice the weight of them.

I thought I heard footsteps approaching. The woman should not be returning yet, unless she had changed her mind and decided to kill the other cat first and write the note afterward. Perhaps she wanted to write the note in cat's blood. It seemed like the type of thing she would do. And I had, more than once, heard men mention how women were as prone to changing their minds as the wind is to shifting direction.

My hiss ordered the other cat to come along. She didn't move, so I did the only thing I could think of. I darted over, and stole the mouse by the tail. I bounded out of the cage with it. She gave chase. Footsteps were definitely getting closer. And now I could hear humming. The tune was, of course, *A-tisket, a-tasket, a green and yellow basket*.

There were gaps between the planks that constructed the shed's walls. I had already taken note of one gap that was larger than the rest. It appeared wide enough for a small cat to squeeze through. Luckily, we were both small cats. Unfortunately, it was on the side of the shack from which the mad woman was making her approach. Timing would be crucial. We needed to dart out through the gap at the same instant the woman opened the shed door and entered.

If I was alone, it would have been no problem. Alas, I was not, and I wasn't about to leave the other cat behind to be butchered. I was a loyal tom.

I stopped before the gap. The other cat stopped to, and tried to snatch back the mouse. I hissed, just a bit, telling her to wait. She hissed back, too loudly.

The woman heard her. "Oh, are my kitty-cats fighting? How delightful. Wait for my little eye to spy. I spy with my little eye." She yanked open the shed door before I was expecting it. I flung the mouse out through the gap, hoping the other cat would instinctively give chase. She did, but she stopped just outside the hole, blocking my exodus.

The woman screeched when she saw the empty cage, door ajar. She made a grab for the axe. I stuck my claw through the gap and gave the other cat a little scratch, to move her furry behind. She leapt out of the way and I darted through the gap. It was a bit of a squeeze for me, after all the cream and sardines I had been enjoying. I was not as fast as I needed to be. I heard the axe swoosh down, cutting the air, as my bottom popped out through the gap, a bit like a cork from a wine bottle.

I yowled as the axe chopped through my tail. My poor, beautiful furry black tail, with the adorable bit of white on its tip. Cats are very proud of, and attached to, their tails, and I am no exception.

Without slowing down, I snatched up the mouse again and raced into the nearest vegetation. The other cat followed. The woman bounded from the shed and gave chase. I caught a fleeting glimpse of her, axe in one hand, the amputated piece of my beautiful tail in her other. I might have sat down and mewled like a wee kitten that had lost its mother, if I hadn't been running for my life.

28-A Dreadful Tail

Sherlock and John did their best to enjoy the fine feast Mrs. Hudson had provided. It was one of her best efforts. Lentil soup, followed by a tender roasted pork-loin, stuffed with prunes, potatoes of course, several properly overcooked, limp, mushy veg, a dill loaf, applesauce, and gingerbread. She had even found the time to bake her famous biscuits, as if the dill loaf and gingerbread weren't enough. They finished the meal with those biscuits, and brandy, despite the fact that the two truly do not pair well together.

John did love his food, yet ate with less gusto than usual. Sherlock didn't have the same appreciation and fascination for what he put in his stomach, but did not want to upset Mrs. Hudson by not doing her meal justice, so he ate more than he had a mind to.

There was not a great deal of conversation while they supped, since their mouths were full and busy chewing. They were a sorry sight, faces cut and bruised from their tussle. And Sherlock was a bit distracted. John Marmalade kept reminding him of Cat Watson's absence by mewling sadly and digging his little claws into Sherlock's ankles, as if to say, *Why are you sitting there stuffing your belly? You should be out rescuing Cat Watson.*

Between courses, John kept sighing, his brow set in permanent wrinkles, like an old man's. Sherlock did not have to be a great detective to know what was bothering his friend. He held his tongue, except for employing it to eat, until they were sated and settled in their customary chairs, brandy glasses in one hand, pipes in the other. John had done a stellar job of putting the room to rights. Only then, meal over, did he try to comfort his friend.

"You're better off without Mary, John," he said, without preamble.

The creases in John's forehead became more pronounced. He slumped deeper into his chair, as if he wished to become a permanent part of the upholstery, and never leave it. He didn't speak one word.

174

It was atypical. John was usually like a woman, inclined to be overly verbose.

Sherlock continued offering comfort. "Mary is a criminal, a crime boss. Her brother is a murderer. Her whole family steal, and worse. Why, she drugs you at the drop of a hat."

John opened his mouth to speak. Sherlock did not give him the chance. "Granted, she does seem to drug you for your own good. Accompanying me to The Regent's Park would have placed your life in great peril. And yes, Mary only drugged you to keep you safe, and yes, she did come and save my life on your behalf, even dragging that murderous brother of hers along as backup. And she wouldn't let Robbie kill me the other night, when he was set on it. She claimed it would have made you sad, and she couldn't have that."

John snorted. "Perhaps it wouldn't have made me as sad as all that."

"Don't be silly, John. Of course it would have. Why, I think you would be more upset by my demise than Mary's, if she was to be killed in the street, out and about, engaged in her criminal activities."

"And you call yourself a great detective," John muttered into his brandy.

Sherlock's sharp ears heard him, nonetheless. "Of course I am. You're much better off here, with me, than with Mary." He thought about her for a moment. "But do you know, she is proving to be much more attractive to me, now that I have gotten to know her nature a bit better. She really is an enticing woman, isn't she? She is not the woman for you, but she is fascinating to me."

John stood up so fast, it was as if the chair he had sought to become a part of, had rejected him, and ejected him from its depths. "Attractive? Enticing? Fascinating? What do you mean attractive? Enticing? Fascinating?"

"You know the meaning of the words as well as I do, John. I am becoming captivated, riveted, fascinated, dare I say enticed, by Mary. Why, now that you have left Mary, I may get to know her better myself. A lot better." Sherlock felt Mary would make a most intriguing case-study. A female crime boss, what could be more captivating than that?

For some reason, John did not agree. He cried, "You can't have Mary. I haven't left her for good. How could I? I love her. Crime boss or not, I love her. She's mine!" He tossed his brandy aside, not even bothering to set down the glass. He did place his pipe in the ashtray, likely not wishing to toss it away, ignite the brandy, and burn down the room he had just put to rights, with a great deal of effort, it should be noted. "I'm going home to Mary, and Gladstone!" John spun on his heel and headed for the door, not even bothering to don his coat.

"You might not have the foul Gladstone any longer, with that crime boss of a wife. She's probably slit his throat and dumped him in the Thames with the fishes. Poor fishes." Sherlock knew it wasn't the wisest, or kindest thing to say at the moment, yet he was sorely disappointed that John was leaving him, again. Choosing a crime boss over him, Sherlock Holmes, almost an officer of the law. Well, no, never that, he was far too intelligent to be a policeman, but an upholder of justice!

"Shut your mouth, Sherlock, before I shut it for you." John flung open the door, then must have recalled it was cold outside. He turned around and lifted his coat off the coat-tree.

"As if you could," Sherlock said, merely speaking the truth.

John tossed his coat to the floor and charged across the room. Sherlock raised his fists and started waving them around, like the boxer he was. John Marmalade yowled in fright and scurried into the kitchen.

Before John's face could meet his fists, or vice versa, as if they both didn't have enough bruises already, Mrs. Hudson screamed, and it was not an everyday scream. Women are inclined to scream when they encounter a mouse or a spider, or spot a bit of dirt on their skirt or slipper, or some such, but this was not that kind of scream. It was more of a, *There's a murderer about to hack me to pieces with an axe!* kind of scream. John stopped charging. Sherlock stopped waving his fists about. John Marmalade did remain cowering in the kitchen.

The two men ran out the door and down the stairs. Mrs. Hudson was in the foyer, still screaming, although the level of loudness had dropped a notch or two, as had the pitch. A small white envelope was clutched in her hand. "Oh Sherlock," she wailed as soon as he reached the bottom of the stairs. She flung herself into his arms, sobbing against his chest.

He patted her on the back and said, "There, there." He glanced at John for help. John was far better at dealing with distraught females.

John said, "What has upset you so, Mrs. Hudson? Pray, tell us."

She thrust the envelope at him, loath to leave Sherlock's arms it seemed. John looked in the envelope and paled. "Oh dear me," was all he said. He traded the envelope for Mrs. Hudson, freeing Sherlock's hands, so he could have a look in the envelope, too.

He did, and felt he might lose his excellent dinner. Cat Watson's tail was inside, or about a third of it. He knew the tail well, with its little wispy white tip. There was no denying who it had come from. "This villain is truly a monster," he stated as fact.

"Uh, Sherlock, did you put out your pipe?" John asked.

"Why are you mentioning my pipe now?" Sherlock cried, uncharacteristically distraught himself.

John pointed up the stairs. Smoke was billowing out through the open doorway of Sherlock's rooms. John Marmalade was trotting down the stairs as best he could, with a bit of rolling. He really was too small to manage them. Mrs. Hudson rescued John Marmalade and hugged him for comfort.

Sherlock thrust the envelope into his pocket and dashed up the stairs with John on his heels. Sherlock's pipe had lit the brandy. The carpet was going up in flames. "Damnation," Sherlock growled and fetched water. John beat at the flames with his own coat, as it was handy. The fire was quickly extinguished. Windows were raised and the smoke was greatly lessened by waving towels about. The room got very cold. The windows were lowered.

Feeling spent and beaten, Sherlock dropped into his chair. Luckily it hadn't gone up in flames. John's chair was barely singed, and perfectly serviceable. Alas, the same could not be said for his coat.

John poured two glasses of brandy, before settling into his blackened chair. He did not hand one to Sherlock immediately. Instead he said, "Before we address other, pressing matters, I need to know, are you in love with my wife?"

Sherlock blinked at him in bafflement. "In love with Mary? Of course not. Where would you get such a cockeyed idea?"

"From you."

"Me?"

John rolled his eyes. "You said you found her most attractive and fascinating, and you wished to get to know her much better."

"As a case study, John. A female crime boss deserves an in-depth study," he stressed.

"Oh. Well, I suppose that's all right then. Here, you may have your brandy now." He extended the glass. Sherlock accepted the drink with a nod of thanks. He did feel the need for it, after seeing what was in the envelope. "Now that that's settled, what does the note say?" John asked.

Sherlock hadn't wanted to read it, for fear of what it might reveal. Silly really. He had to read it, and not reading it wouldn't change a thing. Not reading it could only make matters worse for Cat Watson.

Mrs. Hudson appeared in the doorway, still holding John Marmalade as if he was her ragdoll. The kitten sneezed several times, from the residual smoke. "What does it say, Sherlock dearest?" she asked.

John patted the client's chair and poured her a brandy. She was happy to sit, with John Marmalade on her lap. And happy to have the brandy, lush that she was.

Sherlock pulled the envelope from his pocket. He removed the single sheet. The message was longer than the previous two. Closing off his emotional reaction to the severed tail, he read aloud, "For the man upstairs. I have enclosed a nice present for you. I'll keep the rest of it safe, for now. You owe me a beryl and pearl necklace, and I will take a square-cut emerald ring, instead of a ring of rope around my neck. I don't want to drop down dead. Ha ha. I look forward to our rendezvous at Kensal Green Cemetery tonight, by the garden. Our host will happily open his home, and maybe even his graves, to us. It is the ideal place to meet, and to rest in peace. Do not be rude and snub my invitation, or you will find a paw in the next parcel. Can you stitch your cat back together and make a furry little Frankenstein?" As before, it was signed, *Your boss for now.*

Sherlock folded the paper thoughtfully, saying, "Our monster reads about monsters."

John said, "Kensal Green Cemetery is more than 70 acres in size, and most of it is made up of gardens of one sort or another. How can you hope to find each other? There isn't even a specified time."

"Elementary, my dear Watson. Elementary." He handed over the page.

John read it silently, then shrugged. "It is as you said, or read. Kensal Green is still more than 70 acres."

"Look at the note more closely, John. *By the garden*," he quoted.

John read, sighed, frowned, and shrugged.

"What do you note about the word *garden*?" Sherlock felt like he was leading a horse to water, hoping it would drink, and not simply stand there, blinking stupidly at its own reflection and wondering why there was a horse in the water.

"Well, it's a bit odd that the first letter has been capitalized mid-sentence, when it is not a surname or proper noun," John mused. Mrs. Hudson leaned in to take a look for herself.

Sherlock nodded. "What else do you see?"

John wrinkled his brow. "Uh, the capital *G* is not very curly at the bottom. It looks a bit like a *C*, but *Carden* isn't a word."

Sherlock pointed a finger at John. "True, but it is a name, a surname, which would require it to be capitalized. A name on a gravestone marker."

John cottoned on to where he was headed. "But surely there are a number of Cardens in the cemetery. It is not an uncommon name."

"But only one would be the host of Kensal Green Cemetery." Sherlock smiled triumphantly.

John snapped his fingers. "Yes, of course. George Carden, the barrister who founded the cemetery, after visiting La Cimetiére du Pere-Lachaise in Paris. He wanted an English version of the cemetery. And hoped to stem cholera, of course, when it was believed people caught it from the miasma in the air that wafted off the dead." He chuckled. "People can believe the oddest medical theories. Why, a few quack physicians have even started to question the practice of bloodletting, after 3,000 years of doing it." John could go off on tangents, and now was not the time.

Sherlock said, "Carden died in 1874. He is buried in his own cemetery. It is by his headstone that I am to meet our monstrous villain for this evening's adventure."

"Do you know where is headstone is located?" John asked.

Sherlock sipped his brandy and nodded. "It was mentioned in the newspaper at the time of his death. Oh, and I have read several studies on the outcomes of bloodletting. I am beginning to question its validity myself, and I am no quack."

"You are also no doctor," John shot back.

"Granted, but if I was, I would be an excellent one."

"Not if you didn't bleed your patients, you wouldn't be," John said stubbornly.

Before they got into a debate about bloodletting, one that might see them brawling on the burnt carpet and doing their own bloodletting, Mrs. Hudson said, "I shall fetch the necklace and ring. But Sherlock, how does the blackmailer know all of my jewels so intimately? I never wear the emerald ring, as I think my husband stole it from a royal. Prince George, I believe. I'm not certain, mind, but I have my suspicions. Mr. Turner wasn't the most honest man. That's how he became so wealthy."

"I, myself, have been wondering who might know such intimate details of your jewels. Think, Mrs. Hudson, do you have any idea?"

She mulled it over, while John refilled her glass. "Well, only Mr. Blakely knew such details. One time, I put on all my jewels, and nothing else. Not a stitch. Imagine that, Sherlock." She winked. "He took them off me one-by-one, while I told the story of each. He is the only one who knows ... knew the truth of them all, but he's dead, after falling down my cellar stairs onto that axe."

John raised an eyebrow at Sherlock, who had omitted several key details of Mrs. Hudson's tale, when he had related it to John. "Yes, but you said he saw other women. Perhaps he did not guard his tongue and spoke about you, and about your jewels, to one of them. Did he tell you anything about the other women?"

"Of course not, why, I would have been very jealous to learn he was sharing his affections with other ladies. Well, I was so very angry when I finally found out, wasn't I?" She stroked John Marmalade and said, "He did make mention of a girl, just a passing remark. He said she had a schoolgirl's infatuation for him. He never called her by name, though."

Sherlock lit his pipe, to think. He did not pick up his violin however, as he did not want John to flee or sulk. John and Mrs. Hudson sat silent, aware that his ruminations required an uninterrupted silence. The peace was disrupted when there was a loud scrabbling on the stairs.

"What could that be?" John said, even though it was a sound he should have recognized with greater ease than anyone else in the room. The kitten sprang to its little paws on Mrs. Hudson's lap and arched and hissed. Its fur could not rise. It was dressed, as always, in the wee sweater-vest.

Gladstone barrelled into the room. John leapt to his feet and cried, "Mary!" Except she wasn't there. She must have opened the door and shoved Gladstone inside. John took off running, leaving Gladstone behind. The beast was too exhausted from the ascent up the stairs to follow John, and collapsed by the fire, panting heavily. He let out a fart, as if to christen the rooms with his scent again.

Mrs. Hudson fled, saving John Marmalade and herself. Sherlock was left alone with the foul beast, and he was not at all pleased. Especially when the dog farted for a second time, with greater gusto than the first. If only the hound had been closer to the hearth, he might have gone up in a gaseous ball of flames.

29 - A Sad Homecoming

from The Observations of Cat Watson

I ducked and dodged through the cedar shrubbery, hugging the base of a house that seemed every inch as enormous as Wither Manor. The grounds were more unkempt though, which worked to my advantage. The woman could not traverse the tangled greenery as easily as a small cat. Or two small cats. My feline companion was racing after me, not because I had possession of the mouse, but because of the axe-wielding, tail-chopping madwoman on our heels. I soon abandoned the mouse, needing as much air as possible.

When we reached the front corner of the house, there was a great deal of open lawn between us and the tall hedgerow that marked the border of the garden. In addition, there was a high, wrought-iron fence. There was no-one about at all, save our pursuer. The place had a deserted, as well as a neglected air. The tall hedgerow hid the manor house from the road and any prying eyes.

I had no doubt we would be safe if we could reach the hedgerow and that lovely fence. We could dart right through the bars. The woman, being human-sized, could not. Alas, the fence was simply too far away. We could not risk the open lawn. I had seen the woman run when Sherlock had been chasing her, and she was no slug.

I rounded the corner and stuck close to the front façade of the manor, hoping the other cat would trust my judgement and stay with me. She did. Our pursuer was falling further behind, as we darted through cedar branches. A wide stone stairway led up to the main door, and a spacious stone porch. That grand stairway blocked our path, jutting out from the house the length of two carriages, at least.

I dared to hope there might be a gap beneath the solid, side wall of the stairs, where it met the ground. Earth tended to erode away in the rain, and crack and heave in the winter frosts. Stone much less so, making the two somewhat incompatible and inclined to part company, at least a little bit.

If there was no gap at all, my companion and I would find ourselves trapped in a walled-in, dead-end corner. Emphasis on the *dead*. I scanned what I could see of the base of the staircase as I ran. A cat's eyesight is not as keen as our hearing or sense of smell. Yes, we can see in the dark, but we cannot see as keenly in the daylight as many people do.

Behind us, the axe chopped down on a branch. It cracked off. I leapt forward when I spotted a patch of darkness, where the stonework of the stairs met the damp earth. A crack in the stone, or an erosion gap perhaps? Either would do to save the lives of two innocent cats. I bounded toward it and closer to, saw that it was an entrance of sorts, to the land beneath the stairs. I raced into it, my fur scraping both side. It was a tight fit. The other cat darted in after me.

I was heartily relieved to discover it was a passageway, not merely a shallow hole, which would have surely doomed us. We kept going deeper beneath the stairs, and emerged in a large cavernous space. The stairs were not solid, there was no need for that, as they were sturdily built of fieldstone, timber and cement. We were safe in the cave, but maybe not for long. Every cat knows that an enclosed space, with only one way in and out, is a trap as much as it is a haven.

A bit of light was streaming in through our little tunnel, so I could see quite well. I spotted a second and a third source of light immediately, faint though they were. One clearly led back to the out of doors, on the opposite side of the staircase. The other appeared to puncture the foundation of the manor itself. Curious, I aimed for it and peeked inside the house, through that crack. It was so small, my body could never have fit, but I knew a lot of mice would have been happy to hop inside, and had done so. I could smell them.

I could see into a small portion of the cellar. One gaslamp was burning low, illuminating a thin older man in a heavy wooden chair. His coat was stained with filth and he was not moving. I meowed at him. His drooping head rose in my direction, but slowly, as if it took a tremendous effort. He squinted and mumbled, "Help me. My daughter has gone mad."

His arms were strapped to the wooden arms of the chair, with what appeared to be ribbons. Lots of ribbons. Some of them were even tied into pretty bows. I supposed ribbons and bows could be as effective as rope, as long as they were sturdy and plentiful.

I meowed reassuringly to let him know I understood. I would bring help, if I could escape and get home to Sherlock. I knew I could find the way home. I was no carrier pigeon, although I had eaten one once, yet I had an excellent sense of direction, and smell of course.

I went to investigate the other exit. It was similar to the passage we had entered through, and large enough to allow us to escape out the opposite side of the stairs, if it was safe to do so. I entered the passage first, the other cat sticking close. When we reached the end, I crouched unmoving, listening. There was no sound or movement in the shrubbery outside. Where was the madwoman with her axe? I needed to know exactly where she was, before I exposed myself to daylight and danger.

My ears perked up when I heard sound from inside the house, through the crack in the foundation. A song. The mad daughter had gone inside, perhaps to check on her prisoner—her own father. She was singing to him. "Ring-a-ring-a-rosies, a pocket full of posies, a tissue, a tissue, we all fall down. The king has sent his daughter, to fetch a pail of water, a tissue, a tissue, we all fall down. Do you want some water, Daddy? Or I could make you a cup of tea."

I had heard enough. We were safe to leave. It was almost anticlimactic when we scrambled outside and dashed across the lawn. We bounded through the wrought-iron fencing and I turned toward home. The other cat stayed with me, as if we were part of the same clowder. That is what a grouping of cats is called, though it sounds more like soup. With John Marmalade as a part of it, we would be a very small clowder indeed. Yet, given how quickly I was collecting cats to bring home to Sherlock, we might become a much larger clowder in no time.

Dusk was falling when we finally reached the familiar door on Baker Street. I had been concerned about how we would get inside, since I couldn't open doors or knock with any force. Short of meowing loudly, or finding a partially opened window, I was without ideas. Unless I could force open the window to Mrs. Hudson's boudoir, as the intruder had done, but as luck would have it, such action was not necessary. The front door opened as if an eager butler had been awaiting my triumphant return. Dr. Watson raced out. He spotted me and his eyes widened, "You're safe!" was all he said. He held the door for us. We darted inside, the other cat on my tail, or what remained of my poor tail.

The doctor's mind was clearly fixed on other matters, and he must have had an urgent errand. Before the door had even swung closed, he was dashing down the street, as if he was the one being chased by an axe-wielding madwoman.

As happy as I had ever been, to be home and alive, I was probably prancing about like a show pony, not padding gracefully like a sophisticated feline. I showed the other cat the gap I had discovered to enter the home I shared with Sherlock. She followed me in, and that is when my heart sank. I had not even been gone a day, and Sherlock had replaced me with a dog, and not just any dog.

Gladstone was curled up by the fire, farting. Sherlock was in his chair, smoking his pipe. So, Dr. Watson had moved back in, with Gladstone. I did not have to be smacked across my furry face by a wagging tail to know there could be no place for me now. I mewled sadly. My new friend gave me a little lick of comfort.

I crept out of my once wonderful home. Gladstone didn't even sense us or smell us. Then again, how could he smell anything save the foul air that surrounded him. He was useless. I wondered where John Marmalade was, and hoped Gladstone hadn't eaten him. The kitten was very tiny, after all. I needed to check on him. The obvious place to look was in Mrs. Hudson's rooms, and I knew how to slink inside there.

The other cat purred as soon as we were inside Mrs. Hudson's home. It did smell lovely, of fish and cream. She was just setting down dishes for John Marmalade. He scented me immediately and meowed happily in greeting, bounding over to give me a lick, wearing his little sweater-vest. I admit, I was getting used to seeing him in it.

He alerted Mrs. Hudson to our presence. "Cat Watson!" She clapped her hands in delight. "How did you get in? Never you mind, here you are safe and sound, except for your poor wittle tailkins." She picked me up and squeezed me in a hug. "And who have you brought along. Do you have a wee fluffy-wuffy new friend? You look like twins." She set me down and crouched, to stroke the other cat, who allowed it. She even purred. "Are you both hungry?" Mrs. Hudson asked. I meowed enthusiastically. Despite my heartache, I was feeling half-starved.

The wonderful woman fed all three of us, and fed us well. I did hear Dr. Watson return, his footsteps dragging up the stairs. Clearly, he had not been successful in his errand. I was happy Sherlock had companions, and wouldn't be sad and lonely, yet I could not help but resent Dr. Watson—and Gladstone. I resented the drooling hound most of all. I hated him more than I had ever hated any other dog.

"Does Sherlock know you're back?" Mrs. Hudson thought to ask, when I was washing my face, my belly full and warm. My belly was the only part of me that was not sad.

I hissed, just a bit. The hiss was for Gladstone, not my Sherlock. No, he wasn't my Sherlock any longer, he was merely Sherlock Holmes, Consulting Detective, partnered again with Dr. John Watson. I decided then and there that I would not stay at Mrs. Hudson's. It would make me too sad, to see Sherlock everyday, and not be part of his life, or his detecting companion. John Marmalade and the other cat would have a good home with her. She did not seem inclined to kill cats, only men, and that was merely supposition. I would again make my home on the street. It was where I belonged, especially now that I was missing part of my tail.

Most street cats were missing something: an eye, an ear, a paw, clumps of fur. Yes, I would fit right in with my stumpy tail. Maybe I would rename myself Stumpy. It was a more suitable name than Cat Watson, for a homeless stray. I knew I was indulging in a bout of self-pity, but I felt I had earned the right.

I was saying farewell to John Marmalade and the other, as yet unnamed, black cat, rubbing against them and giving them each a lick, when Sherlock and Dr. Watson tromped down the stairs with all the finesse of two drunken gorillas. I had seen gorillas at the zoo once, when I had ventured far from home. Sherlock was saying, "But where is he, John? Are you sure you didn't imagine seeing him? You were in quite a state."

"Maybe I did imagine him. There was another black cat with him. Do you think it was a ghost cat?"

"Don't be ridiculous, John. There is no such thing as ghosts."

"But what about ghost cats?" Dr. Watson said.

"No, John." Sherlock's sigh could be heard through the door. They sounded like an old married couple, bickering nonsensically. My heart clenched when Sherlock paused by the front door and said, "Alas, I don't have time to search for him. We have to meet our blackmailer in the cemetery, and that is a good hour's walk at a brisk pace, unless we hail a carriage. Or do you feel like a walk?"

John didn't even have to think about it. "A carriage, Sherlock."

"Wise choice. We must conserve our store of energy for whatever this night's adventure holds. You have your pistol?"

"Of course I don't have my pistol. I didn't know I was moving back in when I got here, now did I? I didn't know my wife was a working woman, and a crime boss then," John whined.

"True. Here, take my pistol. I have my baritsu stick, and my wits. That will be more than enough."

"I'll bring a lantern along, in case we need light," John said. There was a small clink as one of the lanterns by the door was picked up.

"Wait, we should use the back door, in case the house is being watched," Sherlock said. The two men did not seem very organized. More footsteps and Sherlock opened the back door at the far end of the hallway. It closed immediately behind them.

I yowled loudly for Mrs. Hudson to open the door—both doors—for me. After overhearing Sherlock's words, my plans had changed. I had also recalled the man tied up in the cellar. He had to be rescued from his mad daughter, and I was the only one who knew of his plight, and location.

I couldn't disappear into the back alleyways yet. I had one last mission to fulfil, at Sherlock's side. He needed me, for I knew a great deal more about our adversary than he did. And a dark cemetery was the type of terrain where I, a stealthy cat, was at my best, while bumbling humans, even clever ones like Sherlock, were at their worst.

30 – The Adventure in Kensal Green Cemetery: A Regrettable Beginning

Sherlock flagged a carriage as soon as they reached a main street, several blocks away from 221B. He scanned for Cat Watson along the lanes, but didn't spot him anywhere. And the cat would not be seen unless he wished to be seen. Had John imagined the cat? Both cats? It didn't seem likely. John was not normally mad. Of the two of them, Sherlock was far more likely to be the mad one.

They climbed into the carriage and Sherlock said to the driver, "Kensal Green Cemetery, and hurry it up."

"Are you dying to get there?" the wizened old driver retorted, with a cackle.

"There's an extra quid in it for you, if you get us there briskly. Alive, and no more puns," Sherlock stressed.

"Sure thing, guv." The carriage rolled off at a brisk clip. Sherlock thought he heard a little thump at the rear of the carriage. Had someone thrown something at them?

No additional thumps followed, so he dismissed it from his mind. He glanced at his pocket watch when they passed under a gaslamp. Nine o'clock. They had plenty of time. He leaned back on his seat, glad his bottom was somewhat healed and causing him little pain. His arm was quite fit, too. "Did you catch up with Mary?" he asked.

"No. She's quicker than I realized. I will go to Mary tomorrow, hat in hand, and beg her forgiveness."

Sherlock frowned. "You are content to return to her? And be the husband of a crime boss?"

"We are none of us perfect, Sherlock."

"True, but we are not all heading criminal organizations, living off ill-gotten goods, and inflicting misfortune and bodily harm on others," Sherlock said.

188

John adjusted his lapels. "I am not at ease with it, but I do love Mary. We are happy together. I am hopeful I can convince her to stop working and stay at home like a proper wife—and give up her life of crime, of course. Do you think she will, Sherlock?"

He shrugged, and not sure John could see it in the dim recesses of the carriage, said, "How would I know? According to you, I lack judgement where women are concerned."

"True. Disregard the question. How shall we proceed when we reach the graveyard?" John asked.

Sherlock steepled his fingers and rested his chin upon the tips. "I have given it considerable thought. In light of how the blackmailer managed to best me through trickery at our last encounter, I am not inclined to play by the rules this time, not that one ever should, when confronting a monster who would chop off a cat's wee tail." His voice broke. He had to get a grip on himself. He cleared his throat. "I must present myself at the cemetery to keep Mrs. Hudson safe, and for Cat Watson's sake ... do you truly believe he was outside 221B?"

"I do, although, black cats do tend to look alike. I have never seen him in the company of another black cat before, and he is supposed to be a prisoner. If he came home, why did he not reunite with you? I am ashamed to say, I did not make note of his tail, or lack of tail. I am not always the most observant of men."

"Truly, John?" Sherlock said, with a liberal dose of sarcasm. It was the lowest form of humour, yet he could not resist. "In that case, I do not believe you saw Cat Watson. I think you saw another black cat. Two black cats."

"They crossed my path, you know. I do hope that is not an ill omen, a portent that our evening will be filled with bad luck," John mused.

Sherlock rolled his eyes heavenward in the dark carriage. "There is no such thing as a black cat causing bad luck, John. Belief in superstition is for the weak minded. As I was saying, with Cat Watson foremost in your mind, you assumed it to be him, which it wasn't. The mind will see what it expects to see. If you are told to watch for a pink pony, you will not notice a dozen blue ones prancing by, but you will spot the pink one. You, more than most men, would overlook a rainbow parade of unicorns, whilst trying to spot a pink pony."

"It is hard to argue with that. I did fail to notice my wife was a working woman and a crime boss, not to mention a dog and moustache hater."

Sherlock inclined his head. "Despite my expert tutelage, you remain unobservant by your very nature."

"Be that as it may, we will be at the cemetery soon enough. Pray tell me how we are to proceed." The sound of his hand brushing over the fabric of his coat reached Sherlock's ears. John was nervous, and reassuring himself the pistol was still there in his pocket.

"Facing an adversary is not like detecting, John. The skills required are quite different. One must react quickly, and cleverly, as unexpected circumstances unfold. As long as we are quicker and cleverer than our blackmailer, we will be triumphant. There are two of us, and I am quite convinced our foe is working alone." He frowned. "On the other hand, it is his or her chosen location, not ours. They have had time to set the stage. That will likely balance the scales. Hopefully it will not tip them to our foe's advantage." A wave of unease washed over him. Why a cemetery? Like The Regent's Park, it was an isolated location, with only headstones to hide behind. At least there would be no fireworks.

The carriage slowed at the main gate into the cemetery, and stopped under a gaslamp. They disembarked. "Gotch'ya here in plenty of time, as ordered." Their driver gave a jaunty salute.

Sherlock paid him, including a hefty tip. The old fellow smiled in appreciation. "The graveyard is a strange place to visit in the dark of night. Make sure you come out alive, guv."

"Let us hope so," Sherlock said.

They faced the vast, dark landscape beyond the entranceway. Sherlock jumped when a small furry body rubbed against his lower leg with a morose meow. They were still beneath the gaslamp and he was able to clearly see the small black cat with the reduced tail.

"Cat Watson!" He scooped the cat up and hugged him. It was a spontaneous reaction, so happy was he to see the cat safe. "If I did not believe in such ridiculous things as miracles, I would credit this to be one. How do you come to be here?"

Cat Watson relaxed and purred happily in his arms, then stiffened and squirmed to be released.

"You've never hugged me," John muttered.

"Well, you are not a cat, are you? And you've never had your tail chopped off."

"I don't have a tail, as you can't have failed to notice, unless you are as unobservant as you claim I am," John snapped.

"Don't be ridiculous, John." Sherlock crouched down and stroked Cat Watson. "How is your poor tail? Does it hurt?" Cat Watson meowed dismissively. "Did the blackmailer bring you here? Or did you escape and find your own way? Amazing cat that you are."

Cat Watson meowed and raised his head to gaze fixedly at the departing carriage. Sherlock recalled the little thump. Cat Watson had ridden on the back of their conveyance, so he had been at Baker Street. Why had he not come home then?

"You've never called me amazing," John muttered.

Sherlock sighed and rose. "Because you are not amazing, John. You are a loyal friend, a stalwart fellow, a capable enough doctor, a dab hand at lighting a gaslamp, and quite efficient at running errands, but you are not amazing."

"Damned by faint praise, indeed." John was clearly in a huffy mood.

"John, this is not the time for histrionics. We have a nefarious and monstrous blackmailer to both elude and capture. Silence and stealth are critical."

"Histrionics! Histrionics?" John cried, with no attempt to lower his tone. "Oh, I will show you histrionics, Sherlock!"

"Stop being jealous of Cat Watson," Sherlock snapped. "Just because he is cleverer than you, is no reason to behave like a hysterical woman. Why, Mary is far more cool-headed than you. She is far more cool-headed than most men, truth be told. And a crime boss! She is a most amazing woman." Sherlock had gone off on a bit of a tangent himself.

John sputtered indignantly in outrage before he said, "So Mary is amazing and your cat it amazing, and I am merely stalwart. Why have you put up with me for all these years, Sherlock? Because I am a dab hand at gaslamp lighting, and you tend to make them explode?" he ranted. "Or is it for all the free medical service? The housecleaning? The tea-making? The errand running? And performing all the menial tasks that your big giant brain finds so bloody tedious?" He finally stopped to take a breath.

It gave Sherlock an opportunity to calm his friend. "Well, you are good at all those things, John, as I have just said. What would I do without you to run errands, and clean up, and do the tedious work that is necessary in many of our investigations? Yet as a doctor, you should know a larger brain would be no more intelligent than a smaller brain.

191

I'm sure my brain is no larger than most men's, or not too much larger. - " Before Sherlock could add the most important bit, that he had been working up to, that the thing he valued most about John was his friendship, and that John was his only true friend, Cat Watson notwithstanding, John cut in, ranting again.

"So you have merely been using me as an errand boy and handy physician and … and gaslamp lighter? Until someone cleverer happened along, like a cat, and Mary. I'd like to see the cat light a gaslamp! No worries, Mary could do it. Perhaps she should be your new Watson. We even share the same surname, so she is already a Watson." John's jaw jutted pugnaciously.

"Mary would make an excellent detecting companion," Sherlock acknowledged. Before he could add that he much preferred to spend time with his friend John, his friend John punched him in the nose. He didn't see it coming, because he wasn't expecting it.

Cat Watson hissed and leapt onto John's leg, digging claws in. John yowled in pain and shook his leg, trying to dislodge the cat.

"Don't hurt Cat Watson," Sherlock cried. "He's already lost his poor tail."

"Again, you put the cat before me. Fine then, clearly I am not wanted here, not when you have a much cleverer companion to aid you." John shoved the unlit lantern at Sherlock. "You might need this. The cat can light it for you." John spun on his heel and marched off, Cat Watson still affixed to his leg. The cat finally disengaged, and hopped down. He padded back to Sherlock, mewling sadly, as John disappeared into the darkness. Their evening's adventure hadn't truly begun, and it had already come apart at the seams.

"He is in a mood, isn't he?" Sherlock said to Cat Watson, who seemed to cast him a frustrated glance. He meowed and started walking in the direction John had taken. It was obvious he wanted Sherlock to go after his friend.

It was what Sherlock wanted to do, too. He took one step, following the cat and John. He did not have the opportunity to take a second. Something rammed into the back of his knees with bruising force. He tumbled backwards, and was caught in a metal bucket of sorts. A wheelbarrow, he realized, as his abused bum suffered the brunt of the impact. Before he could cry out, something very hard bashed him on the crown of his head.

Although he was unaware of it at the time, because he was quite unaware of anything and everything, he ripped yet another stitch out of his bottom.

Sherlock was spirited away, into the cemetery in a wheelbarrow. He was rolled and bumped along a rough footpath, all the way to Carden's headstone, and then the wheelbarrow bypassed it.

The conveyance finally jolted to a stop, and the great detective was dumped unceremoniously into a freshly dug grave.

31 - A Diabolical Plot Untwists

🐈 from The Observations of Cat Watson

I was so fixated on the drama between Sherlock and Dr. Watson, and may I add that it was not the time or place for them to be squabbling so loudly, I failed to attend to other sounds. It was only when I heard a fast rolling wheel that I did take notice. By then it was too late. The madwoman had joined us.

She rammed Sherlock in the back of his knees with a wheelbarrow, caught him in it, and thumped him on the head with a rock. He went limp, head lolling back and long arms dangling down. His knuckles scraped the ground as she wheeled him along the footpath into the cemetery. She even had a handy lantern to light her way. Blood dripped down from Sherlock's head, splatting to the ground and leaving a trail even a human could spot.

My instinct was to follow immediately, and help Sherlock. Alas, although I was clever enough, I doubted I was big enough to do the job. We needed Dr. Watson. I had to alert him to the danger Sherlock was in, before he got too far away. I had to convince him to return to help Sherlock, if I could communicate the urgent message. And if he was willing to do so, after their latest tiff.

As fast as my four legs could run, I went after Dr. Watson. I had no troubling tracking him, but he had travelled surprisingly far. He was marching along at a furious pace, his path lit by the gaslamps along the route. His anger was dictating his pace, and I was quite breathless when I caught up. If I had been a dog, heaven forbid, I would have been panting and drooling, tongue out and flapping about. Luckily I was a cat, and all I did was breathe a bit harder in a dignified manner.

I yowled for his attention, telling him to stop. Dr. Watson's pace didn't slacken in the slightest. I raced in front of him and stopped dead. He almost tripped over me, staggered, and kept going. With a hiss of vexation, I dashed in front of him yet again and yowled as loudly as I had ever yowled. I like to think I sounded like one of those roaring lions I had seen, that time I snuck in to visit the zoo. It was a delusion of grandeur. I was much too small to roar like a lion. He skirted around me and kept going. Dr. Watson was proving to be as stubborn as Sherlock.

Since he would not heed me, I took a running leap and landed on the back of his thigh. I confess, I even bit him, on his bottom, rather hard. I didn't want to, I rather liked Dr. Watson, and when I did have occasion to bite someone, the bottom is the last place I would choose, but needs must. He did not like that and flailed about. He tried to swat me off and gave me a solid bonk to the head. As if the blow knocked some sense into me, I had an inspired idea.

I released his leg and dropped to the ground. I lay there, unmoving, as if I was unconscious. I thought my ploy had failed when he resumed marching away, rubbing his bottom, then his footsteps slowed. He turned around and took tentative steps back. I made sure to lie as limp as if I was dead.

"For pity's sake," he groaned. "Cat Watson, are you okay? I did not hit you that hard, did I?"

Did I look okay? I thought, continuing to play dead—or play knocked-out cold.

He crouched, picked me up and put his ear on my chest. "Still alive," he murmured. He rose with me in-hand, and stood indecisive. "Oh, I expect I shall have to return you to Sherlock, since I can't leave you lying unconscious on the street. He is not going to be happy about this." He started back toward the cemetery.

I kept up my act, so he would keep going. And I didn't mind being carried. I had done a lot of walking and running that day. My tired legs appreciated the respite. When Dr. Watson reached the cemetery gate, he paused and looked around. "Where is Sherlock? Why is the lantern on the ground?" It was where Sherlock had dropped it.

I sprang into action, aware he would need my help from this point onward. He gasped. "Were you playing dead? I don't think you are a cat at all. You are a man in a cat's skin."

No, I was cleverer than a human, or most humans. I padded over to where Sherlock had been whacked on the head. There was a small pool of blood. I crouched beside it and meowed for Dr. Watson to come and have a look. He did. Unobservant or not, he couldn't fail to see it for himself, once I had helpfully drawn his attention to it.

Dr. Watson leaned down and touched it. "Still damp. Is it Sherlock's blood?" I meowed sadly, confirming it. "Is he still alive?" I chirruped an emphatic yes, at least, I certainly hoped so. "The blackmailer got him?" I meowed again, in agreement, and started padding into the cemetery, following the trail of blood droplets. We did not have time to waste.

I glanced back at Dr. Watson, indicating he should follow me. He already knew. He had the pistol Sherlock had loaned him gripped in a tight fist. In his other hand, he carried the lantern he had picked up, still unlit.

As quiet as a cat, I led the way. As loud as a human doing his utmost to be quiet, and failing badly, Dr. Watson bumbled after. There was enough light for me to see perfectly. Alas, the same could not be said for Dr. Watson. I kept emitting quiet meows to guide him to follow me. He stumbled along, tripping every so often, which did not help his pitiful attempt at stealth. At least he wasn't dim enough to light the lantern and spotlight our approach. Then again, the amount of noise he was making was already doing that.

I was the first to spot the lantern up ahead, handheld and swinging about. I heard the madwoman singing one of her songs. It was a lullaby mothers sang to their smelly babies, while pushing them in perambulators in the park, trying to quiet their incessant wailing. I froze. Dr. Watson stopped beside me, in the faint edge of light cast by the madwoman's lantern. He was able to see me as a shadow now.

The madwoman had changed most of the words to suit her purpose, as she was wont to do, yet the tune was undeniable. She sang, "Hush-a-bye Sherlock, in the fresh grave. When the blows fall, you must be brave. When your head breaks, the blood will fall. And down will go Sherlock, so will you all." Her little girl giggle was followed by maniacal cackling laughter.

Sherlock believed our blackmailer worked alone, yet I wasn't so sure. It was as if two separate humans were residing in one body. I couldn't see the detective, only a mound of dirt. And was that a freshly dug grave? I got a sick feeling in my tummy, like the time I had nibbled on a poisoned rat, before I realized it would not be good for me, and vomited it up.

Dr. Watson cast me a puzzled glance, eyebrows raised. "A young woman is our blackmailer," he whispered too loudly, stating the obvious as was his habit.

I slunk closer to our quarry, and he stayed with me. It was fortuitous the woman was singing another stanza, or she would have surely heard his blundering approach. She was not deaf, only mad.

"Hush-a-bye Sherlock, where you did drop. I have my axe, to choppity-chop. When your neck breaks, your head will fall. Down will go Sherlock, so will you all."

Dr. Watson hissed under his breath, rather like an angry cat. It was a truly disturbing song. If mothers sang that lullaby to their babies, the foul-smelling things wouldn't be drifting off to sleep, no matter how tired and whiney they were. Then again, babies were as dumb as dogs, so they wouldn't have a clue what the words meant anyway.

Setting her lantern down, the madwoman tossed a shovelful of dirt into the grave and sang, "Hush-a-bye Sherlock, take your last breath. When the grave fills, t'will be your death. When your heart stops, to hell you will drop. Down will go Sherlock, down will go all."

We crept a bit closer and paused, still in the shadows. "He's in the grave," Dr. Watson whispered to me, as if I hadn't already figured it out. "Let us hope it is one he does not need. Time to confront our blackmailer."

I slunk away, to stay hidden. I didn't trust the tail-chopping madwoman as far as I could throw her, and as I am a small cat, that is no distance whatsoever.

Pistol at the ready, Dr. Watson leapt up and said, "Enough. Stop the shovelling now."

The madwoman clapped her hand over her mouth in exaggerated surprise. She had known he was there. Had she been putting on a performance for him? "Oh, who have we here? Dr. Watson, I presume. Come to rescue your friend, the man upstairs? Well, be my guest." She stepped back and hopped up and down, clapping her hands in delight.

Could any creature on earth be madder than a human who has come unhinged? I thought not. Yet, she was proving very wily in her own mad way. She had been setting the stage, but to what purpose. The fur on my back stood up in alarm.

Dr. Watson moved forward with small cautious steps, pistol never wavering from targeting the madwoman's chest. "Who are you?" he asked.

"Alice Grace. Isn't that a pretty name? Daddy likes pretty little girls who are very well-behaved." Her voice was as sweet as sugar pie. She stopped smiling and her voice changed to be high-pitched and grating. "I am not well-behaved anymore. I am disobedient. I would be sooo happy, except Daddy sent my lover away, into the arms of an old prune. My sweetheart has been gone so very long now, and I can't find him anywhere. Do you know where he is?" She stuck her thumb in her mouth and started suckling on it, as a toddler would do.

I knew where her love's corpse was, and it was no proper cemetery, but this was certainly not the time to mention it. Nor could I, being a cat.

Dr. Watson said, "No, I don't, but I can help you find him. And Sherlock could find him. Sherlock is a clever detective," Dr. Watson's tone was so patronizing tone, I cringed. I half-expected Sherlock to correct John and shout, *World's greatest detective*, from the grave. Alas, he did not.

Dr. Watson continued, "Release Sherlock from that hole and he will find your missing love."

The madwoman pulled her thumb out of her mouth with a wet pop of suction. Her little girl demeanor was shed like a cloak. "It may be too late for that, too late for him. Too late," she said in the screechy voice that would have better suited a puppet—an insane puppet. "Why don't you hop into the grave and check if he's still alive." She hoisted the shovel over her shoulder and stood back.

Dr. Watson cast her a wary glance, and edged up to the hole. He glanced down, keeping the pistol trained on her. The shock of what he saw in the grave turned his face white and made his hand tremble. "You've killed Sherlock," he gasped, and his voice trembled, too.

I knew the madwoman had a nefarious plan in place, I just wasn't sure what it was. And had she really killed Sherlock? I noticed her body tense. I knew she was about to act, in that moment when Dr. Watson was quite undone.

She swung the shovel toward him, intending to knock him out and knock him into the grave with his friend. I was faster, I leapt onto her leg, claws extended. It distracted her aim, her swing faltered. Dr. Watson managed to duck away and fire his pistol. I leapt aside, in case his aim was off.

The shot missed Alice Grace, but not by much. It didn't come close to me. She lowered her shovel to the ground and started pushing the mound of earth back into the open grave.

"Stop that," Dr. Watson shouted.

"No. He is in the grave where the dead belong. You'll be next. And then the old prune. I've let her be for now, saving her for the most deadly, long-lasting fun. And then it will be Daddy's turn. He was going to send me to the insane asylum for being disobedient. Only boys are allowed to be disobedient. Not girls." She stabbed at the earth with the point of the spade, venting her anger.

"Yes, society can be unfair to women—to girls," John said sympathetically, aiming to placate. From what I had observed of humans, it was truth.

"But not my love. He is lovely and doesn't care if I am disobedient. He prefers it. When I find my love, we shall picnic here atop your graves, and laugh. Oh how we will laugh and kiss and touch. And we will wed."

While she screeched, I edged closer to the grave to investigate Sherlock's condition for myself. I stayed low and in the shadows, not wishing to be spotted. Oddly, I could not pick up Sherlock's scent, except for around the wheelbarrow. Was the madwoman resorting to trickery, again?

I risked a quick peek into the hole. There was a body down there, beneath a layer of loose earth. Part of the face was still visible and it did look like Sherlock. Yet, I still could not pick up his scent, although there was a faint whiff of wax in the air.

Alice Grace did spot me then. She darted forward, shovel raised over head. "Bad cat! Bad, bad, naughty kitty. You need a spanking." She swung the shovel down, to crush me flat.

Before I could dart away, which would have been easy enough for a quick and agile cat, Dr. Watson fired his pistol again. This shot did hit Alice Grace. The spade dropped from her hands. She, in turn, fell into the open grave. She landed facedown atop Sherlock, and didn't move. He didn't move either, but I wasn't convinced it was Sherlock, or perhaps I should say, the authentic Sherlock Holmes.

Dr. Watson dropped to his knees at the edge of the grave. He peered down at the unmoving, partially dirt-covered face of his friend, his body pinned beneath the draped, limp form of the madwoman. He started sobbing inconsolably.

I felt further investigation was required. I leapt down into the grave, landing on Alice Grace. She did not react, although she was breathing. I walked across her slender back to Sherlock's still face. I sniffed it. As I suspected, it was made of wax.

Somehow, the mad Alice Grace had gotten her hands on Mrs. Hudson's dummy of Sherlock Holmes, as she had threatened to do. She had invaded Mrs. Hudson's private sanctum, likely hauled the dummy of Sherlock out the window and into a waiting carriage. At least I knew the landlady was unharmed, because Alice Grace had said she was saving Mrs. Hudson for later, as one would save a special treat, to anticipate it all the more. But where was Sherlock, if not in this grave? The dummy had been a distraction, and resulted in a costly delay in finding the real Sherlock.

I had a lot of questions, and I suspected Sherlock was still in grave danger. But first and foremost, I had to prove to Dr. Watson that it was not the real Sherlock Holmes dead and partially buried in the grave.

Since I couldn't use words, I needed proof. I bit off Sherlock's wax nose. Dr. Watson screamed, and then he fainted. I leapt out of the grave, wax nose in my mouth. I walked across Dr. Watson's chest and patted his cheek with my paw, until he opened his eyes. He looked at the nose between my teeth. His eyes rolled back in his head and he fainted, again.

Sherlock was right in his judgement that Dr. Watson was a stalwart, but not necessarily amazing, companion. I patted his cheek again, harder this time. Eventually, he opened his eyes. Before he could faint for a third time, I put the wax nose in his hand. He immediately screeched and flung it away.

Dr. Watson was not making this easy for me. I went and fetched the nose, but not like a dog would fetch a stick that had been thrown. And why would a dog want to chase a stick anyway? Sticks abounded, they were everywhere on the ground. One stick is as good as another, so why waste the energy to chase after one? Dogs, I will never be able to figure out their lack of intellect. Nor do I wish to, but I digress.

I carried the wax nose back to Dr. Watson, who had roused enough to sit. I put the wax nose on the ground, in the pool of brightest lantern light. He blinked at it, then blinked again. Finally, he gave it a proper squint. "No blood, that is odd," he said. I rolled my eyes. He reached out and gave the nose a poke. He grew bold enough to pick it up. "Why, it's wax." He lifted the lantern and lowered it into the grave, all the better to see what was at the bottom.

"Sherlock is made of wax? I know he didn't always act human, or seem human, but still, to be made of wax, that is most unexpected," he said.

Was he joking? Or had his mind been addled by the traumatic events? Or was madness contagious, and he had caught the madness from Alice Grace? If that was the case, I hoped I didn't catch the madness, too.

Dr. Watson laughed then, and I realized it was his poor attempt at humour, perhaps to lighten the somber mood that had fallen over him, when he believed his friend murdered.

Alice Grace sat up then, whimpering and clutching her bleeding shoulder. Dr. Watson raised his pistol. "Climb out." He did not offer to assist her.

She glared up at him. "I can't. I'm hurt."

"Where is Sherlock?" Dr. Watson demanded.

"Why, right here. I'm sitting on him." She ripped off a wax ear. "Did you hear that, world's greatest detective?" she shouted into the amputated ear. "I'm sitting on you, I bested you, I'm smarter than you," she sing-songed, and bit the ear.

"Where is the real Sherlock?" Dr. Watson bellowed, his normally calm nature having fled.

"Oh, him. That Sherlock is buried in a different grave," she said vindictively. "He'll be dead by now, so very long without any air to breathe."

"Where?" Dr. Watson thundered.

I didn't wait for an answer. I started tracking Sherlock's scent, oh, and the wheelbarrow track. The grave I sought was not so far away. Dr. Watson caught up with me, carrying the lantern, and the spade. I meowed to ask him what he had done with the madwoman. He even understood, or guessed my question. "I hit her on the head with the shovel. Knocked her out. She won't be going anywhere for some hours." He wasn't acting much like a physician, and that was fine by me.

I showed him the fresh mound of earth where Sherlock's scent ended. He commenced digging frantically. I tried to help. Alas, my small paws couldn't shift more than a spoonful of dirt at a time. I must admit, if there is one way in which dogs are superior to cats, it is at digging. I was only getting in the way of Dr. Watson's spade, so I withdrew and sat down to wait.

He hadn't dug very deep when the shovel hit something, rather hard. It did not sound like a rock. I realized that there would not have been enough time for Alice Grace to bury Sherlock too deep in soil.

And if he was comatose at the time, a shallow mound of dirt would smother him every bit as effectively as a deep mound. Being one who planned ahead, she had probably pinpointed the locations of all the nearby open graves, freshly dug and just waiting for the bodies to be planted. She did like her madcap schemes.

Dr. Watson tossed the shovel aside and dug with his hands, in the manner of a dog digging with its paws. He cleared the bulk of the dirt off of a body, which when revealed, proved to be Sherlock's. The detective was facedown and unmoving. I had known it was Sherlock from his scent. The back of his head was caked in both damp earth and congealed blood.

"Come on, Sherlock, don't be dead," Dr. Watson cried, turning him over. He laid his ear on Sherlock's chest for the longest time. He did not voice any good news.

I crouched low in the grass and mewled sadly, fearing the worst. It was confirmed when Dr. Watson sat back on his haunches. He gazed at me with teary eyes. "I knew he couldn't be alive after so long without air, yet still I hoped." His little smile was heartbreaking as tears rolled down his face. If I could have shed tears, they would have been rolling down my face, too, wetting all my fur.

Dr. Watson patted his knee and said, "Come here."

I padded over to him and climbed on his lap. He stroked me and we comforted each other as best we could, until we were interrupted.

32 – Misadventure in a Graveyard

Sherlock sat up and brushed earth off his clothing. He shook his head, and dirt rained from his hair. He spat out foul dirt. He blinked dirt from his eyes and squinted about. John and Cat Watson were gaping at him, like two fish out of water—or one fish and one catfish.

"You're dead, Sherlock," John said. "Have you come back as a zombie?"

"There is no such thing as a zombie, John. Shall I lie down and stop breathing, so your fatal diagnosis will be proved correct?" he asked.

Cat Watson bounded over to him, almost prancing with happiness. Sherlock scooped him up. "Do I have you to thank for saving me? And John, of course. I'm sure there was too much dirt for a cat to remove."

John shook his head as if to clear away the cobwebs. "But you're dead, Sherlock. You had no heartbeat. I did check."

Sherlock rose unsteadily and stepped from the shallow grave, still holding Cat Watson. "I had a heartbeat, it was merely very, very slow. I have been training my body for just such instances as this."

"This?" John asked incredulously, motioning at the grave.

"Yes this, or something similar. By sheer will alone, mind over body, I can reduce my heartrate to a mere two beats per minute. Hence, I can survive without a great deal of oxygen for a prolonged period of time, as long as I can be very still and in a trance-like state. And I did have a small pocket of air beneath my face and neck, as the earth is damp and inclined to clump. It was most fortuitous I regained my senses soon after being buried alive, or I wouldn't have known to achieve a trance-like state and reduce my heartrate."

"Fortuitous indeed," John said faintly, still appearing shell-shocked.

"But now I have a headache." Sherlock touched the back of his head. "Did you hit me with a shovel, John?"

Dr. Watson rose to his feet, even more unsteadily than Sherlock, despite not having been deprived of oxygen for long minutes, or knocked unconscious, one or possibly two times. "No, that was the madwoman, the blackmailer, Alice Grace. She hit you on the head. Although, I might have hit you, a bit, with the spade, while digging you out."

Sherlock groped his head. "Yes, two lumps of an impressive size. I didn't have the pleasure, or displeasure, of meeting the blackmailer. I was knocked unconscious, without even a *how do you do,* or a *good evening.* So, where is this Alice Grace? It is high time I met her, face-to-face." He rubbed his bottom and winced.

"She is in an open grave, shot and unconscious, but not dead." John motioned in the appropriate direction. "She is lying on a stuffed dummy that wears a wax face in your exact likeness, in the bottom of the hole."

"Truly? How bizarre. She must have commissioned it. She does go to a great deal of trouble to make her nefarious plans interesting. I must see this. Lead the way." Sherlock motioned for John to precede him.

John did. Sherlock was far weaker in the knees than he would have admitted, and followed like a docile, slightly inebriated lamb, to the side of an open grave. John had spoken truth. The madwoman was unconscious, splayed atop a dummy that wore his face. It was missing the nose and one ear. Regardless, it was undeniably his likeness. The compromising position of the pair in the grave was quite scandalous, as if they were lovers in a bed.

"So this is the villain who bested me. Are you sure she's not dead, John? Why don't you hop down there and check?" Sherlock said.

John grimaced. "Must I?"

Before he could do any such thing, a shrill police whistle rent the air. Lanterns flared to life and closed in from all sides. A number of coppers soon ringed them. Sherlock was delighted to see Gregson amongst their number. "Well met, Inspector Gregson," he said, with more enthusiasm than was his habit.

Gregson looked him up and down. "Still got that cat, I see. You've looked better, Holmes." He picked a worm off of Sherlock's cloak. He peered down into the open grave when his men raised quite a hue and cry, including a great deal of snickering. Gregson's eyes widened.

"Then again, you are looking far healthier than your twin. Poor fellow's missing his nose."

"And an ear. Did the lady nibble it off?" Carron said snidely. Of course he was there, curse him. "And who killed the woman? Why, Sherlock Holmes, here you are hovering over another body, and at the same time lying beneath it. You're all covered in dirt, too. He's the murderer," Carron declared, pointing an accusing finger at the detective.

Sherlock raised one weary eyebrow in Carron's direction. "I am still not the murderer, nor am I sure the woman is dead. Tonight's adventure is quite a tale to tell, although I don't know the whole of it, having been unconscious for an hour or so, and possibly slightly dead for several minutes. Dr. Watson can fill in the gaps, I'm sure, but this is not the place to speak at length." Sherlock hesitated to say more. If Alice Grace awakened and blabbed about what lay rotting in Mrs. Hudson's cellar, it would not turn out well for his landlady. If only the cops had not been so quick to arrive, he could have managed some degree of damage control in regards to Alice Grace.

"How do you come to be here? Now?" he asked Gregson.

"One of the gravediggers summoned us. He said someone has been messing about with his freshly dug graves, burying bodies where they oughtn't. And they made off with his best wheelbarrow. So here we are, and then we heard pistol shots, and have found this." He swept an arm over the bizarre scene. "Who is the woman getting overly friendly with your twin? And how did she die?"

John seemed reluctant to speak, so Sherlock said, "I repeat, I am not certain she is dead. Perhaps someone should check."

"She looks dead," Carron said, as if that meant she was. Well, the fellow didn't bother to check for bullets before waving pistols about like flags, so why would he check a body for a pulse? If left to Carron, he would probably tell the gravedigger to cover up the pair in the hole and be done with it. Problem solved. It certainly would have ended Mrs. Hudson's dilemma.

Gregson surveyed his men and pointed to one of the younger, fitter constables. "Jump in. See if the woman has a pulse."

The young man descended into the grave with obvious reluctance. He left his hand at her neck for some time. "Nothing. Dead."

"Are you sure?" Sherlock asked.

"Positive," the constable said.

"Perhaps a doctor should verify your diagnosis. We do have one right here." Sherlock patted John's shoulder.

"No need. I can tell a dead body from a living one, when it's laid out before me, and has no pulse to speak of," the constable said, and then the woman groaned. He cried out in fear and scrambled quickly up and out of the grave.

Gregson sighed. "Holmes, Dr. Watson, I will hear a complete explanation for all this lunacy, back at the constabulary. With whiskey. Excuse me." He turned to oversee his men and manage the situation.

Two constables hauled the madwoman from the grave. Despite Sherlock's fervent protests, his wax-faced doppelganger was lifted out, along with its ear. His nose was discovered by chance and collected, too. He would have preferred the eerie dummy stay buried, and never saw the light of day again.

All the manhandling revived the madwoman from her diagnosed deadness. She did not revive slowly. She leapt to her feet with startling speed and agility, and a wild wail worthy of a savage cannibal from the deepest forests of Borneo. Before anyone could stop her, she raced into the darkness. There was a disturbing thud, then silence. Coppers with lanterns went to investigate.

Sherlock, John and Cat Watson went along, too. Alice Grace had run headfirst into a large headstone. She was face down on the ground, unmoving. "Is she dead this time?" Sherlock gave John a nudge forward.

John checked her over properly, at length. Cat Watson had been very quiet in Sherlock's arms, but now the cat squirmed to be released. He joined John in examining the woman. John said, "Quite dead, without a doubt this time. She's fractured her own skull, running into the headstone. Probably died instantly." Cat Watson meowed in agreement.

Carron eyed Sherlock suspiciously, likely trying to dream up some way to accuse him of murder, when they had all seen the woman cause her own accidental death. It ended not only her life, but the threat to Mrs. Hudson. It concluded *The Case of the Baker Street Blackmailer*, with a bang, or a skull-cracking thud, as it were.

Alas, it had not been one of Sherlock's better efforts, to be thrice bested by a young woman who was entirely off her rocker, and have his life saved by a cat. Sherlock could claim no victory. They didn't even know the true identity of the madwoman, or her motivations. That aspect of the case still had to be wrapped up, before it could be properly concluded.

Cat Watson helped there. He meowed for Sherlock to follow him out of the cemetery. John accompanied him, too curious not to. Cat Watson led them through the streets, unerringly bringing them to the door of a mansion that was unlit, and from what they could see by the meager light of their lanterns, recently neglected.

Sherlock knocked. No-one answered. Cat Watson meowed more stridently and pawed at the door. Sherlock turned the knob. The door was not locked, so they entered. John immediately lit a gaslamp in the foyer. The interior of the house proved to be as untended as its grounds.

"Where now, Cat Watson?" Sherlock asked.

The cat padded to the rear of the house and pawed at the door to the cellar, obvious by its dank smell. Sherlock opened it. The hinges creaked a sinister protest. "Perhaps we should have brought Gregson along," John commented, when they gazed down into the creepy blackness.

"No. First and foremost, we must ensure Mrs. Hudson's safety. We do not know what messages or clues the madwoman has left behind, ones that might implicate our landlady in dastardly deeds."

"You sound like a penny dreadful," John said, perhaps trying to ease the tension.

"This case has certainly been worthy of one. Shall we?" Sherlock raised a hand toward the stairs. Cat Watson went first, with his cat's eyes. Sherlock and John followed with their lanterns. In the depths of the cellar, they came upon a most piteous sight. A half-starved old man was tied, with ribbons and bows, to a solid dining room chair.

He cried out at their approach. "Help me, help me. My daughter has gone quite mad and tied me up. It is most unseemly."

While Sherlock and John worked to free him, he told his tale. In short, he had sent away his daughter's lover, who he believed to be a gigolo after her fortune. Given recent events, Sherlock knew that man would also be Mrs. Hudson's Mr. Blakely. When Alice Grace would not behave as a proper daughter should, he planned to condemn her to an insane asylum. She didn't like that and proved she was very crafty indeed, drugging him to appear ill, confining him to his bed, keeping him sedated, dismissing all the staff in his name, and lastly, making him a prisoner in his own house for some long time. Months, he claimed, although he had only been consigned to the cellar for a week or two. "I'll see her in an insane asylum for the rest of her days," he cried out at the end of his tale of woe.

"No, you won't. She is dead," Sherlock said.

"Oh, well, that's good then." The man, a Mr. Lostrum, showed no sorrow, only relief.

"Did Alice Grace mention her attempts to blackmail anyone?" Sherlock asked vaguely.

"Yes, some old prune, as she called her. Her lover's next target, I daresay. She was mad with jealousy."

"Did she identify the woman?" Sherlock inquired most casually.

"No, just called her the old prune. Said she would rob the woman of everything she loved. She wasn't making much sense this last year, liked to sing silly songs, like she was a little girl again. Quite, quite mad. Better off dead," he concluded.

They assisted him upstairs to the main part of the house. While John saw to his immediate needs, Sherlock hurried up to the top floor and located Alice Grace's room. He found Mrs. Hudson's broach in a box with several freshly dead mice. Alice Grace had never gotten her hands on any other of Mrs. Hudson's valuables. The necklace and ring were still in his pocket. She must not have bothered to check for them, before she dumped him in the grave.

He went over the room quickly, but thoroughly. He was pleased to find no evidence that would lead back to Mrs. Hudson or 221B Baker Street. The police constables probably wouldn't bother to search, anyway, since the case had already concluded. And most of them were lazy, inclined to do as little investigating as possible.

His mind at ease in regards to Mrs. Hudson's circumstance, he ventured downstairs and out onto the road. He flagged down a passing carriage for hire and sent a message to summon Gregson to the house.

Sherlock and John departed the depressing mansion soon after Gregson arrived, a couple of constables in tow. They would see things sorted, perhaps hire a nurse, or summon back the original household staff who had been dismissed, if they were still without employment. Sherlock was not concerned about the cold-hearted man, who had shed not one tear over his only daughter's tragic end, and had been so willing to pack her off to a madhouse when she did not obey his dictates. Mad or not, she had still been his kin.

208

Cat Watson had been quiet, staying in the shadows, while things were sorted. He padded outside with them. He looked as tired as Sherlock felt. At the bottom of the stone steps, Sherlock bent to pick him up and carry him. Cat Watson darted away from his hands. "Don't you want a ride, Cat Watson? I am happy to be your carriage, until we flag down a wheeled conveyance."

Cat Watson meowed rather sadly and turned away, the shortened tail drooping, ears at half-mast. Something was amiss with the little cat. "Where are you going, Cat Watson? It is time to go home. Mrs. Hudson will reward us with a lovely tea when I deliver the good news, that *The Case of the Baker Street Blackmailer* has been solved."

"Is that what we're calling it?" John asked.

"Yes, don't you think it suits?"

"It's not bad, but I can come up with something better."

Sherlock opened his mouth to argue, then thought better of it. "I have no doubt that you can. John, you are the truest friend a man could hope to have, and I do treasure your friendship over any other."

"Even the cat?" John asked.

"Even the cat," Sherlock said, with a wink that only Cat Watson would see. He knew the little cat would understand, except, the cat was gone. He had slunk away in the mere seconds the two men had been conversing.

"Be that as it may, I am going home to Mary," John declared, his tone challenging.

"I am not surprised. I expected as much." Sherlock squinted around in the darkness, trying to spot a slightly darker shadow in the long grass of the untended lawn. He couldn't. He called, "Cat Watson, you are the truest cat a man could hope to know, and I don't know what has upset you, but please, come back. It is time to go home."

There was no answering meow. John said, "I'll stop by Baker Street to fetch Gladstone on my way back to Mary. I will examine your thick head at the same time, to see if it needs sutures."

"Gladstone!" Sherlock cried.

"That is my dog's name, as well as the name or our prime minister. Did those blows to your head do some internal damage to your big giant brain?" John inquired.

Sherlock gave his head an impatient shake, which did make it ache sharply. He shouted louder, "Gladstone is not staying at Baker Street.

He was merely visiting, without an invitation, foist upon me without my consent. He will be departing forthwith. Come back, Cat Watson."

Still, there was no answering meow. Perhaps Cat Watson was too far away to have heard his words. Or Sherlock was wrong about why the cat was abandoning him, as John had done not so long ago, and would do again today, to return to Mary. No, Sherlock wasn't wrong. Or course he wasn't. It was the logical conclusion, so it was the right one. Cat Watson believed the dog had usurped his home at Baker Street, so he had left, to return to the streets and a life of hardship and deprivation. Poor Cat Watson, he must be so sad. Sherlock was equally sad, already missing the little cat quite fiercely.

"I must find Cat Watson," Sherlock said.

"Is that your new case? Finding a runaway cat?" John asked.

"Yes, that will be my next case, one I will solve. Our next case, if you will help me." He gripped John's arm, needing the support, as much emotionally as physically. When had he become such a ridiculously sentimental and maudlin man?

"Of course I will help you find Midnight Shadow Holmes." John's lips quirked into a smile. "Now, let us get you home as quickly as possible. I fear you may well be suffering from brain damage, as you are not acting much like yourself."

"Am I not? How odd. Let us get me home then. After my head is sewn back together, our newest case will commence." The thought heartened Sherlock, and he went along with John, smiling just a bit, to have his good friend by his side and another crucial case to engage his mind.

From the inky shadows, Cat Watson listened, and he smiled too. He had heard Sherlock's declaration that Gladstone would be departing with John, both to return to Mary. He had been so very tempted to go to his Sherlock then and there. And his tummy was craving a delicious fishy tea. Alas, one must often make sacrifices for those they truly care about, and it was as plain as the fur on his face that his absence was helping to mend the rift between the two men. He would stay away a couple of days, by such time, their friendship would be firmly fixed, as long as they didn't come to blows again. Then he would return to his Sherlock.

Cat Watson was content with his plan, until he saw the eerie shadow. It was tall, taller than Sherlock even, and much wider, almost as wide as that gorilla he had seen at the zoo. Add to that, it had a sinister aspect. Worst of all, it was following his Sherlock in a silent and predatory manner. Cat Watson had rarely witnessed a human move so silently. Sherlock had no clue he was being stalked. Well, he was less than fit. Dr. Watson didn't have a clue either, but that was not surprising. He rarely did.

Gladder than ever to be a small, black, and very clever cat, Cat Watson adopted his crime fighting persona. Midnight Shadow Holmes was on the case. He slunk silently after, stalking the sinister presence that was stalking his Sherlock Holmes.

The End

Coming Soon-
The Adventures of Sherlock Holmes' Cat, Volume 2

Visit SrigleyArts.com for updates,
and to view additional titles by the author.

Books by the author are available at Amazon.com as both
Kindle and paperback books.

On Facebook – Patricia Srigley Author/Artist

Sample chapter readings can be viewed on YouTube.

Made in the USA
Monee, IL
17 October 2024

68223843R00132